AF133248

THE GIRL WITH THE GOOD MAGIC

M. J. CAAN

ᵛINCI
BOOKS

Vinci Books

vinci-books.com

Published by Vinci Books Ltd in 2026

1

Copyright © M.J. Caan 2018

The author has asserted their moral right to be identified as the author of this work in accordance with the Copyright, Designs and Patents Act 1988. This work is a work of fiction. Names, characters, places and incidents are the product of the author's imagination or are used fictitiously. Any resemblance to actual persons, living or dead, places and incidents is entirely coincidental.

All rights reserved. No part of this publication may be copied, reproduced, distributed, stored in any retrieval system, or transmitted in any form or by any means, including photocopying, recording, or other electronic or mechanical methods, nor used as a source for any form of machine learning including AI datasets, without the prior written permission of the publisher.

The publisher and the author have made every effort to obtain permissions for any third party material used in this book and to comply with copyright law. Any queries in this respect should be brought to the attention of the publisher and any omissions will be corrected in future editions.

A CIP catalogue record for this book is available from the British Library.

Paperback ISBN: 9781036704469

The EU GPSR authorised representative is Logos Europe, 9 rue Nicolas Poussion, 17000 La Rochelle, France contact@logoseurope.eu

By M.J. Caan

The Shifter Wars

The Girl with the Good Magic
Enter the Wolf
The Return of the Witch

Paranormal Fades

Midlife Crashing
Midlife Burning
Midlife Rising

Midlife Enclave

Tantric Hexes
Tantric Bindings

Earth's First

Earth's First
Dark Days
A Hero Rises
Rise Of The Acolytes

Singing Falls Witches

Hex After Forty
That Good Hex
How Torie Got Her Hex Back
Hex and Chocolate
Moonlight Hexes
Hex and the Single Witch
Hex Education
Hex After Dark
That Hex Factor

Chapter One

Of all the myriad magical gifts my mother was purported to possess and could have passed on to me, precognition was not one of them. Yet moments before a dead, rotting thing attacked us, I had been working at my family's coffee shop, listening to my best friend drone on, and I had just thought to myself: *Once, just once, I'd love for something exciting to happen in this town.*

"Earth to Allie...you there?"

The snapping of fingers in my face brought me back to reality.

"Sorry," I said. "I was daydreaming."

"In the middle of my read? Wait, were you daydreaming about my future?" Hope said excitedly. She's my best friend and the look in her almond-shaped eyes was way too hopeful for this early on a Saturday morning.

"What? No. I'm sorry, where were we?"

Hope motioned to the sludge at the bottom of her coffee cop. "You were about to tell me that someone tall, dark and handsome is about to waltz into my life, sweep me up into their arms and take me out of this little hole-in-the-wall town. Preferably in a white Lamborghini."

I couldn't help but roll my eyes. "Like I'd let you be part of a Harlequin cliche."

"Well," she said, "what do you see? I mean, what's the point in having a psychic for a best friend if you can't tell me the good stuff before it happens to me?"

"I'm not a psychic, Hope. I've told you that."

"Psychic. Witch. Whatever," she said flippantly.

"Hope! What have I told you about saying things like that when we are in a public place?" I glanced up from behind the counter at the coffee shop to see if anyone noticed. Luckily, nobody had looked up from their laptop, and the fact that most of the patrons had earbuds in helped me to breathe easier as well.

Hope rolled her eyes dramatically at me. "No one pays attention to anything that happens in here. Besides, the tourists come in here for readings, so what's the big deal?"

Trinity Cove was a tourist's destination. Every summer what seemed like a million people came traipsing into our idyllic little town nestled in mountains of North Carolina. They come for the natural beauty of the region; lakes, hiking, quaint bed and breakfasts and access to some of the best furniture galleries in the country. But mostly they come to see the Singing Falls. An hour-plus, depending on the path you took, hike up some of the toughest trails in the region would take you to a secluded lagoon that was fed by a one-hundred-foot waterfall. The water poured down into the natural pool over jagged, protruding rock outcroppings that sheltered multiple caverns carved into a mountainside. Because the rock outcroppings that the water cascaded over were thin and their openings hollow, the sound of the water flowing down was haunting; the echoes created were of varying pitches and constantly changing due to climate and shifts in the topography they ran across.

It also made for treacherous footing along the sides of the fall. Every summer at least one person fell down the steep pitch, breaking legs, arms, and on a couple of occasions, necks.

Still, the undeniable scenic beauty called to people from all walks of life and they descended on the town in droves every year. Their money went a long way to keeping the town's coffers filled, and all of the sleepy businesses in Trinity Cover catered to them during the tourist season. Restaurants advertised the freshest homemade delicacies, even though they were the same meals that could be purchased year round at a much steeper discount. Signs popped up in numerous yards advertising antiques for sale. Every home with an extra bedroom was suddenly a bed and breakfast. Every semi-athletic college dropout that still lived at home with his or her parents was suddenly a canoe guide promising to take you to a secret spot upriver that only the locals know about.

Yeah. That kind of small town.

And I have to admit, I was just as much to blame as everyone else in the town. My Aunt owned the 3 Coves Cafe and Bakery that sat on a prime spot in the center of the town square. I was one of those college dropouts that had decided to live at home while I found myself. I ran the café, and one of my side gigs for summer was to act as the town fortune teller. Instead of tea leaves I would read coffee sludge.

My best friend Hope had just arrived home from her first year of college and had been regaling me with tales of drunken frat parties, all-night jam sessions followed by ditching the class you just stayed up all night studying for.

Oh, and the men. She was convinced that the state college she was attending was where she was going to meet Mr. Right and head off into the sunset with him.

Her badgering look snapped me out of my reverie and I gazed into the bottom of her ceramic cup.

"Nope," I said. "There's nobody in there. But hey, after one whole year away from home, what are you expecting?"

Hope bristled at my tone. It had come out a lot more terse than I intended.

"Well, at least I'm away from home and trying."

Ouch. Touché and all that.

"I'm sorry." Her tone instantly softened. "I didn't mean that the way it sounded." She reached across the counter and placed her hand on top of mine to give it a reassuring squeeze.

"No problem." I smiled. "I kind of deserved that one." I turn and placed her cup in the bin on the back table so it could be bussed into the kitchen and cleaned. Turning back, I smiled again. "But really, why are you in such a hurry to get hitched? You have your whole life ahead of you." I flinched a little. I already knew the answer to that question, but I wanted to see if she would confirm my thoughts.

"It's hard," she said, eyes downcast. "My mom wants to see me in the wedding gown she made for me so bad. I want her to see that as well." Hope's eyes clouded up and I could see her clenched her jaw to stave off tears.

"Hey." Now it was my turn to reach out and grab her hand. "The doctors don't know everything. She beat breast cancer once before and she can beat it this time around as well."

"Thanks for that," Hope said. "I feel like an ass even saying that, considering your mom is…"

"No worries. My mom bailed on Gar and me years ago.

The Girl with the Good Magic

He doesn't really remember her. He was too young when she left."

It was true. My brother Garland, or Gar as he preferred to be called, had long forgotten what our mother looked like. He could remember the stories she told us when he was small, but time had long since erased the mental imagery of her from his mind's eye.

Unfortunately, my mental imagery was as strong as ever. If I closed my eyes I could still picture our mother's face. Not just the green eyes and fire-red hair that I had inherited, but also the tiny curves around her full lips and the lines that danced around her eyes when she laughed. Our mother had been so happy when we knew her. But that was before the madness set in; before she began to whisper about demons and monsters that hid in the woods outside of the house we shared with Aunt Vivian and Aunt Lena.

At least, I had always hoped it was madness.

I came from a long line of witches. Not just any witches, but rock star witches if you believed what my mother had told us as children. According to her, she and my aunts stopped Armageddon from devouring our sleepy little town in the form of werewolves.

While Gar could remember the stories as only bedtime tales, I remembered them as something more: a cautionary tale of what had once nearly wiped out all of Trinity Cover, and could possibly happen again. To Gar, they were heroic and funny. But I was older; to me they were horrific and the cause of night terrors that occasionally would still wake me from fitful nights of sleep.

Our aunts had assured us that the stories our mother told us were just that: stories meant to entertain and frighten children who stayed up long past their bedtime.

While we may have been called witches at one time, my

aunts assured us that moniker was one that was never merited. We might have small gifts, the occasional extra-sensory ability, or a way with certain potions and herbs that did little more than induce euphoria in townsfolk and allowed them to sleep better, but that was it. We didn't fly around on broomsticks. We didn't cast spells.

And we certainly weren't responsible for the destruction of an entire breed of supernatural creatures referred to as werewolves.

The fact is, here in town my family had a certain reputation. We weren't shunned, but we weren't exactly asked over for Sunday dinners either. People here had a grudging respect for my aunts. They were polite to them, some were even friendly, but most stopped just short of crossing the street when they saw one of my aunts heading toward them on the same sidewalk.

They were a little suspicious when I told them I wanted to add fortune telling to the seasonal offerings at the coffee shop, but after they saw the bump in business, they allowed me my indulgences. I wasn't a clairvoyant in the true sense of the word. My medium abilities were mostly the product of being able to read a person's emotional state and combine it with the latest horoscope readings I found online. Add to that a few vague, generic missives from Google and voila...your very own fortune told.

Hope wasn't a tourist however, and she wouldn't fall for the mumbo-jumbo that I spewed to most of the giggling schoolgirls who passed through in the summer. No, she had been my best friend since grade school. She knew what I went through, she knew what the townies whispered about my family, and she knew when to call bullshit on me.

"C'mon, Allie," she pleaded. "I know when you're lying. You saw something. Spill it!"

The Girl with the Good Magic

The truth was I hadn't seen anything, and that was why my gaze had lingered in the cup. Usually there was something; a small spark, or flash of something brief and tiny that revealed itself to me. I may or may not opt to tell the person, but there was almost always something there. That was especially true with the people I was close to. But this time, when I looked into the coffee grinds all I saw was… coffee. I felt numb and cut off from the tiny spark of my vision.

No. Not cut off. Blocked. I opened my mouth to tell Hope that I really didn't see anything, but my words were cut off by the sudden wail of a siren followed by the revving of a car engine as a police cruiser tore down main street, lights and siren blaring. It was quickly followed by the similar sounds of an ambulance as it chased after the cruiser.

"What the…" exclaimed Hope, bolting for the cafe front window.

Just as she reached it, the main door to the shop burst open and Gar came running in, his dark hair wet with sweat.

"Hey, sis!" he exclaimed, his words tripping over themselves. "Guess what? They found a body out by the falls!"

Great. The season was just getting started and we already had our first slip and fall. This wouldn't be good for business.

"Ugh," said Hope. "When will these tourists learn the rocks there are signposted 'No Climbing' for a reason?"

"Not this one!" said Gar, excited. "This one was an animal attack!"

Both Hope and I snapped to attention immediately.

"What?" I said.

"Yep," Gar replied. "I heard that whoever it was had their throat ripped open and their chest torn apart."

I swallowed the lump that made its way into my throat. I clutched at the pink stone jewel I wore around my neck, the one my mother had given me for luck on the night she disappeared. I was overtaken by a sense of dread like I had never felt before. I sank back against the counter, hardly able to register the patrons that were suddenly rushing from the shop and running in the direction of the wailing sirens.

Chapter Two

I locked the shop door with a sigh after the last customer had exited. I could feel the slight buzz between my eyes that indicated a potential migraine was on the way. "Great," I said to myself aloud. "Just what I don't need."

"What don't you need?" Hope's voice caused me to jump. I had forgotten she was still here and had just gone to the restroom.

"Migraine," I answered.

"I'll help you clean up. That way you can close sooner and get out of here."

Before I could pretend to protest she had already walked around behind the counter, picked up a bus bin and started clearing the tables of the few saucers and coffee cups that the patrons had not left at the counter.

"Thanks, but that's really not necessary. I'm sure you have some place to be."

"Nope. We haven't seen each other in months. We have so much to catch up on." She stopped what she was doing and wheeled around to face me. "Unless you're telling me to go because you *know* there is someplace I need to be! Am I destined to meet Him tonight?!"

I knew she was just yanking my chain, but I also knew that part of her was dead serious. Rather than answer I changed the subject.

"So why didn't you go up to the trails and see what was going on with the rest of the town?"

"Once you've seen one mangled body you've seen them all," she miffed.

I couldn't help but laugh. "Honestly, the rumor mill must have been working overtime with this one. God knows how Gar heard it before the official reports. I mean, c'mon...an animal attack?"

"Well," Hope said, turning to me, "you know what that really means, right?"

"What?"

Hope rolled her eyes dramatically. "Please, I've watched enough *Supernatural* to know that animals never attack and kill people in real life. It's always a cover-up for something really nefarious. Like vampires, werewolves or some other bloodthirsty creature."

"Yeah, right," I say. "This is Trinity Cove, not the Hellmouth."

"Not if you believe the stories we grew up with as children. Don't you ever wonder why all the parents in town would never let their kids play outside after the sun went down? And why we weren't allowed to go outside at all during certain times of the month?"

"Probably because this was pre-internet days when pervs weren't lurking online but rather were cruising around in white vans, snatching kids."

Just then my phone rang and I couldn't stifle a little

The Girl with the Good Magic

moan as I looked at the caller ID. I picked up before it could go to voicemail.

"Hi, Aunt Viv," I said, looking over at Hope. "Yes, I'm fine. I'm still at the cafe. Hope is here with me, helping me close. We'll be heading out soon, and I'll call you when I'm on my way home." I paused, looking over at a smirking Hope. "Aunt Viv, it's literally a five-minute walk home. I don't need…yes, all right. I"ll see you soon."

"Let me guess," said Hope, "she's freaked out by the animal attack."

"'Freaked' isn't the word. She's sending someone to pick us up and drive us home."

"I'm sure she got all the good dirt on what happened," said Hope. "For someone that no one really talks to in this town, your aunts seem to know all the good gossip."

It was true. My family kept to themselves, but still managed to be on top of everyone's business. While I didn't want to alarm Hope, if there was anything supernatural going on in the area, chances were my aunts had already sniffed it out. Maybe that was why they were so intent on my being escorted home. Had they made the same call with Gar? If anyone needed protecting it would be him. He was powerless. Men weren't born with the power of witches. At least that's what my mother had always said. They could acquire it in other, less pleasant ways, but she had declined to explain what exactly those ways were. Aunt Vivian always said it wasn't true and not to listen to her. Men belonged to another pocket of the supernatural, she had said. They couldn't cross over into the corners occupied by witches.

The knock at the door distracted me from the espresso machine I was wiping down. "Sorry, we're closed," I said into the air.

It was dark outside and I could only make out the form

of the person standing on the other side of the locked door. Another knock, this time more determined. Hope was closer to the door and peered out the window.

"It's a cop," she said. "He's holding his badge up to the door."

"Geez. Aunt Viv has taken getting us a ride to the extreme."

Hope moved to answer the door, and just as it cracked open it hit me: the smell of earth and rotted flesh accompanied by a wave of dark magic that made my stomach reel.

"Hope no!" I shouted, but I knew it was already too late.

Before she could react, the thing standing outside had burst in. The force of the door swinging open threw Hope across the room and over two of the tables. She crashed to the floor, unconscious. The sight of my best friend being hurt like that filled me with a white hot rage. I reached deep inside myself and grabbed that rage. Calling it forward, it manifested itself in a ball of blue flame that I hurled at the creature even as it charged at me.

Even as the creature was struck in the chest by my power, my thoughts raced as I tried to identify just what was attacking us. It looked like a human, a large, solidly built male. But I knew that when it came to the supernatural, looks could be deceiving. Whatever it was, it was only wearing the skin of a man. Underneath it reeked of death and darkness.

I dove behind the counter, looking desperately for anything that I could use as a weapon. The fireball I threw probably surprised me more than it hurt my attacker. I'd never been able to manifest my magic like that before. I could levitate objects and charge other items with magic, but I'd never been able to create something like that out of thin air.

I was too afraid to risk a peek over the counter to see where the creature was or what it might be doing. But then I remembered Hope lying out there, helpless.

"Shit!" I was sitting with my back against the counter, and looking around, I saw the silver cake knife lying on the floor. Knowing my aunt, it was probably real silver. That was a plus for what I was about to do. Silver has certain innate properties that make it both ideal for absorbing the right kinds of magic and for being anathema to supernatural constructs. I had no idea what that blue fireball I threw was, but other than the initial contact it didn't seem to have done much to the creature.

I crawled to the far end of the counter and chanced a quick peek. Whatever that thing was, it was lumbering to the opposite end of the counter, where the cash register sat. I winced as it grabbed one end of the counter and ripped up half the bar, throwing wood, glass, register and granite counters toward the ceiling as it shuffled around, looking for me.

"Okay, so you're strong, but you don't seem very smart."

I crouched, circling around the front side of the counter, trying to sneak up behind it, cake knife at the ready. How did this thing even get into the cafe? My aunts' wards were top notch. Anything giving off the kind of dark magic this bad boy was reeking of should have set them off, given me some kind of warning. That told me that maybe this thing wasn't a supernatural creature, but something that probably has a contained burst of magic inside it as a power source. It smelled dead, so that meant someone probably animated a corpse and sent it after me. That's big time mojo.

But I couldn't focus on that right now. That thing was definitely strong enough to kill me and Hope, and that wasn't happening on my watch.

I concentrate and focused my will on the knife I was carrying. As I approached the creature, the cake knife began to take on a blue tint, glowing with the magic I was forcing into it. Just as I reached the creature, I heard a small moan. Hope was starting to wake up and had begun to move around. The zombie immediately spun in her direction and realized I was standing right behind it. Faster than I would have expected a dead thing to move, it swept me up in its arms and immediately started to squeeze.

I screamed in pain and raised the knife over my head. Had to do this before it crushed my spine, and judging from the pressure it was expending, that would happen in a matter of seconds.

With a yell, I plunged the knife down and into the creature's exposed neck. The silver, augmented by what little magic I have, was enough to pierce the flesh. But more importantly, it created an opening in the skin, a vent to release the magic that was powering this monster. What I did was akin to cutting the gas line on a car, only on a far more dramatic scale.

The zombie dropped me and staggering backward as black steam hissed from his torn flesh. The magic that animated him was evaporating, and with it, so went the monster's corporeal form. It fell to its knees before falling face forward onto the ground. The scent of rotted flesh breaking down for a second time was beyond nauseating. I retched as the smell hit me and instinctively buried my face in my elbow to ward off the fetid stench.

I could hear Hope coming to, dragging herself up to a sitting position. In the distance I could make out the sound of sirens getting closer. As much as I hated to do it, I needed to get rid of the body.

I looked at the decomposing mess before me and muttered a quick incendiary incantation that melted it to so much slag, and then caused even that molten goo to evaporate. By the time Hope was looking around and clearing her head, I had moved to her side, trying to comfort her.

"What the...?" she mumbled.

"Hey, take it easy. Help's on the way."

"What the hell was that?" she said, rubbing the back of her head.

"Some coked-out druggie. Barged in, messed up the place, looking to take what little cash I had on hand, then ran back out. He's gone now." Not a lie. Not exactly, at least.

"Jesus, Allie. Are you okay? Did he...?"

"No, no. I'm fine. I think all my screaming scared him off."

I returned one of the knocked-over chairs to its upright position and slowly helped Hope to her feet before gingerly seating her. A knock at the door got my attention and I turned just in time to see a police officer stepping through the ruined opening.

"Ma'am, we had a report of a disturbance here," the officer said, looking around. I saw one hand hovering near his holster, which made me more nervous than being attacked by a zombie for some reason. Plus, his reliance on his gun told me he was not a supe. Still, I keyed up some magic and had it at the ready just in case.

"It's okay now. Some guy just burst in here, knocked all my shit over trying to break into the cash register, then ran back out," I said, trying to defuse the situation.

I watched as the policeman turned his head to the side

and said something into a communication piece attached to the shoulder strap of his bulletproof vest.

He then stepped over to Hope and examined her head.

"Don't move, ma'am. An ambulance is on the way to take a look at you," he said.

"I don't need that," Hope replied. "It's just a bump. I feel stupid just sitting here like this. But can you make sure my friend is okay?"

I looked at the police officer and read his badge. Hunter.

"I'm fine, Officer Hunter," I said. "Thank you for getting here so quickly. I think it was the sound of your sirens approaching that scared him off."

"Did you get a good look at him?" Officer Hunter said.

"No...it all happened so fast. He was big, dressed in some type of large jacket and a cap I think..." Careful here, I tell myself. Don't back yourself into a corner.

"Oh my God!" said Hope. "I just remembered. He had a badge that he flashed at me when I looked out the door!"

"What?" said Officer Hunter. "Are you sure?"

"Well, it all happened so fast," I interjected.

"Yes, but that's why I started to open the door to begin with," said Hope. "Remember, we thought it was someone your aunt had sent to pick us up. I started to open the door...and then...then it gets fuzzy. But I know for a fact he had a badge."

Officer Hunter was busy scribbling in a pocket notebook he had pulled out of his vest.

Before he could ask more questions, the ambulance pulled up to the street in front of the cafe.

"Oh, good," I said, looking at Hope. "You really should have them check you over, as hard as you must have hit your head when he knocked you over."

"Yeah," she replied, rubbing the back of her skull. "As long as they don't try to cut my hair or anything. I'm not having my summer do messed with."

Officer Hunter smiled as the paramedics walked in with bags and stepped back to give them access to Hope. I watched as he strolled around the cafe looking at things, examining the broken counter and making more notes in his little book. Definitely not good.

"We're just going to take her in for a couple hours of observation," said one of the paramedics to Officer Hunter. "She seems fine, but you never know."

The fact that this particular medic was about six-two and solid muscle was probably the reason that Hope wasn't putting up a fight. If anything, she was gazing at the first responder dreamily and rubbing her head even more.

For once I was happy to see her man lust rear its ugly head. Maybe it would keep her from focusing too much on the details of what had just happened here.

"I'll call your parents," I said. "I'll have them meet you at the hospital."

I watched as the medics loaded her into the back of the ambulance before turning to the officer as he exited my busted-up coffee shop and bakery. I really wanted to follow my best friend and make sure she really was okay, but I had a more pressing conversation to have with my aunts.

"So," said the officer, "I think I have enough for now, but I may have some follow-up questions."

Of course you will, I think.

"And I really don't think you should be walking home if that was what you were planning," he added.

"How'd you know?"

"Your friend said your aunt was sending someone to pick you up. No need. I'll drop you off."

I opened my mouth to argue, but the look he gave me silenced all objections.

"Fine. Just let me lock up and grab my purse." This was going to be a long night.

Chapter Three

If there was one thing my aunts were known for, it would probably be scaring the beejeezus out of the town folk, but that would only be if you asked the town folk. But no, that's not it. It would be their southern hospitality when it came to making strangers feel welcome in their home. Because truth be known, only strangers would come and sit in their home.

The house was a sprawling custom-built contemporary in the style of the old Victorians that used to dot the landscapes of North Carolina before the age of the McMansion: two floors of gracious living plus a full basement that ran the entire length of the home. The main floor and the basement opened onto sprawling decks that overlooked a picturesque backyard of mature trees and a babbling creek.

The home was part of an enclave of homes that sat up a winding series of roads along the top of a ridge. They were known as "back deck homes" because they all commanded such beautiful views of the woods, and neighbors would often converse with one another in the evenings while enjoying a glass of wine, waiting for the grills heat up.

The fact that they enjoyed such peace and solitude while only a short forty-five-minute drive to a major city never ceased to amaze me. The fact that Trinity Cove itself was almost considered a suburb of the city was one of the perks that made living here tolerable. We were the only access point to Singing Falls, so all traffic flowed through us. The ridge where my aunts lived ran above the roads that circled around to the falls, so that meant for the most part I got to miss all the congestion moving through the main streets. Until I had to go in to work, that is.

So having said all that, it stands to reason my aunts would invite Officer Hunter in for some tea, and they weren't about to take no for an answer.

"Oh, I'm sure the officer has more…rounds to do or something," I tried.

"Actually I'm officially off the clock," he replied. "But I don't want to be a bother this late at night."

"Nonsense," replied Aunt Vivian. "I insist you come in for some tea. My sister just put on a fresh pot and it's the least we can do."

"Well…" He hesitated. "I have always wanted to see inside one of these houses."

"Well, that settles it then," said Aunt Viv, ushering him inside the door. "Come on in and I'll show you around."

Like most officers, he wore one of those ridiculous broad-rimmed hats. I'd always wondered what the purpose of those was other than to funnel rain into your car when they stopped you during a storm and leaned down to ask for your license and registration through your barely cracked window. Whatever its purpose, he was kind enough to remove it as he stepped through the entryway. His head immediately craned back as he took in the twenty-five-foot ceiling in the expansive great room. To his left, stairs ran up to the second floor, spilling into the exposed loft area. The great room opened directly into the massive kitchen, complete with sixteen feet of granite island in the middle of the space. Beyond that was a set of French doors that led out to the deck overlooking the woods.

"Wow," he said. "This is far more impressive on the inside than the outside would lead you to believe."

"Well don't just stand their gawking," Aunt Vivian said, "come on into the kitchen and get you a cup. It's a beautiful night. We can drink it on the deck."

She gave me a look that said *don't even think about ditching*, and smiled as we all walked into the kitchen where Aunt Lena was just removing a kettle from the large, six-burner gas stove. She had already taken out a selection of teas and had them lining the island.

"Pick whichever you like, dear," she said, waving a hand over the selection. She had also placed four cups on the island as well as some sugar, honey, and lemon.

"Oh, I have no idea what's good," replied Officer Hunter. "Why don't you surprise me?"

Aunt Lena's eye browns arched in surprise and she couldn't help but chuckle slightly to herself. "Oh, now that I can do."

I frowned at my aunt as I moved to pick out some tea. Aunt Lena was the more somber of my two aunts. Her face was almost always contorted in a frown or some other mask of disapproval, yet here she was playing hostess to someone she had most likely never laid eyes on before tonight. I looked questioningly at Aunt Vivian and she just smiled at me, her gray eyes dancing in the soft overhead lighting.

I just shook my head and picked out some Earl Grey for myself. Whatever my aunts were up to was between them. But I hoped they realized that the more time they wasted with this guy meant the more time was passing before I could tell them what happened at the coffee shop. Which meant any possibility of tracking the black magic that was capable of raising a dead man from his grave was slowly slipping away. Aunt Vivian took the officer by the arm and escorted him out onto the deck, remarking all the while about how beautiful the night was.

As soon as they were out of earshot, I whispered urgently to Aunt Lena.

"Aunt Lena! I don't know what is going on here, but I really, really need to talk to you and Aunt Vivian! Something really weird and scary just happened to me tonight!"

"Shhh!" she practically hissed, her perma-scowl returning at once. "We can chat later! Right now we have a guest to attend to." She suddenly smiled mischievously. "A rather handsome guest, wouldn't you say? Plus, I didn't see a ring on his finger."

I actually felt myself blush at her comment. Dear Goddess, please tell me this isn't why they are doing this? Are my two aunts actually trying to set me up with a town officer? Suddenly I wanted to set my cup back on the counter and bolt for the stairs and the safety of my room. Aunt Lena must have sensed what I was thinking because she fixed me with a look that said, "I'll turn you to stone if you take one step out of this kitchen."

I sighed. Fine. The sooner this charade was over with, the faster I could get down to real business with the aunts. I turned on my heel, gave my aunt one last look over my shoulder, then walked out to the deck.

There was a large gas grill against the rails opposite the doors. Beside that there was a large six-person dining table covered by an even larger umbrella decorated with an array of hanging lights. Walking past that, I came to an intimate seating area bathed by warm, flickering outdoor candles. Aunt Vivian and Officer Hunter were sitting there talking quietly.

"So," I heard Aunt Vivian say as I sat down in a chair opposite the two of them, "you were just about to tell me your name. Unless you want us to remain so formal with you."

"Oh, no, ma'am," he replied. "My name is Cody. Cody Hunter."

Of course it was. I'm thankful that the flickering light hid my eye roll.

"Well what a beautiful name. So strong and manly," my aunt added. "Don't you think so, Allie?"

Jesus.

"I guess," I replied. "If you're a regular on a CW show."

I smirked, confident that my aunt wouldn't catch the reference, but equally confident that the good officer would. Before either of them could say anything, Aunt Lena came up beside us carrying a tray with a few more mugs arranged on top. She handed one to Aunt Vivian and another to Cody Hunter before settling down on a small loveseat next to us.

"Lena," said Aunt Vivian, "this polite young officer's name is Cody. Cody Hunter."

"Really?" said Aunt Lena. "Are you related to the Hunters over on Simmons Lane, or the Hunters of Trinity Drive?"

"Trinity Drive," Officer Hunter replied. "My family has been in this area for several generations."

"Oh, we are quite familiar with your family," said Aunt Lena, sitting back. "Drink your tea while it's hot, dear."

He smiled and raised the cup to his lips, blowing lightly

across the surface of the liquid before sipping gingerly. "Wow, that's really good." He took another sip, this one a little bigger.

"So I'm surprised that you and Allie don't know one another from school," said Aunt Vivian. "Were you in the same classes?"

"Honestly I don't remember, Aunt Vivian," I said.

"Oh, I remember you," said Cody. "You were a grade ahead of me and ran with a different crowd. We had an economics class together but that was it."

Great. I barely remember Economics, let alone who was in the class with me. Despite myself, I glanced at him a little closer and searched my memories. Nope. He was not bad-looking to be honest; his square cut jawline and brown eyes matched his name. But I certainly didn't remember him from school. Despite his assertion that I ran with a crowd, nothing could have been further from the truth. Other than Hope, I despised being around other teenagers.

"Interesting. Allie had a knack for keeping to herself. That could explain why she is still lacking in the social graces to this day," said Aunt Vivian. It was almost as if she were reading my mind. Hell, for all I knew she probably was.

"So where's Gar?" I asked, trying to steer the conversation away.

"He's in his room playing video games or doing whatever it is that young men his age like to do," said Aunt Lena. "Don't you go bothering him now; you just sit right here with the grown-ups and talk to this handsome young man."

I could feel my cheeks burn as Cody's eyes wandered my way. I immediately began drinking my tea, turning my body slightly away from his gaze.

"Oh, that's okay," said Cody. "I'm sure Allie has other

The Girl with the Good Magic

things on her mind than sitting here chatting with me. I mean, why should tonight be any different from any other time we've run across each other?"

I immediately spun around. "You mean the one class we had in high school four years ago?"

"No, no," he said, holding up a hand. "That's not what I meant. I come into your coffee shop almost daily. I see you around town quite a bit actually."

"Stalk much?" I didn't mean it; it slipped out before I could edit the thought.

"All right, that's enough," said Aunt Vivian. Her voice has taken on a slightly different edge, one that Cody wouldn't recognize but I did.

"I think I should be going," said Cody, moving to sit his cup on the small coffee table in front of him.

"Nonsense," said Aunt Vivian.

Now I was really annoyed. It would serve them right if I just got up and went to my room without telling them what happened. Let them figure out there's a rogue witch somewhere in town raising the dead.

"Finish your tea first and then you can be on your way if you'd like," said Aunt Vivian, her voice becoming just a little more singsong.

Cody obeyed, lifting the cup to his lips and taking in a couple of large gulps. That was when I noticed his movements. He was a little sluggish and off-kilter, an almost imperceptible sway settling into his shoulders as he placed the now empty cup down. I glanced again at Aunt Lena and notice her lips were moving. She seemed to be speaking, or at least mouthing words silently to herself.

Oh no. She wouldn't dare! She was casting, working some type of spell on Cody! She must have drugged his tea as well. That would explain his sudden lack of coordination.

"So that was some nasty business with the animal attack that everyone was talking about today," said Aunt Vivian casually. "Were you out on that call? It must have been so scary."

"Oh, ma'am," Cody started, "I'm not really allowed to talk about official business…"

"Oh, come now," my aunt continued. "This isn't business if it's just among friends. I mean, Allie here is your friend, and she is my niece. I'm sure neither of us want to see anything bad happen to her; so all I'm asking is that, if you know there is anything bad happening around here, you could tell us so we can protect ourselves, right?"

I glared at Aunt Vivian, but bite my tongue. Part of me wanted to see how this played out.

"Well…I guess that's true," said Cody, his words beginning to slur ever so slightly.

I glanced over at Aunt Lena. Her lips were moving at an even faster clip now. Her eyes had gone ghostly and gray under the strain of the magic she was pulling.

"Cody." Aunt Vivian leaned in. "Was there a body found at Singing Falls today?"

"Yes."

"Was it a fall from the rocks? An accidental death?"

"No."

"Was it an animal attack?"

Cody hesitated, his eyelids at half mast. "I…don't know."

Aunt Vivian looked at her sister briefly and then continued. "What do you mean? Surely the coroner has some idea."

"It looked like an animal did it, but there isn't anything in these parts that would do that to a body."

"Explain," said Aunt Vivian.

The Girl with the Good Magic

"The throat was torn open, so bad that most of the neck was missing. The head was hanging on by a strip of skin. The spine and larynx was tossed aside next to the body. The chest was mangled, but not by teeth. It looked like the ribcage had been split open by hand...or claws. The heart was missing, but other than that, the body had not been chewed at or eaten."

I clamped a hand over my mouth as I felt a wave of nausea hit me.

"Were samples taken from the body?" Vivian asked.

"Oh yeah. We found some weird hairs around the neck wound. They also took tissue samples and blood from around the body just in case some of it came from whatever did it. Working theory is it was a bear attack. One must have wandered down from the high country. At least that's what we are supposed to tell everyone."

"What's the unofficial theory?"

"No one will come right out and say it, but everyone is whispering that maybe *they* are back. You know, the werewolves."

I gasped audibly and Aunt Vivian shot me a look. I knew not to speak aloud; it can break the delicate spell Aunt Lena was weaving. I let my eyes apologize before my aunt continued with Cody.

"Cody, you have been so helpful. I want you to do one last thing for me. As soon as the reports come in from the coroner and the lab, would you be a dear and bring them to us here at the house?"

Cody frowned, but then nodded in agreement.

"And Cody, as soon as you do that, you will forget all about having done so. You will also forget that this conversation ever happened. We had tea, made small talk, and you enjoyed your time with us and my niece. That's all, okay?"

"Okie dokie," he replied cheerfully.

Aunt Lena leaned back, cutting off whatever spell she had cast. Aunt Vivian snapped her finger sharply in front of Cody's face and he was instantly aware and back to being his normal self.

"Oh wow," he said, looking at his watch, "where'd the time go? Thank you ladies for such a wonderful evening and that tea…I definitely need to pick some of that up. But I need to be going. Busy day tomorrow."

We all rose and thanked the young officer for his help and walked him to the door. He nodded again, placing the wide-brimmed hat back on his head, and headed down the drive to his car.

I turned to my aunts after shutting the door and couldn't control my excitement.

"Holy shit!" I exclaimed before I could stop myself. "When are you guys going to teach me the good stuff like that?"

"Allie!" said Aunt Lena. "Language!"

Chapter Four

I headed back to the cafe the next morning after stopping in to check on Hope. Other than a serious headache she was no worse for the wear. Thankfully her memory was a little more fuzzy, and she was taking full advantage of the light pain pills they had given her. The doctors had told her a couple days of rest and she'd be back to normal.

Good. That gave me a couple of days to try and get handle on what was going on around here without having to worry about the safety of my best friend. I let my mind wander back to the previous night's events. I had filled my aunts in on what had happened at the coffee shop. For some reason they weren't impressed by the fact that I was able to create my first manifestation of magical force to defend myself. They also didn't seem to be terribly upset over the fact that I had been attacked by what appeared to be a zombie freshly risen from the grave.

"Obviously you were mistaken," said my Aunt Lena. "The trauma of it all must have scared you so deeply your mind played tricks on you."

"Tricks?" I replied. "I'm not a child, Aunt Lena. That was no trick. The smell was real and everything about it just felt...I don't know, rotted and dead. And it was so strong..."

"Well there you go," said Aunt Vivian. "Zombies aren't very strong. They mostly just shamble around bemoaning the fact that they can't really do anything to anyone other than bite them."

"Well yeah, if you go by *Walking Dead* lore," I replied. "But what if this was different? What if *The Walking Dead* has it all wrong and those are just some dude's mish-mashed ideas about what zombies are?"

"Allie," said Aunt Lena, "enough already. It was probably some dope fiend looking to rob you of enough cash to get his next fix. I've heard men on angel dust can be very strong."

"Angel dust?" I said. "Yes, that might by plausible. If this were 1975!" I took some deep breaths trying to calm my nerves.

"Honey, believe me, there are no such things as zombies. They don't exist," said Aunt Vivian.

"Oh yeah? Well you also said there are no such things as werewolves either and that all the stuff Mom used to tell Gar and me about how she helped eradicate them was just her being delusional. Yet when Cody mentioned the word you didn't seem to think he was so crazy. And for that matter, most people also don't believe in witches, yet here we stand."

Aunt Lena whirled on me, her eyes blazing.

"We are agents of light and nature," she said. "Don't ever forget that. We are not creatures forged out of darkness and the mad ramblings of a ..."

"Sister!" interjected Aunt Vivian. "Have a care lest you confuse the child." Her words seemed to strike a chord with my other aunt, who immediately fell silent. I looked at her closely and she avoided my gaze. Best believe I made a mental note to have her finish that sentence the next time we were alone.

"Allie," said Aunt Vivian as she took on a much calmer and more soothing tone, "we are worried about your safety. There is obviously something going on in this town, something not of the supernatural variety, but of the everyday, mundane, violent male variety, which if you ask me is far deadlier than any perceived supernatural threat could ever be. The three of us come from a very old line of witches. We can be very powerful. But even we can't raise the dead. To my knowledge there isn't anyone out there left that can do such things."

"Left?" I said. "You mean at one point someone could have done this?"

My aunt hesitated before answering. "Perhaps at one time. But such a manipulation of the natural forces was outlawed many generations ago. Such old and dark magic died out long before you were born. Whatever is going on out there is the work of man. Or, as Officer Cody will come to realize, an animal that has wandered too far from its feeding grounds, driven to attack someone out of fear and desperation."

I looked at Aunt Lena and she smiled, nodding her agreement.

"But I must say," added Aunt Lena, "congrats on manifesting a hex. That takes real skill, and the fact that you did it without instruction means you're a natural when it comes to magic."

"A hex? You mean that blue ball I created?"

"Yes, dear. It's called a hex. It seems you're a natural at it, just like your mother," said Aunt Vivian.

"Does that mean you're going to start teaching me more magic and spells? Like what you did to Cody tonight?"

"That," said Aunt Vivian, "was a necessary evil. Subverting free will is something I never want to see you mess around with. We would never do such a thing if it weren't imperative that we know what they know."

"By 'they' you mean the norms?" I asked.

"That's a vulgar term," replied Aunt Lena. "Your brother is a 'norm,' you know. Not his fault he was born one of the only males in a line of female witches."

I shuffled my feet and didn't meet her eyes. "But you're saying that there could be something out there we need to be aware of? Something…that's not norm?"

"Maybe," said Aunt Vivian. "Either way, we need to know what to be ready for. Just in case."

That was all I had been able to get out of them. I didn't see them on my way out of the house. It was just as well. Zombie or crazed crackhead, they would not have wanted me coming back to the shop alone until they knew what was really going on. I just wanted to get back to some kind of normal rhythm, and the best way to do that was to go back to work. Plus, I wanted to try some residual tracking spells I had been working on to try and pick up any trail that thing could have left behind.

I wasn't exactly sure it would work. It was a spell my aunts had taught me to locate mundane items, like car keys and my student IDs as a child. But it was all about moving energy around, attaching it to a signature that was imprinted on your mind, and then following that energy to the item. Granted, I had no idea if it worked on a living, or in this case an undead, being, but I figured it would be worth a shot. Especially since the creature was so prominently fixed in my mind.

The first thing I did was probe for Aunt Viv's wards to make sure they were still in place. Not that they had been the least bit helpful last night, but it was a little reassuring knowing that they were still up and guarding the shop from any potential mystical threat.

I locked the door behind me and surveyed the damage from last night's fight. In the light of day, it didn't look quite as bad as I thought it would. There were only a couple of chairs and tables that had been tossed aside, and a few broken cups. The worst damage had been done to the counter bar and display case. The zombie, which I was sure was what the creature was, had busted the counter all to hell. I'd have to call the insurance adjusters for that and file a claim. It would mean closing up shop for a couple of days, but we would manage. I had already called the two summer high-schoolers who were scheduled to come in today and told them what happened. They pretended to be bummed but in reality were probably just as happy to have a couple days off at the beginning of their summer vacation.

Mess aside, I made my way behind the counter to do what I felt needed to be done.

I walked over to the spot where I had immolated the zombie. That spell alone had nearly wiped me out. Creating normal fire was hard enough, but magical fire was on another level entirely. It consumed everything that it was focused on, but did no damage to the surrounding areas. In the zombie's case, it was literally eaten by the flames, but they didn't so much as singe the wood flooring beneath him. This was the only part that I altered when I told my aunts about the attack. I told them that the creature had burst into flames when I stabbed it, releasing the dark magic. I had no intention of telling them that I had created a mystical conflagration that had destroyed all evidence of the creature. I wasn't ready for them to start asking questions about just how much I had been practicing the arts.

If they had their way, I wouldn't know any magic. But magic was innate for me. If they didn't teach me how to control it, there was no telling what could happen. Not long after my thirteenth birthday, I started having nightmares that I couldn't remember, and during those dreams, my latent abilities would flare out of control, damaging lamps, mirrors, and furniture in my bedroom. It all came to a head one evening during a particularly violent nightmare when my aunts came into my bedroom to find the curtains on fire. That was when they decided it was time to help me at least control my magic, the idea being that by giving me tiny incantations that would require great focus, it would bleed my magic so that it never became too pent up. For the most part, it worked. But as I grew, I started experimenting.

Plus I discovered the internet. You'd be amazed at what you can find out in chat rooms and on forums. Granted, there was a lot of bogus nonsense about magic posted all over the web, but every now and then I'd find a little nugget of truth, or meet someone online who knew a thing or two about spells and how they worked. That knowledge, coupled with my natural abilities to channel magic, had helped me grow my abilities.

Far more than what the aunts knew about. Or at least I hoped they didn't know. Only Gar knew what I was up to, but he had always kept my secrets, just as I had always kept his.

I swept all of that out of my mind and concentrated. I reached down inside myself and pulled at my magic. Closing my eyes, I built a mental image in my mind of the creature that attacked me. I call to the magic and invoked a spell of retrieval, focusing on the spot where the zombie lay before I had lit its ass up.

Technically there was nothing left for my magic to track, but maybe, just maybe I could latch onto the signature of whatever had raised it from the grave. If I could, then maybe I could follow that and find out who, or what, was capable of creating zombies. For a second I hesitated as a thought chilled my spine. What if I did find the source? Then what? I was a witch with the barest understanding of magic. What was I going to do if I ran into someone with the power to command the dead?

Stop it, Allie.

I pushed that thought from my head and focused on the task at hand. First things first. I sent my magic into the ether, trying to grasp onto something, anything, that didn't belong in my shop. I was about to give up when I felt it: a small tug at the filament of magic I was tethered to. It was almost imperceptible, like the feel of a fish nibbling at your bait and sending the slightest shiver up your line and into your pole, so slight that at first you aren't sure you really felt it, until it happens a second time, only slightly harder.

Whatever it was it had my attention now. I zoned in, focusing on the tiny, wiggling little worm trying to scurry back into a rotting apple.

"Whatcha doing?"

The suddenness of the voice coming from behind me was like having a bucket of cold water dumped over my head. The shock snapped my tenuous connection with the spell, severing any link that I was fishing for. The worm, apple and entire damn orchard disappeared.

"Goddamnit!" I said with a start, spinning around.

Standing behind me, just inside the door, was Officer Cody Hunter.

"What are you doing here?" I asked, "and for that matter how did you get in?"

"The door is pretty smashed. The knob doesn't turn, but it's off the frame enough that all you have to do is give it a push to open it."

I looked over his shoulder and see the door sitting open. It never occurred to me that it could be damaged, but after seeing the job that zombie did on the counter, I shouldn't be surprised that he had also managed to fuck up my door. I walked around from behind the counter to stand in front of the officer.

"Are you sure you should be in here alone?' he asked. "What if the robber were to come back?"

"Oh, so now it's a robber. My aunts think it was some kind of crazed druggie looking for a quick fix."

"Well, your aunts could be correct in that. Places like this are seen as easy targets. They have cash onboard, low-tech defenses and…no offense, usually have inexperienced high-schoolers or women working at them."

For some reason hearing that made my internal temperature shoot up. Had he really just said that?

"I'm sorry, did you just blame the victim of an attack for that attack?" Please let him say something smug, 'cause there's a forty-eight-hour itching spell I read about that I was just dying to try.

"No, not at all," he stammered. "I meant that you have to always be aware of who might see you as prey. I mean… not prey, but a target." He scratched his head before continuing. "I mean…it's the training. We get all these facts drilled into our heads and sometimes they just leak out. But I assure you I didn't mean that as an insult. If anything, you look like you can handle yourself."

Did he just blush? Despite myself I almost smiled at his discomfort.

He held up his hands, palms out. "Before you say anything, I meant that you don't look like someone that would be afraid, even after the encounter that you had here last night."

That did make me smile. For the first time I noticed that he was not wearing his police uniform and annoying wide-brimmed hat. His dark hair was ruffled and standing at odd angles, but seemed to fit his strong, etched features. He was dressed like someone from the city however, wearing a purple and blue gingham shirt and khaki-colored Chubby's. Definitely not what I expected from a local. He caught me looking and cleared his throat.

"What? You were expecting blue jeans and a wife beater?"

I frowned. Whatever I may have been thinking was gone. "I hate that term. Why not just call it a tank?"

Now it was his turn to look away. "I'm sorry. To be honest, I hate that term too. It just came out."

"You have that problem with a lot of words it seems. Maybe you should get that checked." I turned to head back to the counter but stopped when I realized that I still didn't know why he was here.

He must have been able to read the unspoken question in my eyes through my annoyance.

"Oh yeah," he said, flinching, "I wanted to bring you this." For the first time I notice the cloth messenger bag slung obliquely across his body. He reached in, pulled out a plain manila envelope and stepped toward me, holding it out in front of him.

"What's that?" I eyed the package suspiciously but made no move to take it.

"It's the coroner's report on the blood and tissue samples from the body up at Singing Falls. Oh, and we got an ID on it as well, so I figured you guys would need that as well."

For once I was actually speechless. I felt like a buffoon when I realized I was literally standing there with my mouth open.

"What?" he said. "Your aunt told me to bring it to you when I got the results. I was on my way up to your house when I drove by and saw you working in here. Hey, speaking of your aunts, what did they do to me last night? I felt really weird. At first I wasn't sure it happened when I woke up this morning, but then I remembered what they wanted. How'd they do that?"

"You're not supposed to remember anything other than the key command they gave you. After fulfilling it you should forget everything," I stammered.

"Figured as much. So is it true? The things that some people whisper about your family. Are y'all really witches?"

He looked around, wrinkling his nose.

"Oh yeah, I meant to ask you last night; what is that smell in here? Smells like you burnt something up really, really bad."

Chapter Five

I found my aunts sitting on the deck enjoying a midday cocktail.

"Here you go," I said, dropping the envelope on the table in front of them.

"What's this?" Aunt Lena said, eying the package.

"It's the coroner's report you asked Cody for last night."

Both of their eyes widened as Aunt Vivian picked the envelope up and opened it.

"How did you get this?" asked Aunt Lena suspiciously.

"He brought it to me," I answered, crossing my arms in front of me. "At the coffee shop."

"What? He was supposed to bring that here," said Aunt Vivian.

"Yeah, and from what you told me he was also supposed to forget doing it and everything that happened last night," I said. "But that didn't happen. He remembers all of it."

"Not possible," said Aunt Lena, looking at her sister. "Either the spell or the tea alone would have wiped his memory. The combination of the two should have completely blanked him. Are you sure?"

I nodded, my attitude changing when I noticed the look of concern on my aunts' faces. "What's wrong? And please don't say there is nothing to worry about. Obviously something is going on."

They looked at one another before Aunt Lena let out a long sigh.

"She's not a child anymore," she said to Aunt Vivian. "And as we said, we can't protect them forever."

"Protect us from what?" I asked. "And by 'us' I assume you're talking about myself and Gar?"

"And others," said Aunt Vivian cryptically.

I pulled out a chair and sat down at the end of the table.

"There is no way that young man should have been able to shake off that spell," said Aunt Vivian. "Are you sure you cast it correctly?"

"Of course I did," replied Aunt Lena. "Are you questioning my skills?" Her eyes squinted at her sister.

"Well, you're no spring chicken," said Aunt Vivian. "You're not the witch you once were, you know."

"How dare you! My casting has only gotten stronger with age and you know it. I'll show you…"

"Okay, enough," I interjected before this conversation completely derailed. "Let's focus and stay on subject here. First, you're admitting that you did work magic on Cody last night and for some reason it didn't work. Any thoughts as to why?"

They exchanged looks, and for a second I could almost swear they exchanged some type of non-verbal communication as well.

"The spell your aunt cast was one that not only compelled him to speak the truth, but should have also acted as a veil over his mind as well," said Aunt Vivian. "It should have prompted him to follow the commands he was given, and then forget it ever happened. The tea he was given acted as a mild relaxant to make him even more susceptible to suggestion. He had information we needed and there was not time to be subtle about getting it."

"Okay, so just how powerful are you?" I asked. "And while you're opening up, are these learned skills or were you born with them?"

"A combination of both," Aunt Lena said. "The potions and herbs we use are learned. The spell used to subvert human will is learned as well, but it is bolstered by a witch's will."

"The magic that runs in our family is deep and powerful," said Aunt Vivian. "It's both learned and intrinsic to us."

"So who taught you?" I asked. "And why didn't you teach me?"

Aunt Vivian took in a deep breath and looked out over the railing at the rolling treetops around us. The breeze whispered through the canopy of old growth as it made its way across the wooded landscape.

"Your mother never wanted you to learn," she replied quietly. "She was afraid to have you pulled into our world, and made us promise that we would not bring you into this. She said that there was no longer any need for us to practice and therefore there was no need to involve you in the lore."

"That was her parting request before she left us," said Aunt Lena, her eyes growing misty.

I didn't say anything as I thought through this. They didn't often speak of my mother. It was a painful subject for them and I knew they missed her terribly. Plus, while I still had memories of her, Gar didn't, and they were always wary of bringing her up around him. As much as I wanted more information about her, I sensed that this was not the time.

"So what's changed?" I asked. "Why did my mother say there was no longer a need for magic?"

"That's a longer story," replied Aunt Lena. "One that we will tell you, but first, we need to look at this report."

I started to argue, but kept quiet as Aunt Vivian pulled the contents of the envelope out and laid them on the table. There were pages of printed reports along with myriad pictures accompanying them. She flipped through the pages until she found what she was looking for.

"Cause of death, excessive trauma to the torso and neck consistent with animal attack," she read. She turned a few more pages before continuing. "Tissue and hair samples removed from the wounds were type and cross matches with…" She paused, reading silently.

"With what?" I asked.

She looked up before continuing. "It says there is an eighty-four percent chance the hairs are canine, but of a strain that can't be one hundred percent identified. There is a chance the samples were contaminated due to the presence of human DNA in the torso samples, but animal DNA was found in samples from the throat."

The pictures that accompanied this section of the report were stomach-churning close-ups of the victim's rent chest and slashed throat. I swallowed the lump that I felt rising in my own throat and looked away.

"So then it really was an animal attack," I said.

"Appears so," said Aunt Vivian.

"Damnit!" I shout and was immediately sorry for the profanity in front of my family members. "I'm sorry for that, but after all these years I can read you both. Neither of you believe that. What are you not telling me?"

"The report is probably correct," said Aunt Vivian, "but it's also wrong. It states the only way there could be contamination of this order is if one of the police officers, or whoever found the body, messed with the crime scene. But what they aren't assuming is that it could be the same person."

I let that sink in for a second before responding. "But you said there are no such things as werewolves."

"Well...what I should have said was there is no such thing as werewolves *anymore*."

"So then the stories my mother told us were true? She killed all the wolves?"

"She might have had a little help," said Aunt Lena with a twinkle in her eyes.

"But I assure you, Allie, this was not a werewolf. There is one obvious explanation we are overlooking," said Aunt Vivian.

"What's that?" I ask.

"That this was done by a man with a large dog. The dog could have killed this person and then the man harvested his organs."

I arch an eyebrow at them both. "Let me guess, in order to feed his angel dust addiction?"

The look they gave me let me know neither of them was amused.

Aunt Vivian flipped more pages until she found what she was looking for.

"It says here the victim has been identified as an Alexander Tilden from Queen City, North Carolina. A native."

"Does that name ring a bell?" I asked.

"Perhaps," said Aunt Lena. "It does sound familiar. We should go look into it." They both got up, gathered the paperwork and headed for the door that led into the kitchen.

"Wait, that's it?" I asked. "That's all you're going to say? What about that thing that attacked me last night? What about the fact that Cody not only shook off your spell but he could smell..." I stopped, aware of what I almost said.

"He could smell what?" Aunt Vivian said, looking closely at me.

"He could smell something in the coffee shop," I added. I was careful not to tell an outright lie because that was something the two of them would have been able to pick up on immediately. "I told you that thing that attacked me smelled dead. Why would he be able to smell that?"

"Hmmm," said Aunt Lena. "Maybe there is more to the good officer than meets the eye."

I almost snorted. "Yeah. Like a Decepticon."

"More like someone you need to keep an eye on until we can figure out what is going on," said Aunt Vivian. She turned to face me, smiling warmly. "Allie. You have a lot of questions, rightfully so. I promise we will answer them all as soon as we know a little more about what is going on. But until then, I need you to be smart. Stay close to the house or the coffee shop. Both are well warded. Find your brother and make sure he stays put as well."

I knew there was no point in arguing with her, so I just nodded.

"And Allie," said Aunt Lena, "until we know more about him, stay away from that officer. Even though he is very cute."

With that, they both disappeared into the house, no doubt headed for their study. I walked into the kitchen, filled with more questions than answers. I opened the refrigerator, took out a bottle of water and sipped it slowly as my mind raced. I had an idea, one that the aunts wouldn't like and which they certainly would never allow me to attempt.

Of course, what they don't know can't hurt them. It might hurt me after they found out, but for now it was worth a try.

I scooped up my keys from the entryway table where I had dropped them and ran to the foot of the stairs.

"I'm headed back to the coffee shop. I need to make sure everything is secure for the day if I'm not going to be there," I called up the stairs. No answer. Good; that meant they were plotting God knows what in their study. I slipped out the door and bounded to my car, only to find the passenger seat occupied.

"Gar," I said, "get out. I need to run back down to the shop. The aunts said you need to stay in the house until they're convinced all is safe."

He looked at me, his eyes twinkling as he smirked. He didn't have my red hair, but we had the same green eyes, and his shone mischievously.

"What they said was for you to look after me."

"Were you eavesdropping again?"

"No. I was on the bottom deck and couldn't help but overhear your conversation. I wasn't trying to listen, so technically that's not eavesdropping."

"Gar, I'm not going to argue. I won't be gone long, so just wait inside until I get back."

"C'mon," he said, "we both know you're not going to the shop. I may not know where you're going, but I guarantee it's not there."

I eyed my little brother carefully, trying to gauge just what exactly he may know.

"Wherever you're going," he continued, "I want to go as well. You know the aunts always know when we lie to them. This way, when they ask if you kept an eye on me you can truthfully said yes."

I hesitate, considering this option only for a briefest of seconds before shaking my head.

"No dice." I said. I open his car door and motion for him to get out. "Get out now or I'll tell them what's on your computer browsing history."

Instantly I can sense the change in his demeanor as he narrows his eye to slits and stares at me.

"Go ahead," he said, "and I'll tell them what's on yours. I'm sure they'd love to know where you're learning about magic and how to cast spells!"

We stared at one another, deadlocked. Finally I slammed his door shut and hopped behind the wheel.

"Put your seat belt on and you're not to breathe a word of this to either of them, agreed?"

He nodded emphatically and buckled himself in.

"Where are we going?" he asked.

"Singing Falls. I want to get a look at the spot where the body was found."

"Hells yeah!" he shouted excitedly as we pulled out.

"Gar! Language!"

Chapter Six

We made the drive to the outskirts of town in silence, me focusing on the road, Gar staring out the passenger window in silence, watching the scenery whiz by. More than once I was tempted to ask him just how much he had overheard. What I really wanted to know was just how much he knew about my extracurricular studies.

"How come they never talk about Mom?" he asked out of the blue without turning to face me.

"Honestly, I don't know. From what I can tell, they have always had a strong relationship as siblings, so I'm not sure what happened."

"Is it because of the witchcraft or the fact that she said she killed all the werewolves?" he said.

"Gar...you know those don't exist, right?"

"Which one? The werewolves or the witches?" This time he turned in his seat to face me. I could feel his eyes burrowing into me.

I didn't say anything; instead I just gripped the wheel harder.

"That's what I thought," he said, answering his own question.

Neither of us said anything else until I pulled into the gravel parking area that opened onto a maze of trails that headed into dense, old growth woods. There were only a handful of cars in the lot. Word of the dead body had probably spread like wildfire and was keeping the peepers away. Only the truly hardcore hikers or the hardcore curiosity freaks were venturing up to the falls today. I glanced over at Gar as we shut the car doors.

"I'm still not sure this is a good idea," I said. "You being here I mean."

"Well I'm certainly not staying in the car at this point," he answered.

We headed toward the main pass that would take us up to the falls. It was about an hour and a half hike from where we were and I started to worry about the daylight.

"Not that one," Gar said. "The west passage opens up where they found the body." He pointed to a break in the shrubbery opposite the path I was going to take.

"How do you know?" I asked.

"Because that's where all the action was happening when I came by yesterday. It's also where your boyfriend the cop was taken, along with some of the paramedics."

I ignored his grin and refused to give him the satisfaction of a reply.

"Plus, it's a quicker route to the falls. Unless of course you want to be up there when it starts getting dark…" His tone became a lot more serious, and much as I may have wanted to, I knew arguing that point was useless. I shrugged and we both headed for the west passage. We passed the sign marking the beginning of the trail that stated the west passage was the most difficult route and was for experienced hikers only. We had both made the hike countless times so we weren't deterred by the warning.

Once we were on the path, we were immediately greeted with the changing light as the forest canopy intertwined high above our heads, diffusing the light and reducing visibility by several degrees. Five minutes into the hike and the only sounds we heard came from the frogs, a few chirping birds, and the restless creaking of tree branches shifting around us. The western-facing path took a very steep, vertical ascent up the mountainside. Whereas the other passes offered a more circular and scenic route, this one was the straight line from point A, the lot, to the falls, which resided at point B.

We made our way up the trail, careful of the footing and using the outgrowth of tangled vines and tree roots that sprouted from the sides of the mountain for handholds. I looked back at Gar to make sure he was doing all right. Not that I should have worried; he was in excellent physical shape. He was one of the co-captains for the cross country track team and this was probably little more than a light practice day for him. I wished it were that easy for me. A half hour into the march and I was starting to huff. Serves me right for never doing anything strenuous, I thought. The climb was steeper than I remembered, but the good news was that it would also shave off about a half hour on the time it would take to reach the base of the falls. I stopped to catch my breath at a small break on the trail and waited for Gar to limber up beside me.

"I'm sorry," I said between gulps of air.

"For...?" He seemed genuinely perplexed.

"For saying that I would tell the aunts about your internet searches."

He immediately glanced away, a small blush creeping

across his features. He mumbled something I didn't catch as he obviously struggled to find something, anything else, to talk about.

"I would never say anything," I added, grabbing him by the elbow to make him face me. "It's no one's business but your own."

"I don't know what you're talking about," he said, running a nervous hand through his damp hair. "I mean, yeah, I might have looked up some things as a joke...but that's it."

I could tell he was becoming too uncomfortable and decided to drop the matter. I changed the subject as we continued our hike.

"Okay," I said, "so ask me."

"Ask you what?"

"Whatever you want. We've always had each other to rely on. That shouldn't change now. The aunts might keep us in the dark, but we sure as shit shouldn't do it to each other."

He didn't hesitate. "Are you practicing magic spells that you learned online?"

"Sort of. I've met some people in chat rooms that seem to know a thing or two about magic. Real magic. They're helping me and guiding me toward some resources."

"So you and the aunts are not the kind of witches I see on reality shows? The type that talk about spirituality and nature and all that BS, right?"

"No. We are the real thing. At least as far as I can tell."

"Can you ride a broom?"

"Don't be ridicules, Gar," I said as I turned to face him.

"Well I don't know. I have no idea what a 'real' witch is and what they can do."

We climbed a bit farther before he spoke again. "So, what can you do?"

"Little things come easy to me. Kind of in an innate way. Like, I can levitate small objects and move things around with my mind."

"TK? That's cool."

"TK?"

"Yeah, telekinesis. But not sure that would be considered magic."

"Okay, how about this?" I stopped walking and held out my hand, palm up. Concentrating, I breathed out a quick incantation and then added a sin gel word. "Light!" A glowing sphere of blue light, about the size of a basketball, materialized in the air, hovering above my hand.

"Now that's cool," said Gar, reaching out to touch the orb. Before I could stop him, the silence around us was broken by the sudden sound of snapping branches to my left. It was so loud we both looked in that direction and the orb I created fizzled and dissolved with the break in my concentration.

"What was that?" asked Gar. He looked around, then back at me, his eyes wide. "And why is it suddenly so quiet?"

I realized he was right. Every ambient sound from the forest had gone silent. No chirping, no frogs; even the wind seemed to have died.

"It's the woods," I said. "They just go quiet every now and then." I started moving again, and this time Gar hurried to match me step for step.

"You think? I mean, don't you think it's weird that everything is all fine and good until you called up your little glowing ball thingy, and then, poof, everything goes quiet. What was that anyway? What does it do? Oh, and what was in the woods? Do you think whatever you just did attracted it?"

I don't answer as I pick up the pace. Even though I know he didn't mean to, his words gave me a cold chill that ran down my back and drenched me in sweat.

"We need to hurry up," I said. "I want to get there and back before it gets dark." Now I was giving myself a chill. "How much farther until we reach the falls?"

"We should be coming to a clearing, and then the falls are on the other side of that. From what everyone was saying, the body was found against the rocks at the very base, where the swimming hole meets the cliffs."

In the silence, I realized that we could indeed hear the hum of the falls. We were close. Good; the quicker I did this, the better. We broke into the clearing and I was more than a little grateful for the sunlight that was suddenly streaming down on us. Even though it had moved farther away and was beginning to dip in the sky, it did a world of good for my courage. We crossed the small field quickly and headed for the wooded section ahead of us which would open up to a natural swimming hole created by the falls cascading down the rocks.

No matter how many times I had seen the falls, the sheer beauty of the formation always overwhelmed me. Out of the pool, the rocks rose in staccato formation roughly one hundred feet toward the sky. The water that flowed from the top crashed downward, hitting the jutting rocks at various angles while refracting the setting sun, splitting the light into a million phantom rainbows. The hum from the falls vibrated like someone running a wet finger lightly around the rim of a fine crystal glass. It was hypnotic and deadly at the same time. Many college lovebirds had fallen to their doom trying to climb the slick rocks to the apex.

We started to make our way around the pool to the base of the falls. The rocks there were slippery, and the cool spray of mist coming from the falls soaked my hair and clothes. I look back at Gar to make sure he was still behind me.

"It has to be in this area," I said, pointing to a flattened stretch of rocks that ran beneath and behind the falls. It was a great spot for selfies, and I had to admit I'd taken more than my fair share of them from that spot over the years.

We reached an area of rock that had circles in various diameters spray-painted in white along its surface. That had to be where the body was found. Unlike on television shows, they didn't do chalk outlines of bodies in their death poses anymore. I briefly wondered if they had ever really done that before shaking the morbid picture out of my mind.

"What are you going to do?" asked Gar.

I took a deep breath and turned to face him.

"You know that thing that attacked me in the shop?"

"You mean the zombie?"

I narrowed my eyes at him. "How do you know that?"

"I heard you discussing it with the aunts. So was it a zombie?"

"I think so. Anyway, earlier I tried a spell that would locate the source of the magic that created the zombie. It was working, but I was interrupted before I could complete it. I'm going to try something similar here; a revelation spell. Hopefully it will show me what really happened."

I tried to manage a reassuring smile, but I'm pretty sure it came out as the facial equivalent of a shoulder shrug and a glance toward the sky for strength. I could feel that he really wanted to ask me if I knew what I was doing, and since I didn't want to lie to him I said nothing. Instead I set my resolve and turned my back, letting him know that now was not the time for any discussions.

Okay, Allie, what exactly are you planning here? I thought.

The tracking spell was based on an incantation meant to unearth that which was hidden. By all rights, that spell shared all the basics with a revelation spell. It was all a matter of removing impurities to let the truth shine through. Or so I had read. I reached inward, willing my magic to bubble to the surface to do my bidding.

"Well," said Gar, "as creepy as that sounds, I'm kidding of stoked to see what you can do."

"As am I," came a third voice across the opening.

We both whirled around to face two men standing on the opposite side of the water hole. One man was slight of build, dressed in black on black, jeans and a tee shirt. His hair was crew-cut, almost to the point of being bald. His bright eyes seemed to sparkle in the fading sun, but I was pretty sure that had to be trick of the light dancing off the water.

The man standing beside him was mountainous in comparison. He had to be all of six feet seven inches and built like a tank. Muscle rippled on every inch of his exposed flesh. And when I say "exposed" I mean exposed. He was naked, except for a leather collar around his neck. Attached to the collar was a chain leash that was gripped tightly by the man in black. The naked man was breathing hard, his body covered in dark, wiry hair, and he seemed to be sweating profusely. Needless to say, I was struck speechless by the sight.

"Who the fuck are you?" said Gar, sounding far more confident than I could have at the moment.

"Who I am is not important. But you," said the lean man in my direction, "are the one whose magic I felt sing out in the woods just a bit ago. I wondered at the source of it, and now I see. Good to see witches returning to the area; it's been so long since I got to do this." His smile widened into a frightening rictus.

"What are you talking about?" I stammered, moving protectively in front of my brother.

His smile disappeared as he reached a single hand up to the fastener on the chain and unclipped it from the larger, much more naked man's collar.

"Kill," he said calmly.

The larger man's demeanor changed instantly. There was a low, menacing grumble that quickly became a rumbling growl that reached Gar and me across the water. The man opened his mouth to reveal very large, very pointed teeth begin to descend from his cracking jawline. I watched in horror as he began to shift and charge at us across the rocky lip that surrounded the water.

Chapter Seven

"Gar! Run!" I screamed as I turned and made a mad dash toward my brother.

Luckily this was the one time Gar didn't argue or offer some sort of smart-ass retort. Instead he turned on his heels and ran in the direction I was headed. We ran the opposite side of the water as the shifter, trying to make for one of the trails before whatever it was caught us. I chanced a glance to the side to see where the creature was. The giant of a man had finished his shift and I was terrified to see a gigantic black bear loping along the water's edge, already making up the stagger on us.

Adrenaline kicked in as shock wore off as we hit one of the trails. I could feel the ground tremble beneath us as the bear began to close on the two of us. Gar ran off the trail, and I followed, hoping the densely packed woods might slow the beast down. The low-hanging branches scratched and grabbed at my face. I barely noticed as we barreled ahead. I wasn't about to look behind me, but the roar of the bear and the shaking of the ground told me it was gaining on us. We leapt over a downed tree and scampered into a thick cluster of smaller saplings, zigzagging through the grove. I could hear the bear roar, followed by the sound of smashing trees and logs. It wasn't running around things the way we were, but right through them.

Fuck! I didn't wake up this morning planning to die, and I sure as shit didn't plan on dying by being ripped apart by a supernatural. It was clear we weren't going to outrun the beast. My lungs were burning and my legs weren't far behind. Maybe, just maybe, I could give Gar a chance however.

I took one last look at the fleeing backside of my little brother and then turned to face the bear.

I gasped when I realized just how close it was to us. It was closing the last few yards between us at an impossible pace. It slobbered and roared as it stretched out a massive paw with razor sharp claws toward me.

"Shield!" I screamed, holding both arms out before me. It was instinctive, and I wasn't exactly sure what would happen, but I could feel my magic rushing up and prayed it would at least buy Gar enough time to get clear of this.

I felt a strange, humming sensation coming from behind my belly button and a sudden pressure behind my eyes. Then, my hands began to glow and the air in front of me shimmered blue. The bear crashed into it head first. It was too close and coming in too fast to avoid the collision. The impact knocked both of us in opposite directions. I wasn't prepared for the hit, didn't have the slightest clue what would happen. The shield blazed, flaring brightly when the bear struck. It felt like I had been hit as well. I was knocked off my feet and hurled backward about ten feet, but the bear was obviously a little more worse for the wear. It was repelled up and back, landing in an earth-shaking heap on its side.

I was dazed and my ears were ringing from crashing to the ground like that. I felt Gar's hand on my shoulder, shaking me. Goddamnit, why hadn't he kept running?

I rolled to a crouch, motioning for Gar to keep running, but he kept tugging at my arm, making it clear that he wasn't going anywhere without me. I looked over at the bear and saw it was beginning to limber to its feet as well. Eyes that were dark and brimming with hatred and hunger raked over me as it pawed the dirt, preparing to charge. I stabbed my hands out again, this time using my telekinesis to grab only a couple of small boulders that were lying to either side of the carnivore. I lifted them and charged them with my magic. I had never done this before without touching the object, and had never dreamed of charging something so big, but fear was proving to be an excellent catalyst. The large stones glowed blue in response and slammed together on either side of the bear's large head. It howled in pain, but was shaking the blow off as it once again prepared to charge.

My arms felt like I was trying to lift them through quicksand. Whatever magic I had managed to call on was most likely all I had. Definitely shot my wad as my pounding head refused to let me concentrate enough to even try forming another shield.

The bear lunged at us and I could smell the fetid rot of its breath as those massive jaws opened wide to clamp down on one or both of us.

"Get down!" I heard as something rushed past Gar and me to stand in front of the charging animal. Just as the bear was about to make contact, a boom so loud it drowned out the massive creature's roar cut through the air.

The Girl with the Good Magic

Officer Cody Hunter had dropped to one knee in front of us with a shotgun braced against his shoulder. He fired point blank into the bear's gaping mouth. The explosion stopped the monster dead in its tracks. But momentum carried it forward, crashing into Cody as the massive black bear fell on top of him.

I screamed as Gar and I rushed to Cody's aid. He was dazed, lying on his back with the bear's massive, now bleeding head sprawled across his torso. The bear was so big that I wasn't sure Gar and I would be able to pull the officer out from under it. We managed to get him free and helped him to his feet. He was winded, but had the presence of mind to retrieve his shotgun from a few feet away where it had been tossed.

"You two okay?" he asked, his breath coming in short gasps.

"Thanks to you," said Gar.

"Where...how...how did you find us?" I asked, confused.

"Your little brother here texted me that you guys were on your way up here," he replied. "I had a feeling you might need some company."

Before I could cast a scolding glance in Gar's direction, my vision was filled with the incredible large form of the black bear rising onto its hind legs.

"Look out!" I screamed too late as it swept one gigantic paw through the air. A red mist spewed into the air from behind Cody as the claws shredded through his shirt and skin. His body arched as he dropped his gun and his eyes were comically wide as he slowly fell to the ground. His back looked like ground hamburger meat with dollops of mayo dropped throughout.

He hit the ground face first just as the bear dropped

down onto all fours and advanced on us. Moving far quicker than I thought I could, I swept up the shotgun and placed the barrel directly under the beast's snout. The recoil of the weapon going off threw it out of my hands, but it also threw the bear backward as half of its face disappeared in the blast.

I dropped down on my ass, stunned. Gar had rushed over to the officer's side and I could tell from the look on his face that he was about to be sick. I crawled over to the bloody mess that had only moments before saved both our lives.

"Shit!" said Gar. "What do we do?"

"I...I...don't know!" My mind wasn't firing on all cylinders and part of me was starting to think—no, to hope—that none of this was real; that maybe I was home in bed, dreaming. But then movement out of the corner of my eye caught my attention and snapped me back to reality.

It was the bear. One paw was starting to twitch. I looked at the mangled head of the creature and watched in dismay as the blown-out top of the creature slowly began to reform. It was regenerating. Slowly, but it was regenerating nonetheless. I grabbed Gar by the shoulder and pulled him away from the creature.

"We have to go, Gar!" I shouted.

But it wasn't his voice that answered.

"You bitch!" came a cry. I looked over Gar's shoulder just in time to see the man in black come into the clearing, carrying the bear's chain in one hand.

Fuck! This couldn't be good, but before I could move my nose wrinkled at the smell of burning ash and the strong stench of sulfur.

Gar and I both wheeled around in time to see the air behind us shimmer and split apart. A small, circular tear was forming. It started out the same size as a frisbee and then widened, the edges glowing fiery red until it was about five feet in diameter. Aunt Vivian stepped through, straddling the breech and motioning for us to come to her.

"Bring the officer!" she shouted. "And get a move on; I'm not sure how long we can keep this open!"

Gar and I scooped Officer Hunter up, throwing one of his arms across each of our shoulders, and dragged him toward Aunt Vivian. We reached her and she helped us drag him into the portal. I chanced a look back just as the man in black was approaching the bear. He crouched down next to the behemoth and gently rubbed its back. He looked up at me, eyes filled with hate and tears just as the air in front of me slammed shut and I felt my body pulled backward.

Chapter Eight

The feeling of being turned inside out and upside down at the same time only lasted for a split-second. Or it could have been an hour. I had the distinct sense of time stopping and restarting a couple hundred times before we were suddenly standing in the aunts' study. Officer Hunter was still supported between me and Gar, and the sudden rush of vertigo that hit me made me buckle under his weight. I might have dropped him had Aunt Vivian not been there to help hold him up.

"Over here," said Aunt Lena as she cleared the pillows off a large couch that sat against one side of the room. "Lay him here."

Gar was able to place him on his stomach on the couch. I got my first real look at his injuries and gasped, covering my mouth with my hand. Gar was speechless, his mouth hanging open as he stared at the river of red that was pouring out of Cody's back and spilling down onto the study floor. I had no idea what to do. I had taken a rudimentary first aide class in school, but I don't think it was meant to cover what to do in the event of a were-bear mauling.

"It's okay," said Aunt Vivian. "He's going to be fine. Your aunt and I are going to get him fixed up." She took me by my elbow and started escorting me toward the study door. "But right now I need you and Gar to do something for me."

She hurried over to a tall cabinet in the corner of the room and removed two clear bottles filled with a milky white substance. She motioned for Gar to join us as she made her way back to me. Over her shoulder I could see Aunt Lena applying clean towels to Cody's back that she had retrieved from the connecting bath.

"Take these—" Aunt Vivian shoved the bottles at my brother and me "—and go shower with it. Apply it liberally and then wash it off. I don't want that creature tracking your scent here."

"It can do that?" I asked.

"You reek of magic right now. Don't argue, just do as I say. Quickly!"

Gar and I exchanged looks but did as we were told. I heard his bedroom door slam as I hurried into mine, passing through it to the bathroom.

To be honest, the shower was just what I needed. The hot water soothed my knotted muscles, and whatever was in the elixir Aunt Vivian gave us smelled pretty bad, but it also worked its way into my body and helped relax me even more. I did as she asked, covering myself in it and then rinsing it away.

After drying off I decided not to mess with my hair, opting instead to just pull it back into a ponytail before making my way back up the stairs to the study. Gar was already inside, his hair also wet and plastered to his head. How the hell to guys shower so fast? He seemed none the worse for wear and was looking at the still form of Officer Hunter on the couch.

"Is he..." I started, but couldn't bring myself to finish the sentence.

"He's fine," said Aunt Lena. "Or at least he will be after a few hours' sleep."

I stepped over to the couch and as I drew closer I could see that he was indeed breathing. Shallow and slow, but breathing nonetheless. His back was covered in white cloths, so I couldn't see just what the aunts had done, but I was pretty sure it was something that would not have been found on WebMD. The fact that there was no blood seeping through the bandages testified to that.

I looked over at the aunts and they both looked extremely tired.

"Gar," I said, "can you go put on some tea for Aunt Vivian and Aunt Lena? They look like they could use it."

"What? Of course...absolutely," said Gar, practically running from the room.

"Okay," I said, "how is he really?"

"Like I said, he's going to be fine," said Aunt Lena. "The wounds he sustained were life-threatening. Had we not gotten him here so quickly he would have surely passed away from them. As it is, the healing spell we used was barely able to stitch him back together. It's still trying to heal the internal damage he suffered."

Aunt Vivian walked over to me. "Now, young lady, care to tell us just what the hell happened?"

"Not here," interjected Aunt Lena. "He needs some uninterrupted downtime." She motioned in Cody's direction.

We headed downstairs to the large table in the kitchen

where Gar and I spent the next thirty minutes giving them the rundown on everything that happened from my ill-fated decision to visit a crime scene, up to the moment that they appeared in a portal and whisked us away to safety. For once I didn't leave anything out, deciding that the full truth was long overdue in coming out.

After vomiting all of that up, the four of us sat around the table in silence. I sipped my tea, waiting for the inevitable tongue lashing that I knew was on the way.

"Allie. Garland," said Aunt Vivian. We both looked up, red in our eyes. "Are the two of you okay?"

I couldn't hide the shock, and I slowly nodded.

"Then that's what matters," Aunt Lena continued. "The why of your decision-making and the what were you thinking are all secondary at this point. What you did was very brave."

"And rash," added Aunt Vivian, but the softness of her tone belied the harshness of the words. "But yes, we can deal with anything that happens moving forward. As a family." She gave Aunt Lena a look and nodded. "No more secrets. It's time we all sat down and had a very long, very frank discussion about things."

Aunt Lean was nodding. "About damn time."

"First, how did you find us?" I asked. "Gar, did you call them as well?"

He shook his head emphatically in response. "What, do you think I'm crazy?"

"Then how?" I said, glancing at the aunts.

"Do you think you are the only one that can use a tracking spell?" replied Aunt Lena with a smirk. "In this case, the spell was embedded in the magic you were practicing."

"What?" I asked. What she just said made no sense to me.

Aunt Vivian smiled at me before speaking. "Do you really think that there were strangers on the internet that were teaching you magic, child?"

I opened my mouth to reply, but for once I had no idea what to say.

"The fact that you were researching magic online let us know just how serious you were about the craft. You know Anna Witenhouer, our neighbor a few houses down the street? She teaches computer science and has proven invaluable in helping us."

"You've been snooping on me?" I said, unable to hide my shock and anger. Out of the corner of my eye I could see the color start to drain from Garland's face.

"No, no," said Aunt Lena quickly. "We would never spy on you. We have nothing but respect for your privacy. Long ago, we had certain keywords flagged on the computers for your own protection."

"Yes," added Aunt Vivian. "It's a new world now. When we were your age, our mother booby-trapped the cabinets that had certain tomes and potions in them so she would know what we were getting into. This was the electronic version of that."

I could see Gar relax a little when I glanced in his direction.

"So...all those spells I looked up? The online covens that were helping me learn?"

"All us," said Aunt Lena proudly, waving her hand to indicate herself and her sister. "While most of what you find and read on the internet is utter rubbish when it comes to true magic, you were digging into areas you shouldn't have.

So we decided to lead you to certain, safer aspects of the craft."

"Yes. If you're going to dabble, we needed to know what you were doing," said Aunt Vivian.

"Let's just say you were riding with training wheels," said Aunt Lena. "But now, in light of what's happening, it's time for the trainers to come off."

"And that means we need to tell you and Garland everything," said Aunt Vivian.

Despite finally hearing what I'd been waiting for most of my life, I couldn't shake the sudden feeling of trepidation that swept over me.

Chapter Nine

We all sat around the large dining room table with fresh cups of tea. Aunt Lena assured me it wasn't laced with anything and that they would not be tampering with our memories. I felt like a heal for even having to ask that, but hey, lessons learned.

"So first, why were you so adamant that I wasn't attacked by a zombie?" I asked. "You almost had me doubting my own eyes."

"Because you weren't," said Aunt Lena. "What attacked you was not a member of the walking dead."

"You were attacked by the same type of creature that nearly killed the two of you today at the falls," added Aunt Vivian.

"That was a shifter, right?" said Gar.

"Correct," said Aunt Vivian. "What attacked Allie in the coffee shop was a shifter that had not been able to complete its transformation. It was stuck in the gray zone between forms. When a shifter changes from form to form, the body it is wearing temporarily dies in the transition. For most shifters the change happens nearly instantaneously, so you don't notice. That rotting smell you picked up on was the decaying dead flesh of the creature's humanity. It was stuck and couldn't complete the shift."

"Why?" I asked, simultaneously intrigued and grossed out.

"That's part of a much larger topic," said Aunt Lena.

"You said no more secrets," I reminded them.

"Very well," said Aunt Lena. "Shifting is a form of magic that was forbidden many years ago. As part of that forbidding, a spell was created that undid, or blocked, the magic that flowed in this world that allowed shifting to happen. When shifters were cut off from that free-flowing magic, they were stuck in the form they occupied. Some were in human form while others remained in their animal states."

"So I was attacked by a bear shifter in the coffee shop as well? But what...it was a shifter in training?"

"Something like that," said Aunt Vivian. "The spell that prevents shifting is starting to unravel. Either it is decaying, which I doubt, or it is under attack by someone intent on breaking it. I believe that the creature that attacked you was the first attempt by whoever is behind this to bring shifting back into the world. They didn't quite get it right. Until today."

"Are there other types of shifters? Other than just bears I mean?" Gar weighed in.

"Yes. There are all manner of animal shifters out there," replied Aunt Lena.

"Including werewolves?" Gar said.

"Werewolves are a breed unto themselves among the shifter populace," said Aunt Lena.

"They are the only shifters capable of taking on a

hybrid form of animal and man, while retaining all the intellect and instinct of both. They are the alphas and omegas of the shifter world, and therefore the most dangerous," said Aunt Vivian. "But they are also not something you have to worry about."

"Why's that?" asked Gar.

"They are extinct. Shifters are born, not created. That holds true even for werewolves. The last remaining werewolves were erased from the population long ago," said Aunt Lena.

"How do you know that for sure?" I asked, eying the aunts suspiciously.

"Because we, along with your mother, killed them all," said Aunt Vivian matter-of-factly.

"I knew it!" cried out Gar. "All those stories our mother told us about how she destroyed the wolves were true!"

"But why?" I asked. My memories of my mother were always a little fuzzy, but I remembered the stories she told, stories that involved great magic and spells that defeated great evils, those evils being werewolves. But growing up years later, I always thought they were just stories. Even though I believed in our family magic, I didn't believe in monsters.

"And how?" added Gar. "How exactly did you kill all the wolves?"

"The old-fashioned way I'm afraid," said Aunt Lena. Was that a bit of sadness that had crept into her voice?

They were both silent as we sipped our tea. I could sense that it wasn't the right moment to rush them. After a couple of minutes, Aunt Vivian spoke up.

"Magic," she began, "is not what you see on television or the movies. It isn't something that someone studies for years and learns. Its origins are supernatural, and like all things supernatural, you're either born into it or you aren't. In our case, magic has flowed through this family for generations, passed down from mother to daughter."

"About that," said Gar. "Why no love for the men?"

"Males belong to a different point on the mystical spectrum," said Aunt Lena. "Much of the magic we witches perform is grounded in nature. We draw our power from Mother Earth itself. Men are cut off from that maternal connection based on their nature. But magic can present itself in strange ways, so you never know." She added a wink, and Gar smiled back at her before settling back to sip more of his tea.

"So we come from a long line of witches then?" I asked.

"Yes. And we have always been here, in this same town, for many generations," said Aunt Vivian. "You see, Trinity Cove has been home to magic for years beyond remembering. The town is built on the conflux of ley energies. Ley lines, ley tides, ley rhythms, and ley stones. It is what allows magic to thrive and flow so effortlessly here."

"Wait, if that's the case, then why are we the only witches in town?" I asked.

"Oh, we aren't," replied Aunt Vivian. "Witches have lived here dating back to the first colonies that came over to the new world."

"Before that," chimed in Lena.

"Yes." Aunt Vivian nodded. "Quite true. But the practice of magic has all but disappeared in the last generation. Your generation."

I felt a blush creep up my neck as I fidgeted with my tea cup, purposefully avoiding eye contact with anyone. "Why?" I mumbled.

Again Aunt Lena and Aunt Vivian exchanged serious looks.

"Go on," said Aunt Lena, "tell her."

Aunt Vivian took a deep breath before continuing. "Long before you were born, when your mother and the two of us were small, witches raised their daughters in the age old practices of witchcraft. It was tradition. Magic itself flowed freely here in the Cove. We lived peacefully, not harming anyone or anything."

"And it wasn't just us," said Aunt Lena. "We lived side by side with the shifters and other magical folk as well. Trinity Cove was ground zero for all manner of supernatural, and we all abided by certain unspoken rules and we lived in peace."

"But surely not everyone was a supernatural," said Gar.

"No, no," replied Aunt Vivian. "There were more humans than supernaturals, of course. Some of them knew about us; some of them didn't want to know and looked the other way. But we all tolerated one another equally. And then that changed."

It wasn't as if we weren't wrapped up enough in her tale, but her sudden ominous tone grabbed Gar and me in a visceral grip. "What happened?" I asked.

"Our quiet little hamlet was shattered by the arrival of a man; a warlock unlike any we had ever seen before," said Aunt Lena.

"I thought men couldn't be witches?" said Gar, beating me to the punch.

"No, we said men can't be born into magic," replied Aunt Vivian. "Certain men can take magic from other sources, control it, shape it, use it for nefarious purposes. But they aren't born with it. They can't tap into it naturally. Think of them as having an arcane gas tank that they can fill and top off with magic. But it's a limited amount, and once they use it, it's gone. They have to fill up again."

I felt a pit forming in the bottom of my stomach, but I had to ask anyway. "Where do they fill up? I'm guessing the local Exxon doesn't sell the kinda high test they need."

"You would be correct," said Aunt Vivian. "For men like that, we were Exxon. Warlocks steal our magic and hold it captive, twisting it into something obscene and unnatural. The type of arcane arts they practiced was forbidden ages ago, but the laws that governed witchcraft never stopped them. They fed on us, bleeding us dry of our magic and enslaving certain witches to use as living conduits for them to tap into magic whenever they needed.

"Centuries ago, there was a great war, a rebellion if you will, between a handful of witch clans and these warlocks. The battle was brutal and long, with heavy casualties on both sides of the war. But in the end, the witches prevailed, decimating their captors. The witches, through their connection with the power of Mother Earth, were able to cast a spell that created powerful allies for them. Through potent magics they were able to allow humans to tap the eldritch energies around them for short periods of time. These humans were then able to take on animal forms yet retain the intellect they possessed as humans. They loved the new powers we gave them, and in return pledged their allegiance to us and agreed to help overthrow the warlocks who kept us as living, mystical batteries."

"Combined, our power was too much for the warlocks," said Aunt Lena. "They were defeated and the witches that had been held in bondage were freed."

"What happened to the warlocks?" I asked.

"They were put to death," answered Aunt Lena.

I winced at the casual way she had replied. "Just like that?"

Aunt Lena narrowed her eyes at me and continued.

"Believe me, girl, taking a life, *any* life, is something a witch takes very seriously. We are grounded in nature. Killing is anathema to us. But these monsters, these warlocks, were perverting the natural course of things. They were using out power to commit heinous acts against mankind. They bonded themselves to our magic in a way that left us no choice. Only death severed the bonds."

"Plus, the act of binding a witch to a warlock resulted in the death of the witch over time. It was a slow and agonizing way to die, being drained of one's life force. It was death by a thousand magical pinpricks," said Aunt Vivian. "Between the witches and the shifters, the warlocks were destroyed once and for all. But the effect of that battle reverberated throughout our history, forever changing the practice of witchcraft. It drove us back into the closets, so to speak. Those of our kind who survived vowed to never again live in the open as they had been. Many abandoned the practice completely out of fear that doing so would only attract more warlocks. Turns out that fear was not warranted. More warlocks never showed up on our shores. It was whispered that the last of them had been wiped out, and the secrets of enslaving witches died with them. Even so, our numbers dwindled to near extinction levels. Soon, we were thought to be the creations of imaginative writers and storytellers, passing on into the realm of fiction."

"And that was how we wanted it," said Aunt Lena. "Obscurity suited us well. Over the generations, witches settled in small communities, blended in with the human inhabitants, and lived quiet, solitary lives. For the most part, their magic died out as practice stopped and the craft was no longer passed from mother to daughter. No woman wanted to see her daughter potentially become an errant victim of a warlock, even if a warlock hadn't been seen or heard from in centuries."

"So one of those settlements was here? Trinity Cove?" I asked.

"Yes," said Aunt Vivian, nodding. "Our family line is directly descended from the original witches that led the rebellion against the warlocks. We continued to practice here, and so did the ones who settled with us."

"And what about the shifters?" asked Gar.

"It was our lineage that cast the spell that created them. They were allowed to keep their powers, and in return pledged their loyalty to us witches forever. They lived in secret as well, keeping close proximity to the witch communities."

"Something doesn't add up," I said. "If the shifters are allied to the witches, why would one of them attack me?"

"Because," came a voice from the stairs, "she hasn't told you the best part yet. Tell them what you and your sisters did." It was Officer Hunter. He was standing on the stairs with the blanket draped over his bare shoulders as he tried to steady himself. His dark eyes were narrowed and staring at the aunts. "If you're going to tell her, tell her everything."

Chapter Ten

"Young man!" said Aunt Vivian sternly. "You should not be up just yet."

Gar and I rushed to the policeman's side to bolster him up as he took a tentative step off the last stair and onto the hardwood floor. I draped one arm over my shoulder and Gar did the same. Though I tried to block it out, I was reminded of what had transpired only hours earlier when we had dragged him through the woods in the same fashion. He was very warm to the touch. Fever was running through his body, and the effort of walking was making him shiver in our grasp. We made our way to the couch that sat just outside of the kitchen and eased him down. I was only slightly annoyed at Aunt Lena making certain that the blanket draped around his upper body slid between the couch and his wounded back.

"Officer..." I started before catching myself. "Cody. You shouldn't be up. You need to rest so you can heal."

"I think I'm healing just fine all things considered," he replied, indicating his back. I caught a glimpse of it before he lay back and was shocked to see that while the wounds were angry and white, the bleeding had stopped and the flesh was already starting to knit back together. "No doubt a courtesy of whatever the two of you did for me," he continued, nodding at the aunts. "Thank you for that."

"You're welcome," replied Aunt Lena.

I was surprised by her answer. I expected them to dodge having anything to do with healing him, give him a cup of tea laced with God knows what, and send him on his merry way with a wiped memory. The fact that they acknowledged he at least knew something above the norm was going on was encouraging and frightening at the same time.

"I'll get another blanket," said Gar, heading for the guest bedroom down the hall. I realized then that the officer only had on a pair of red, stained pants. He was bare from the waist up. The sheen created by the layer of sweat only caused the definition in his abs to stand out even more. His olive-toned skin was on full display. The only hair on his torso was a small dark line that started lightly above his belly button and dove in a straight line into the waistband of his black underwear. I swallowed and looked away, thankful when Gar showed up with a blanket and covered his half-nakedness.

"What exactly did you do?" he asked.

"A combination of potion and spell," replied Aunt Lena. "One meant to heal and soothe the spirit. Under normal circumstances it would not work this fast. You were attacked by a supernatural being, and in all honesty I wasn't sure it would work at all. You are very lucky."

"Well, I'm grateful, that's for sure," he replied. "But don't let me interrupt. I believe you were about to tell Allie the second half of your tale." He leaned back, resting his head fully against the large teal throw pillows.

Aunt Vivian narrowed her eyes at him as she made her way to the large sitting chair opposite the couch. Gar and I sat on the oversized ottoman between the two while Aunt Lena made her way back into the kitchen to put on another kettle of water for tea.

"Your family has been in the Cove for as long as ours has," Aunt Vivian said to Cody. "I assume your parents told you tales of our kind?"

"And my parents' parents before them," he replied. "My mother is one of you, isn't she?"

Aunt Vivian nodded before continuing. "Yes, your mother is a witch. While outing her to you is not for us to do, I am afraid that right now we don't have a choice."

"Wait," I said, "where is your mother? All through school we only ever saw your father."

"Oh, so you did notice me," he said with a twinkle in his dark eyes.

I tried to ignore my blush as I continued, "I just mean I don't remember ever seeing your mother at any of the school events we attended."

"My mother left us a few years after my sister died," he said. "She drowned in our pool shortly before I was even born. My mother blamed herself because she had left the back door open accidentally while she was doing laundry. When she found my sister, it was too late. She never got over the guilt of that, and eventually it proved too much for her, so one day she abandoned me and my father and moved out west when I was a toddler. My father is the only parent I've ever known."

"I'm sorry," I manage to say. "I had no idea."

"It's okay," he said. "Like I said, it's been awhile. I've come to terms with what happened."

"I am sorry as well," said Aunt Vivian. "I knew your

mother well, and I know that when your sister died, so did a part of her. She wanted so very badly to be the mother you needed and deserved. In the end, she opted not to expose you to a lifetime of her sadness. She wanted more for you, and she felt that as long as she was hanging around, weighing you down, the darker your future would become. As a witch, losing her only daughter was more than she could bear. So she did the unthinkable and abandoned her child. I can't imagine the strength and the weakness it took to do that." I looked up expecting to see her focused on Cody, but was shocked to see she was staring at me as she spoke. She smiled and looked away, turning her attention to Cody.

"Did your father tell you about your mother?"

"Yes," Cody replied. "He was angry at her for walking out on us. He told me everything when I was old enough. He hated witchcraft, blamed her disappearance on you and your kind. He said it wasn't the death of my sister that caused her to leave us, but it was the stress of keeping secrets that did it—one secret in particular."

"What is he talking about?" I asked. "We said no more secrets, remember? So what's he talking about?"

Aunt Vivian cleared her throat before speaking up. "As I said, we lived in peace and harmony for generations after the destruction of the warlocks. The witches that survived and wanted to continue the craft lived in communities where they looked after one another and protected one another. Here, in Trinity Cove, there were only a handful of witches. We lived with the shifters and built this town into a haven of sort for supernaturals. We grew complacent, and with that complacence came a false sense of security. We dropped our guards.

"And before we knew it, he was among us." She

stopped, shifting her weight and gathering her thoughts before continuing. "A warlock had found our Cove, drawn by the immense flow of eldritch energies within the ley properties around us. But this warlock was different. He came prepared. He was armed and protected by talismans against our magic. He used silver collars to bind us; silver is one of the few metals with innate qualities that can be manipulated to disturb magical rhythms. Before we knew what was happening, he had taken some of our number and retreated to a cave behind the Singing Falls. There he leached power from the witches and used it to create more talismans, talismans that were designed with one purpose: to pervert the age old magic that we used to create the first shifters."

She paused to see if we had any questions. Aunt Lena brought in a tray with fresh brewed tea and passed the cups out to all of us before returning to the kitchen, all without breathing a word. The air in the room was heavy with tension, and I waited patiently for Aunt Vivian to continue.

"This warlock was far different from the others that came before. He was savage. Calculating. Cruel. The things he did to the witches in his control were unspeakable. But nothing prepared us for the monsters he created. He created hybrid shifters that could halt their shift in midtransformation, trapped between a man and an animal. He preferred the wolves for this twisting of our magic, creating great, hulking beasts that walked on two legs with ten times the strength of a wolf, and none of the wolves' fears or sense of restraint. They were savage monsters loyal only to their dark master.

"He used these creatures to tear through Trinity Cove on bloody rampages when the moon was full. The werewolves ravaged the other shifter clans, decimating their numbers and driving them deep into the mountains far from Trinity. Humans were slaughtered by the dozens and witches were captured and taken back to the warlock. After a while, there were only a few witches left. We knew that our time was limited, and we also knew that once the warlock was finished with Trinity Cove he would move on to the next community and the next after that…drinking them dry of magic, and making slaves of our sisters.

"Those of us who remained were the most powerful of the covens. We gathered together with a few of the humans we trusted and came up with a plan. We knew that we had to fight back, just as our ancestors had. Taking out the warlock wasn't the problem. Together, we witches were more than a match for a single man wielding stolen power. No, the warlock wasn't the challenge. It was his guardians, his nightmarish werewolves that were the issue. They were fast and strong. Their fangs and claws would rip us to shreds before we could get close enough to finish off their master. So we came up with a rather grim plan. Desperate times called for desperate measures.

"Your mother, Lena and I met with the remaining few witches in the clan in secret at night and agreed on a course of action. We knew that the wolves were at their most lethargic during dusk and dawn, the nether time when it's not dark, but no longer light either. The magic within them would settle before shifting along with their body to one form or the other. Most of the werewolves reverted to their human form during the day, but some of the more powerful creatures could maintain their lupine forms at all times. They were the ones that warded over the warlock until nightfall.

"We gathered here, in this very room, seven witches, and eight humans. We didn't dare tell the rest of the Cove what we were planning lest they attempt to stop us. A few of the residents had fled, leaving everything except what they could carry. But that was before the warlock decried that if anyone else left Trinity Cove before he had completed his... business here, he would have his wolves hunt them down no matter how far they ran, and peel their skin from their bodies inch by inch. So no one left. The humans knew it was only a matter of time before all of the witches were either dead or captured, at which time the warlock would pull up stake and leave. They turned a blind eye to us. That was the beginning of the hatred for our kind that can still be felt to this day.

"But that hate was one-sided. The witches knew it was our responsibility to protect the humans and destroy this madman once and for all. So we met on a night when there was a quarter moon, when the pull on the wolves would be the weakest. We waited until just before dawn, when we knew they would be resting in the caves that surrounded Singing Falls. And then we cast a spell, one that consumed so much of our energy that two of our sisters were rendered powerless forever. It was a spell of undoing. We reversed the spell that allowed shifters to exist."

The silence was deafening. "You can do that?" I asked.

"Normally it would not have been possible," said Aunt Vivian. "But remember, it was our ancestors that created the spell in the first place. My sisters and I were the three most powerful witches in the Cove. Your mother was the most powerful of the three of us, so together, we were able to undo the spell that allowed humans to walk as animals.

"The wolves were swept up in the spell. It locked them in their weaker human form. Overcome by the lethargy the magic created, they dropped where they stood, falling in piles one on top of the other. That was when we, and our human comrades, crept into the caves and killed them. We walked through the human pile and drove pikes through their hearts, killing each before they could cry out and rouse others. We moved through the cave structure until we came to the last passageway, deep in the tunnels that ran behind the falls. That was where we thought we would find the warlock, and put an end to this terror once and for all. But it wasn't him we found…"

Her voice trailed off, and I thought I could see tears reflecting in the light. She leaned back, closing her eyes.

"What did you find?" asked Gar.

Aunt Vivian took a deep breath and opened her eyes, staring at us.

"We found a room where the walls had been lined with wooden torches and the floor was covered in the pelts of various woodland animals. It was plush and deep and somehow made the cave room incredibly intimate. Lying on the pelts were…were…babies. A dozen of them, just lying there quietly. It was eerie the way they made no noise as we walked into the space. They were awake, looking around, stretching, trying to roll over. They were only days old, but so alert; bright eyes were open and I swear they watched us…tracked us as we moved.

"My sisters and I could smell the magic they had been bathed in; they were werewolves, but there was something different about them as well. They had yet to go through their first shift. In breaking the spell we had trapped them in human form; a form that had never known the dark kiss of transformation."

She stopped talking, letting her words dangle in the air.

"What happened?" I asked, wide-eyed.

"Go on," said Cody when Aunt Vivian remained silent for a second, "tell them what happened. Tell them how you and your sisters callously slaughtered a room full of innocent babies!"

Aunt Vivian instantly snapped to attention. Her frame became rigid as she snapped around, focusing her attention on Cody. The flower vase on the table behind the couch burst into shards of glass, spilling its contents across the hardwood floor. I could feel the magic leap up in Aunt Vivian, like a dragon poised to unleash liquid napalm.

"Vivian!" shouted Aunt Lena, rushing into the room. "Control yourself!"

Instantly I felt the magic recoil and wind down, retreating back to the otherworldly pockets Aunt Vivian had summoned it from. I looked at Cody. His face was pale, and his eyes, though defiant, were not quite as set in anger as they had been a second before.

"Is that what you think happened?" said Aunt Vivian, swallowing hard. She didn't wait for an answer. "No, nothing even remotely close to that happened. Where did you hear that?"

"My father was there! He told me!" cried Cody, struggling to sit up.

"Your father was indeed there," replied Aunt Vivian, "at the beginning. He didn't have the stomach for battle. He could barely enter the caves; he begged to stay outside swigging from that silver flask I'm betting he still carries around in his jacket pocket!"

I looked at Cody, watching the blush spread across his handsome features. I'm sure that wasn't the effect my aunt intended for her words to have. I was thankful that when she spoke next, her words were much softer, almost apologetic.

"I'm sorry," she said, "but it's true. And that is no reflection on the character of your father. Not everyone was cut out for what had to happen that day. So you can't believe the words of a man who was not there to see what happened.

"As I said, we stood there in shock, taking in the sight. There was no debating what to do. We were close to the warlock, so finishing him off was the duty of the witches. We left the shifter babies to the humans. They took all of them out of the cave and made their way through the mountain and back down to the Cove.

"My sisters and I, along with the other witches, made our way through the caverns until we finally came upon the warlock. He wasn't what we expected. Truth be told, none of us had ever actually seen one or really heard a description of what they looked like."

Her pause here had the expert timing of a master storyteller.

"Well?" said Gar, unable to hold in his curiosity any longer. "What did he look like?"

"He looked like you, darling," she said, looking at Gar. She smiled at the shocked look on his face. "Not in the physical sense, but in the normal, all American young man type of look. He wasn't menacing, or old and smitten. He was just a young man, barely out of his teens. Where he studied the practice of magic from, we never got the chance to ask him. Despite his youth, he was brimming with hate and darkness. I could feel the black magic rolling off him in waves as he attacked us.

"He knew what we had done. He felt the mystical and the physical deaths of his werewolves and in return he had drained everything out of the witches he still held in captivity, leaving only soulless husks in their wake. He used that magic to attack us directly, hurling black waves of power at us that meant to fry us where we stood. But he made one mistake with that.

"He attacked us with magic that had an inherent flaw. As dark and twisted as it was, we could still sense what was at the core of his spells. It was the singsong power of our sisters. We were able to tap that power and redirect it back at the warlock. The fight went on for what seemed like hours, but in reality may have only been minutes. Our combined strength was able to deflect his attack, and he responded by doubling and redoubling the energy of his power. But that had the desired effect. Unlike us, his power supply was limited. He had no new reserves to draw on once his stolen magic was spent. Without his wolves to take us out, he quickly grew too weak to fight, and once spent he slumped to the ground.

"We surrounded him, magic at the ready, and prepared to deliver the death blow. But it was your mother who stopped us," she said, staring at me. "She said that if we killed him, there was nothing to stop another warlock from taking his place. Instead, she devised a way to trap him in the cave: a spell that would cause his body to become ethereal, a living spirit with no power and no connection to the living world, sealed inside that cave forever. We used his own talismans, the ones he had crafted to make his wolves, to act as binders for his spirit. We also used the same talismans to create a forbidding; a wall of magic that worked with the ley energies in Trinity Cove to disrupt the flow of magic here. While we can access and draw on our natural power, it is all but impossible for a non-witch to tap into our energy source again; so effectively, warlocks can't exist here anymore."

"In theory," Aunt Lena said. She had returned from the kitchen in the midst of Aunt Vivian's recollection and I had almost forgotten she was in the house. "The spell we cast that day was something no witches had ever attempted. To create a forbidding that trapped the spirit of a warlock and acted as a warning for others who may have followed in his footsteps? We have no idea what we really did."

"Wait, so are you saying that warlock is still up there in some cave behind the falls?" I asked incredulously.

"By now he is no more than a remnant if his spirit has not succumbed to the darkness of the nether realms," said Aunt Vivian. "The spells we wove were meant to cleanse and hold. Without a body, and nothing to anchor him to the physical world, he is trapped in limbo. He's neither here nor there, but somewhere in between the world of the living and the dead, with no hope of ever walking in either. He is no threat to us."

"What about the shifters?" Gar asked. "I mean, you said you undid the spell that created them? So...?"

"There have not been shifters in the world since that day," said Aunt Lena. "They shouldn't exist."

"But what about the one that almost killed Gar and me today?" I asked.

"Wait," said Cody, "shifter? You mean that bear I shot?"

"Wasn't a bear," I said as Gar nodded in agreement. "Just minutes before you arrived we watched a man turn into that bear and come after us. So if shifters don't exist anymore, how do you explain that? Or the one that attacked me in the coffee shop?"

"It was definitely a shifter that attacked the three of you today," said Aunt Lena. "That was why we wanted you out of the room when we treated the officer. We had to examine the magical signature that was left within his wounds. It was unmistakable; definitely a shifter attack. But we can't figure out how."

"After all these years, how is this happening?" said Aunt Lena. "Perhaps the spell is wearing thin. That can happen, you know."

"Not likely," said Aunt Vivian. "Magic exists outside of the individual that cast it. That's why it is able to maintain itself long after the creator of a spell has passed. No, more likely than not, it is being eroded by someone or something."

"Another warlock?" said Aunt Lena. "Perhaps someone has found a way around the forbidding."

Aunt Vivian nodded. "That would be the most likely explanation. Someone is seeking to break the wards we put in place. It's the only reason that shifting could happen again. Small cracks are appearing in the forbidding, and that's brought the power to shift back into the world. Whoever, or whatever, is doing this is still working to find a way through the wards. That's why the shifter that attacked you at the coffee shop couldn't completely transform. The bear, on the other hand, was able to complete a shift. Still, that doesn't explain why it was attracted to you."

"The man that was with the shifter said something about sensing my magic. I had just conjured a small ball of light to show Gar when they popped up."

"Of course," said Aunt Vivian. "Whoever the man with the shifter was, he must have sensed your magic and sought it out. The fact that you are a descendant of the original magic that created the forbidding made you stand out even more. Whoever they are, they are seeking the source magic to break the spell that forbids shifting and keeps the warlocks at bay."

"That would explain why they were at the shop as well," said Aunt Lena.

"Wait, why would that be?" I asked. "I had not used any magic when that thing attacked us."

"Hmmm," said Aunt Lena. "Perhaps it was attracted to the stone."

Aunt Vivian looked at her sister before speaking. "Yes. That could indeed be it!"

"I'm confused," I said. "What stone?"

"Your mother created a necklace out of the last talisman the warlock had," said Aunt Vivian. "It was made from a ley stone that was bathed in the same magic as that which created the forbidding. It's the necklace she gave you the night she disappeared. She said it was so that, no matter what happened in the future, it would keep you blinded to the vision of any warlock. It also bound your power for your own protection. Which is why you should not have been able to manifest it the way you did today. But if whoever is trying to break the forbidding spell is looking for a way to undo the magic, they could be drawn to any remnants of the original spell, in the hopes that it would help bring the shifters, and by extension the warlocks, back into existence."

Both of my aunts looked at me as I sat there in silence. My hand had automatically gone to my neck, reaching for my necklace.

"Allie," said Aunt Lena, "where is your necklace?"

I swallowed hard, aware of the look of horror that must have crept over my face.

"Oh God. I gave it to Hope to wear that night she was taken to the hospital. I gave it to her to wear for good luck."

Chapter Eleven

"C'mon, c'mon," I said. "Pick up the phone!"

We were speeding toward Hope's house in Cody's patrol car. I wasn't able to talk him out of coming, but at least I had been able to convince him not to call anything in to Trinity Cove police department. If what we had heard was true, and based on everything that had happened in the last forty-eight hours I had no reason to believe it wasn't, then this was not the type of thing to get the police involved in.

I kept quiet as we made our way across town to where Hope lived. She was in a gated community that was built around a pond, about fifteen minutes from the ridge where I lived. I kept glancing over at Cody. One, to be sure he was still conscious, and two, because I couldn't quite shake the image of those six-pack abs he was rocking under his bulky tee shirt. He caught me looking once and smiled.

"How are you so calm?" I asked before he could question why I was sneaking looks at him, "and are you sure you're up for this? I men, just a few hours ago you were bleeding out on my aunts' couch."

"I'm not going to lie: my back feels like someone is throwing lit matches on it every time I breathe. But whatever magic they used to heal me is definitely doing the trick. Besides, no way was I letting you come over here alone or with Gar. That kid's got balls, but I've got a gun, and as we saw today, that seems to do the trick."

"Or at least it slows shifters down," I said, "so that's good to know. So why weren't you freaked out by everything you heard back there?"

"Because most of it I've heard, in one form or another, all my life. You should know, there are a lot of tales that circulated around town and around school about your family. And you."

I turned to look out the window without responding. Of course I knew about the rumors swirling around my family's name. It was one of the chief reasons that I was such a loner throughout school. I was popular for a couple of years in grade school, but that was before the other girls were old enough to hear what their parents were saying about my aunts. Once that started, everyone shunned me out of fear. Everyone except Hope. She pretty much danced to her own drumbeat and didn't let anyone make up her mind for her.

Thinking about my best, and probably only, friend made the knot in my stomach pull itself even tighter. I fidgeted, wanting Cody to drive even faster than he was.

"We're almost there," he said, almost as if he could sense my feelings. "Try her again on the phone."

I did as he asked, only to get the same result. It would ring and ring before going to voicemail. She would never stray more than arm's length from her cell, and I highly doubted she would have let the battery die. I didn't want to think about any alternatives as to why she wasn't answering. My anxiety picked up as we made the turn off the main road onto the street that led into Hope's development. It was an upper-class gated community, and the fact that there wasn't a guard on duty at the gatehouse made my heart start to hammer. Then, when I saw that the gate leading into the community was slightly ajar, my heart went into full-scale triphammer mode.

"Shit," I said, already focusing on the worst. Suddenly I wished my aunts had come with us. But they had a lot to look into on their end to try and find a spell that could help them uncover who, or what, we might be up against. No, for better or worse, it was up to me and Officer Hunter to make certain Hope was all right.

Despite my anxiety I understood why we drove through the wooded neighborhood so slowly. I could feel Cody peering deeply into the shadows of the well-manicured lawns and watching for anything that didn't belong to separate itself from the shadows. I directed him to Hope's house and he killed the lights as he coasted to a stop on the street just past her driveway. I had no idea why he didn't just pull into the drive, but I chalked it up to being some sort of cop thing.

"Stay behind me," he whispered as we exited his patrol car. I noticed he had drawn his gun and held it in both hands, barrel pointed down as we advanced slowly on the front door.

"Are you crazy?" I said. "Put that away before you hurt someone!"

"And are you forgetting how fast that thing in the woods moved?" he replied.

"Fair enough," I answered. I didn't have a gun, but I did draw up some magic and held it vibrating in my fist. What I would do with it, I had no clue, but I wasn't about to be taken unaware for the third time in as many days.

The Girl with the Good Magic

I approached the front door and looked at Cody. Once he nodded, I rang the doorbell. The house was a one-story mid-century modern. The middle section was all glass and offered an almost unobstructed view through the house and out to the pool in back. The land then sloped away, diving down into a table of trees that led to the large pond that the community was centered around. Cody took a few steps to either side of the large windows, peering in as I rang the bell again. This time I punctuated the ringing with a few hard knocks with the palm of my hand on the wooden frame.

"Hope!" I yelled. "It's me, Allie! Let me in! Are you home?"

I ignored the frown Cody gave me and banged again at the door. This time my adrenaline kicked in and I was to the point of actually kicking the door when it suddenly swung open. I stopped my hand in mid pound just before it would have collided with Hope's annoyed face.

"Girl!" she said, not bothering to mask her annoyance. "What in hell is wrong with you beating down my door like that?"

I wanted to rush in and hug her, but instead I just stood there with my mouth hanging open. "You weren't answering your phone," I finally stammered. "I was worried about you."

Hope softened, smiling sheepishly at me. "Well, if you must know I was kinda busy. My parents are out and I invited that cute EMT over. You know, the one that showed up at the coffee shop the night you were robbed."

I couldn't say I was surprised, but at least she was okay. I stepped in and then noticed her looking over my shoulder.

"And who have we here?" she asked, arching an eyebrow.

"This is Co...I mean Officer Hunter," I said. "He investigated the crime scene at the coffee shop and was just dropping by my place to fill in some final details when I mentioned that you weren't answering your phone. He offered to give me a lift over to make sure you were all right."

"Mmm-hmm," Hope said, turning on her heels to head into the house. "C'mon in. I was about to take a dip. Wanna join?" She gave Cody a wry smile and me a not too subtle wink.

"No," I said, following her into the house with Cody at my back. "We just needed to make sure you were okay. Umm, hey, do you by chance still have my mother's necklace I gave you?"

"What? Oh yeah, of course. You know I would take care of that."

"I'm sorry to come over so late, it's just that...I mean, it's all I have from her and I didn't think I would miss it as much as I do," I said.

Hope stopped and turned to face me. She took my hand in hers and squeezed gently. "You don't have to explain anything. I'm honored you let me wear it. It's over here on the mantel. I didn't want anything to happen to it after I got home from the hospital."

She retrieved a small, intricately carved jewelry box from above the fireplace, retrieved the silver necklace with a teardrop-shaped pink stone attached to it and placed it in my hand. I closed my fist around it and instantly felt more settled and focused. That was when I noticed that the magic I had called up seemed to fizzle and run away from me, like something I could see moving off in the distance, but it was just out of arm's reach.

That was also when the sliding doors that led out to the pool exploded inward in a shower of glass.

Chapter Twelve

I threw my arms up, instinctively protecting my face from flying shards of glass. I barely had time to make out three figures rushing into the room before feeling Cody's hand on my shoulder as he shoved me behind the large couch to our left.

"Get down!" he shouted, drawing his gun. Suddenly I was very thankful he had brought it, and if we survived this I intended to make sure he never parted with it again.

Hope screamed as she dove behind the couch with me, her hands covering her ears.

"What the fuck?" she shouted. Her entire body was trembling, but right now I couldn't think about that.

I needed to call up some magic and help Cody get us out of here. That was when I felt it. The magic I reached for was gone. Damnit! Now what?

Cody rolled out from the opposite end of the couch where Hope and I cowered. I heard the rapid fire of his gun but couldn't see what he was firing at. Then I heard a grunt and the sound of two bodies colliding. Cody was hurled backward with one of the intruders on top of him. The two men tussled, crashing over the console table with books and family photos arrayed on top of it. I heard the clatter of Cody's gun as it flew from his hand, sliding across the floor.

"Stay here!" I said to Hope. I jumped up and bolted from behind the couch. Magic or no, I wasn't going out hiding behind an oversized sofa. There was a large fireplace across from the couch that anchored the large, open space. I tried to block out the horrible sounds of Cody trying to fight off his attacker as I raced for it and grabbed one of the iron pokers. Before I could turn around I felt arms clamp around me from behind and a man pressed his face next to mine as he locked me in a perverse reversal of a loving embrace.

"We just want the stone," he grunted into my ear. His breath was hot and foul across my face, like he'd been chewing on used, days old trucker socks. I suppressed a gag and let my head slump forward before rocketing it back with all my strength to slam the back of my skull against his face. He swore loudly, but the blow made him let go of me as he cupped his broken nose. I spun around to face him and brought the fire poker up and around, connecting with the side of his head. He went down in a heap, and that was when I realized he was dressed exactly like the smaller man that had attacked Gar and me at the Falls.

I turned to see the second man advancing on me, again wearing the same pants and shirt.

Shit! Did that mean the crazed-looking one that Cody was struggling with was another shifter? I reached for my magic again, and again came up empty.

"All we want is the stone," said the second creeper, taking a step toward me.

"Well, come and get it," I said, gripping the iron poker tighter and raising it like a baseball bat. Not that I had ever held a bat, but I had seen it done enough at Gar's games that I had a pretty good idea how to swing one.

I heard a grunt followed by a cry of pain and looked over to see Cody standing toe to toe with his attacker. He kneed the man in the groin and followed up with a right cross that landed on the man's jaw with a loud pop. It didn't seem to matter. If anything it just pissed off his attacker even more. He once again lunged at Cody, this time taking him to the ground and pinning him there. Cody placed his forearm on the man's neck to keep him as far from his face as possible. Jesus, that thing was trying to *bite* Cody! And was he growling as he gnashed his teeth at the officer?

My distraction, quick as it was, had given the creeper time to take another couple steps toward me. His eyes went from me to the poker I gripped and then back to me. Then the fucker smiled at me. He smiled and his lips started moving. No words, at least none that I could hear, came out, but his lips were moving incredibly fast. I started to get dizzy, and suddenly the poker I held in my hands started to get heavier. It felt as heavy as a bowling ball, and then double that. I let it drop to the floor as the room started to spin again.

Magic. He was using some type of incantation and it was totally fucking me up.

The creeper moved closer until he was standing over me.

"Give us the stone, and I'll let the policeman live. And your cute little friend."

Fuck. I noticed he didn't say anything about sparing me. Whatever—this wasn't about to go down like this. My stomach was churning, but it wasn't from the mystically induced vertigo attack. It felt more like a visceral reaction to something. Whatever spell he was using on me, I could feel it clawing away at my insides, invading all the little nooks and crannies in my mind. It was making me ill. No, it was pissing me off.

Just then, a loud bang caught both of us by surprise. I looked to the side just in time to see the crazed man that was trying to make a meal out of Cody's face flung to the side. A large, gaping wound appeared in the side of his chest. Standing next to him was Hope. Her arms trembled as she struggled to hold onto Cody's gun. It was still pointed at the man as Cody struggled to his feet. I felt myself start to recover slightly. The sound of the gunfire had been just the distraction I needed.

The anger I felt at being violated tore its way out of me. It felt like I was being hit by a hot wind that was blowing across a construction site, picking up bits of debris to scour my skin. My rage was stronger than whatever magic he had used on me and I shrugged the spell off. I picked up the poker and swung it knee height, striking his left leg. I wasn't sure if the yelp I received was from the pain of the blow or the surprise that I shook off his raggedy ass spell. Either way, I was not in any mood to play.

The creeper collapsed to the floor and was rocking back and forth holding his shattered knee. I stood over him, looking down. I still had my necklace in my hand and held out up in front of his watery eyes.

"This is what you want?" I said, my anger again flaring up. I threw the necklace down onto the marble fireplace.

"No!" the creeper shouted, sensing what I was about to do.

I raised the poker over my head and brought it down in a two-handed, overhead blow onto the pink stone, shattering it into a million pieces. The sound of breaking rock was masked by the violent explosion accompanying it.

Eldritch shards of light in green, blue and red burst out of the broken necklace in all directions. A shockwave of pure magical energy bloomed upward, spiraling outward and knocking everyone in the room off their feet. The house rocked violently as the wave of energy passed through it like a thunderhead.

I staggered to my feet. My head felt numb and there was a roaring in my ears. What the fuck had I just done? I looked around to take in the damage and was amazed at what I saw. Other than the broken furniture caused by Cody's fight, and the busted back door, everything else seemed to be all right. From the mystical explosion I had expected to see the roof of my friend's house completely blown away.

I looked for Hope and saw her lying on her side, still trying to recover from being rocked by the blast. The gun lay beside her and she was instinctively feeling for it with one hand as she forced herself to a sitting position with the other. I made my way over to her and stooped down to help her up.

Suddenly I froze in place. Every instinct I had went off, warning me of danger. I spun around to face the couch, fists clenched. I didn't have a weapon on me, but something had pushed me into fight or flight mode. A deep growl emanated from behind the couch and the hairs on the back of my neck stood up. I saw a hand reach up and grasp the back of the couch in a shaky grip, the fingers stretching and elongating as the nails became inch-long claws. I could feel Hope's terror as she scrambled away from the piece of furniture, placing her back against the wall. I moved with her, trying to stand slightly in front of her protectively.

The hand that gripped the couch dug into it, shredding the top of it before beginning to exert enough pressure to toss the four-hundred-pound piece of furniture end over end into the great room and away from the crouching figure.

My voice caught in my throat and I could feel my eyes widening as Cody stood up, his jaws elongated into a snout complete with razor sharp fangs jutting down. His back arched and he threw his head back, howling in rage at the ceiling as his clothing tore away from his rapidly expanding body. His howl became a scream of terror as his eyes glowed yellow and fixated on the two of us. He dropped to all fours as the man disappeared and the shift to wolf became complete.

Chapter Thirteen

I stood there dumbfounded while Hope screamed.

I wasn't exactly sure what I thought a werewolf would look like. But in my mind's eye, whatever picture I had imagined did not match the great shaggy beast that stood before us. Cody no longer stood on two legs. He also didn't have a furry, snarling, fang-filled face, and he wasn't waving his arms around menacingly like Lon Chaney in the classic movies. What stood in front of us was a five-foot-tall black wolf. It looked incredibly powerful; its haunches rippled with muscles, and the dark hair was long and thick. All of that was capped off by a set of gleaming yellow eyes.

Yellow eyes that at this moment were fixated on the two of us.

Hope swung the gun up, pointing the barrel right at the beast's face. I managed to knock her arm to the side just as she squeezed off a shot. The bullet ricocheted off the far wall and I was barely able to stop her from trying to squeeze off another round.

"Hope, no!" I said.

Not that I blamed her; the wolf in front of us was a terrifying sight. But now I felt different from before. I could feel the magic in the room; I could feel it all around us. Whatever had been blocking me before was gone. It felt like all my senses had just awakened for the first time. I could smell and taste the magic on the tip of my tongue. I reached out, probing at Cody with my new senses.

But Cody wasn't there. There was only the wolf and an animalistic hunger that I had never before imagined. But beyond the hunger I could also sense confusion. Cody may have been gone, swallowed up by the beast that stood before us, but I also sensed that the wolf didn't know its own self; it wasn't sure what it was and why it was here. It was as unsure of its purpose and why it had been called forth as we were. Maybe I would be able use this to my advantage—provided, of course, that I could keep Hope from shooting the damn thing.

The wolf let out a low, rumbling growl. It began to circle, never once taking its yellow eyes off of the two of us. I reached down and called up some magic, channeling it into my right hand in the form of a blue sphere just in case he decided to pounce. Calling on the magic like this was new and instinctive. I wasn't exactly sure what to do with it, but tapping into it felt like the right thing to do at the moment.

It also triggered a change in the wolf's body language. It was as if the wolf could sense the magic, and its demeanor changed accordingly. Saliva began to drop from its mouth in long silver strands. Yes, there was no doubt I was being perceived as a threat. It stopped pacing and squared up, facing us directly. I saw the muscles in its haunches tense as it prepared to spring. In a flash it leapt into the air, all claws and two-inch fangs headed directly for us. I barely had time to raise my hand and hurl a bolt of magic at the dark blur. Blue fire struck it in the center of its chest and hurled it backward, deep into the room. The snarl emanating from the creature told me that it was more angry than it was hurt.

Jesus, is it even possible to hurt a werewolf?

"I know you came here with that thing," said Hope, "but whoever he was, he now wants to eat us. And not in a good way." She cowered farther behind me and I could sense her looking around for the gun. She was right. This wolf would definitely be the end of us both if given the chance. Once again the wolf stalked toward us, this time more cautiously, but fangs still bared nonetheless. It seemed to be focused on the glowing sphere surrounding my hand. I held up my other hand palm out and slowly recalled the magic. Once there was no glow I held up both hands and slowly took a step toward the creature.

"Cody," I said. I spoke in hushed terms the way I'd seen Caesar do on *The Dog Whisperer*. "Are you in there? I don't want to hurt you any more than you want to hurt us." I was advancing on the wolf, keeping my tone and my body language open and non-threatening. "If you're in there, you have to stop this. I don't know what is happening, but you have to fight this."

Even though I didn't want to, I could feel my magic snaking out and probing gently at the wolf. It wasn't something that I was in control of, but at least it wasn't as aggressive as before. I could feel it; whatever had triggered Cody to become this wolf seemed somehow familiar to me. I pushed that feeling aside as I focused on trying to soothe the savage beast. I took a tentative step forward and he seemed to mirror my actions by taking a small step backward. The sheer size of the wolf was impressive. I could hear the wood floors creaking under his massive weight.

His head lowered and his ears seem to go back just a little. I could see his nostrils flare as he sampled the air between us. I made sure to keep my magic shielded, trying not to provoke another attack.

"That's it, that's it, just relax. No one to hurt you."

"What are you doing?" said Hope in a whisper. "That thing can take your arm off at the shoulder if it wants to."

"Be quiet," I said without turning around. I never once took my eyes off Cody, but his eyes seem to break contact the more I stared. If I could just somehow reach the man inside the wolf, maybe, just maybe, I could get him to shift back. Course, I had no idea how shifting worked, so Hope could be right. Maybe I was about to lose my hand. As I got closer I stretched one hand out. Instinct told me that, like any animal, he needed to get my scent, and maybe if I touched him he would know that I didn't mean any harm.

I almost had him. But then the click of the gun cut the tension between us. Hope might as well have thrown scalding water on him. Instantly his growl became an inhuman roar and once again he lunged. This time I was ready. Again I called on my magic and formed a shield. Cody struck the glowing bubble and bounced off, once again careening toward the far wall. This time I reached out with my mind and commanded the bubble to become an extension of my arm. I pinned him against the wall in a grip that he struggled and howled against. He flailed with his claws and gnashed with his teeth at the invisible barrier that held him in place. I knew I couldn't maintain this for long. His strength was unimaginable, and I had no idea how long a first-time-conjured shield would hold up. Sweat was soaking my forehead as I drop my arms and fell to my knees.

Turns out newbie shields don't last long at all. It felt like a freight train was running through my brain. I looked up just in time to see Cody charging me. He leapt through the air and landed straddling me, his jaws mere inches from my face.

I reacted instinctively, grabbing the sides of his neck with my hands. Surprisingly, the fur was very soft. I was sure he was about to bite me, and part of me felt guilty for hoping that the blood splatter from my carotid would at least ruin that fine pelt. But as the fates would have it, that wasn't meant to be.

As soon as I made contact with Cody, something changed. I imagined the shock that ran through me was what it would feel like if I grabbed a live wire. The jolt of energy that coursed through both of us was palpable. My eyes closed as my brain was suddenly flooded with a myriad of images. There were too many to decipher, and the sudden onset felt like the start of a migraine. Apparently Cody felt the same thing. He howled, this time in real pain, and fell away from me.

I forced myself to open my eyes and looked to the side just in time to see Cody writhing in pain next to me. Just as I didn't understand what I had just seen, whatever Cody saw was having an even greater impact. It was forcing him to shift. I watched in awe as fur begin to melt off of him in glowing clumps, the skin beneath becoming smooth and once again taking on Cody's olive Mediterranean hue. His form began to contort and shrink, returning to the more familiar human aspect. Cody's paws became hands and feet, his fanged snout receded back into his face, and tall, pointed black ears once again dissolved into human lobes. The sound of his bones contracting and retreating sounded like little pops of breaking glass carried out in concert throughout the room. A few spasms later and the more recognizable human form of Cody Hunter was lying on the floor next to me.

I stood up and looked down at him. He was curled in the fetal position as small moans escaped his lips. I reach for the blanket that had been knocked off the couch and used it to cover his nakedness. He was shivering, and his teeth chattered even though we could both see the heat rising from his body. We stared as he slowly started to come around. He sat up clutching the blanket around his shoulders and cleared his throat. His voice was scratchy and deep when he finally spoke.

"What happened?" he whispered.

Hope and I looked at one another.

"You really don't remember?" I said.

"I remember fighting with that crazy man. I remember Hope picking up my gun and shooting him," he said. "Oh God! You shot a man. With my gun!" He looked at Hope. "But you also saved my life, so thank you."

"Well," said Hope, "I may have shot a man, but you just tried to eat…"

I jabbed her in the ribs just enough to shut her up before turning my attention to Cody. He was adjusting the blanket around his shoulders, and looked down. For the first time, he noticed that he was naked.

"What the…?" he said.

"We have a lot to discuss," I said. "But we also don't have a lot of time right now."

A scraping sound, like someone dragging themselves through glass, caught our attention. Turns out that was exactly what it was, as one of the men dressed in black tried to drag himself across the back of the room through the broken French doors. It was the one I had hobbled. I walked over to him and placed the sole of my boot on the back of his crippled knee. He screamed out in pain, rolling over onto his back.

"And just where do you think you're going?" I said. "We've got some questions, and I'm thinking you might have some answers."

His pursed lips and the set of his jaw made it clear that he wasn't going to talk. That was until I dug the heel of my boot into the front of his knee and gave a little grind. The yelp of pain it elicited told me that his resolve might not be as firm as he pretended. I removed my foot and squatted down so I was closer to his teary face.

"Who are you?" I said.

The hate blazed in his eyes, but to my surprise he opened his mouth and smiled.

"It doesn't matter if I tell you who I am or if I don't," he said. "They know who you are and they know where you are. Do you really think I'll be the last one to come for you?"

"What do you want with her?" said Cody. He stepped up, the blanket wrapped around him as he stared down at the man who was clenching his teeth to hold back the pain. "Who sent you to do this?"

At Cody's approach, the creeper's entire demeanor changed. I saw his eyes widen in fear—real fear. It was as if he were looking past Cody and seeing something deep inside the officer. That gave me an idea. I look from one man to the other I stood up.

"You know what he is," I said, motioning to Cody. "So you're going to tell me exactly what's going on here or I'll let my friend here take you out back and have a special kind of word with you."

"How did you do it?" the creeper said. "There hasn't been one of his kind here in many years. And on a night with no full moon, that's particularly impressive."

"What's he talking about?" said Cody.

"She's the witch," said the creeper. "Why don't you ask her?" His smile drew back into an evil grin. Then his brow furrowed and understanding seemed to wash across his features. "Unless of course you don't know." That last statement was directed at me. "You don't, do you? You have no idea what you've just done."

I could sense Hope walking up behind us. This time I didn't tell her to drop the gun as she stood next to Cody and me.

"Why don't you tell me what I've done?" I said.

"I won't have to," said the creeper. "We are the Order of Nine. We serve the Grey Seer, Mallus, and he is coming for you. You just broke the last ward. You have made his job so much easier." With that he sneered through the pain and laughed at us once again. The laughter broke apart as he was racked with spasms of pain. He looked at Cody and coughed. "And you, I almost feel sorry for what is going to happen to you."

I felt it even before I saw his lips begin to move and invoke more magic. I felt the heat rising all around us, and I instinctively reached down and grabbed my own magic, drawing it up to form a shield. We watched in horror as the creeper slowly began to dissolve. Whatever spell he had called upon was eating away at him as well as his two comrades. It was the same immolation spell I had used on the intruder's body at the coffee shop. Part of me shivered at the realization as we watched the bodies burn to ash.

Chapter Fourteen

"Well," said Hope. "That was all horrifying."

For a split-second, part of me wanted to see if I could figure out a way to wipe her memories. But I had no idea how magic really worked. It was instinctive, I got that, but something like this I would think would require almost surgical precision. Besides, when the aunts tried that on Cody, it didn't work.

"Are you okay?" I asked.

"What the hell just happened here?" said Hope. "My parents are going to shit when they see this place."

Looking around, I could see that the house did look in pretty rough shape. There were overturned pieces of furniture, broken coffee tables, and of course the demolished French doors. Actually, the whole thing gave me an idea.

"When are your parents coming back?" I said.

"It's their anniversary," said Hope. "They'll go to dinner, then spend the night in the city and be back tomorrow."

"Perfect," I said. "You had a party. And it got a little out of hand with a couple of the guys. You called the cops, they handled everything. You're very sorry, and this will never happen again."

"Jesus," said Hope. "I don't know; I've never been in this kind of trouble before. And besides, that doesn't explain any of the shit that just happened and went down here tonight." She glanced at me questioningly and motioned in Cody's direction. "And what about him? Are you going to explain that?"

The "he" in question had been examining the body, and stood up to walk over and stand next to us.

"You know I can hear you," he said. He had shifted the blanket from around his waist and now wore it like a towel. I couldn't help but avert my eyes even though I wanted to let them linger on his flesh. "Is someone going to tell me what's going on?" He watched as Hope and I exchange gazes uncomfortably. Hope slowly maneuvered away from him to stand behind me. "And why am I naked? Also, why are you so freaked out around me now all of a sudden?"

"I'm so freaked out because you're..." Hope began.

I cut her off for she could finish that quote. "She's freaked out because you're naked."

Hope scowled at me, but she didn't say anything else to the contrary.

"Hope, why don't you see if there something in your dad's closet that will fit Cody?"

She gave us both the side eye, but then nodded and bounded down the hallway toward the master suite at the back of the house.

"There is one thing that I need from you," I said, turning quickly to Cody. "I need you to fill out a police incident report stating that there was a party here and that a couple of drunk frat boys got out of hand and caused some damage."

"Allie, I can't do that. You're asking me to falsify an official report."

"Would you rather I tell them what really is going on here?" I said. "Good luck explaining that."

"I couldn't explain it if I wanted to. Because I still know what's going on. You're asking me to do something like this, then I'm asking you to tell me why."

"Fine. But not here. Let's just take care of this and head home to my place. I'll tell you everything on the way that happened here. We are going to need to consult with the aunts."

"And you better start with why I am naked. Was it at least for a fun reason?"

The look that I gave him told him that it was anything but fun. Before I could even reply, Hope came down the hall carrying a gray tracksuit that was several sizes too big for Cody. She handed them to me, still refusing to get too close to Cody.

"All right," I said. "Cody's gonna do this. He'll file a report, you just stick to the story. No matter what your father says, no matter who comes to visit you, stick to the story."

"There won't be any more visitors, right?" Hope said. "I mean none like these, right?"

"I wish I could tell you definitely no. But honestly, even I'm not sure," I said. "But I want to try something. My aunt had been able to place wards, protective spells, around our house and the coffee shop. It was meant to protect the space from being invaded by any type of supernatural force. I may not be able to re-create a spell of that magnitude, but I can at least leave some type of mystical booby-trap. If anything supernatural happens here it'll let me know. And no matter what, leave your phone on."

Hope nodded and looked from me to Cody. She narrowed her eyes as she walked with us to the front door.

"I will call you first thing in the morning," I said. "We have a lot to discuss."

"Girl, you ain't never lied."

We were halfway back to my aunts' house before Cody spoke. I was on the verge of telling him what had happened, but honestly I was still trying to digest it myself. How could I explain to him that he had shifted into a wolf when I wasn't even sure that that was possible to do? I'd seen it with my own eyes, but more importantly, I had felt it with my magic. Magic to a degree that I didn't even know I possessed was suddenly talking to me, whispering into the back of my brain, but I wasn't quite able to discern what was being said. It was as if the magic were speaking to me in a different language, a language that I once understood but could no longer remember.

"Allie," Cody said, "why do I have a mental image in my brain of me being on top of you and you looking terrified?"

I took a deep breath. "Because you were on top of me. You were actually about to bite me."

I was watching him out of the corner of my eye. I could see him grip the steering wheel a little tighter, but he didn't seem surprised.

"So that part was real too?" he said.

"Yes. You turned into a wolf, Cody." The words sounded ridiculous coming out of my mouth, but Cody wasn't laughing. "Are you a shifter, Cody?"

"Until today, I didn't even know what a shifter was. Not really at least. I mean, we had all heard stories from my parents know about the Big Bad Wolf waiting in the woods to carry us away if we stayed out before it got dark, but nobody really believed that."

"Hell of a day. You find out you're shifter and I find out I'm a witch."

"But I thought you knew you were witch," Cody said.

"No, there's a difference. I knew that I could practice witchcraft, that I had a gift for it. At least that's what I was always told, that magic ran in our family, but this was something completely different from that. It's like the magic was a part of me, not something that I called to and shaped to my will. It felt like it was coming out of me. I've never experienced anything like that before."

"It looks like we both have questions that we're going to need answered. And honestly, your aunts are the only ones who I know of who could be of any assistance to us at a time like this."

That was exactly what I was afraid of. Whatever had just happened, whatever he had just experienced, was completely foreign to anything I had ever been hinted at by my family. Sure, I had dabbled in magic for a while, learning a few things here and there, but that was it. I didn't have a spellbook, I didn't have a broomstick, I didn't have a crystal ball. I didn't even know if these things were the types of objects that witches even truly utilized.

"My shift was connected to your mother's necklace. I don't know how, but when you broke that necklace I felt like something inside of me break at the same time. That's the last thing that I remember until I woke up on the floor next to you with all these weird flashes of pictures of violence and memories of rage inside my head."

"I sensed it too," I said. "I was acting purely on instinct. I would have never, ever in a million years wanted to destroy that necklace. It's the only thing that I have that reminds me of Mom. But every instinct I had at that moment told me that it was the right thing to do. I felt like I had been pushed into fight or flight mode, and I chose fight."

I looked away out the window, watching the trees and the streetlights go by as I waited for the lump in my throat to settle and the steam in my eyes to dry. It hurt thinking about my mom and knowing that I had possibly lost the last connection I had with her.

"It wasn't just your shift that was connected to the necklace," I said. "When I destroyed it, it also removed whatever chains had been binding my magic. I don't know how to explain it, but I felt free and terrified at the same time."

"Didn't your aunts say that your mother had bound your power?"

"Yes. Apparently she did it to protect me."

"What did he mean about… something about a last ward? What exactly is a ward? I heard you mention that to Hope as well."

"A ward is a spell of protection. It creates a wall between two objects that you want to keep separated."

"So the one you put on Hope's house will keep all of these things out?"

"Honestly, I have no idea. It was something I've only read about but never thought I could actually do. In theory it should keep out any type of supernatural creature. But I don't think that those men were supernatural. I think they were using magic, but they were definitely human."

We continued on in silence for a few more minutes before I spoke again. There was something that I had to know.

"Cody," I said, "what did it feel like?" He knew exactly what I was talking about. There was no reason to further explain my question.

"I can't really explain it, because the flashes of memory

that I have are more visceral than visual, if that makes any sense. When I first came to lying there beside you on the floor, I had no memory of anything that led up to that point. But in the time since then I've been getting bits and pieces flashing into my mind, but it's more the feelings that I remember when I was in that state."

He swallowed hard as he turned the wheel of the car and guided us onto the road that led to my aunts' house. As we pulled into the drive, he eased the car into park and looked over at me before opening his door.

"What I felt," he said, "was an overwhelming sense of hunger. I was starving. To be truthful about it, I still am. I hope your aunts have a full pantry."

Chapter Fifteen

Part of me was hoping that the aunts would be asleep when we made our way back to the house. The other part of me prayed that they would be awake. As luck would have it, they opened the door just as I reached to place my key into the lock. The look on at Lena's face told me that they knew something. And the fact that she grabbed me and gave me a full body hug only reinforced that.

"Allie, what happened?" said Aunt Vivian. "We felt so much pain and fear coming from you. And a tear in the fabric of magic."

"Where's Gar?" I asked. I didn't want to have to talk about this in front of him.

"He's in bed, asleep," said Aunt Lena. "We can talk in private."

They both looked at Cody, leaving it to me to decide just what "private" meant.

"First things first," I said. "Cody really needs to eat. Do you think we can whip something up for him?"

Aunt Lena frowned but nodded. She made her way into the kitchen and began rummaging through the refrigerator. Cody and I sat down on the couch in the front room as Aunt Vivian made her way to the back room only to bring back a heavy blanket to place around Cody's shoulders.

"Thank you," said Cody. "I don't know why I suddenly feel very chilled."

Aunt Vivian looked at me but didn't say anything. I looked at Cody and tried to force a smile. Just a couple of hours earlier he had been generating enough heat to warm up a small room, but now I could actually see him starting to shiver.

"It's your body readjusting to going from one form to another," said Aunt Vivian. "You'll get used to it."

"No offense, ma'am," said Cody, "but this is something I don't plan to ever get used to."

"How did you know?" I said.

"You might say I could smell it on him. It's the mystical equivalent of a wet dog walking into the house," said Aunt Vivian. "I can smell you too."

Whether she meant it to or not, that last statement stung. I felt the blush creep up my neck and I looked away to distract myself from the pointed stare she had fixed me with.

"What did you do, Allie?" she continued. She sat down on the chair opposite the two of us and leveled her gaze at me.

I swallowed hard, but before I could say anything, Aunt Lena called from the kitchen. She was taking a pan off the stove and placed it on the large center island. She quickly divided some pasta primavera onto two plates and shoved them at Cody and myself. She then turned to the stove and removed two chicken breasts that had been warming in the oven. Rather than divide them, she placed them both on a single plate and placed them in front of Cody.

"Something tells me you're going to need the protein," she said.

I picked at my food. Cody devoured his. As we ate, I relayed the evening's events to my two aunts, who were listening with rapt attention. By the time I was finished reciting what happened, I was even more exhausted. All of the adrenaline had burned out of my system, and all I could think about was climbing into bed. But I needed answers— answers that only my aunts had.

"Wow," said Aunt Lena. "Where to begin?"

"That's pretty easy," I said, trying not to sound annoyed. "Is Cody a werewolf?"

Aunt Vivian eyed Cody before addressing us. "Cody is a shifter. The fact that he shifted into a wolf form...I can't say what that means."

"The bigger question here is why was he able to shift at all? There have been no shifters capable of doing that for decades," said Aunt Lena.

"As I've said," continued Aunt Vivian, "your mother was extremely powerful. She was the primary engine that drove the spell that bound the shifters, effectively wiping their kind out of existence. By rights, she would be the only one capable of undoing that spell."

"Or her direct descendant," added Aunt Lena as all eyes turned to me.

"What does that mean?" I asked.

"It means that you are your mother's daughter. You inherited her gifts. You inherited her magic. You broke the necklace that she created to bind your power. In effect, that could have temporarily broken the spell she cast that halted shifting." Aunt Vivian spoke quickly, making statements that left little room for discussion or doubt.

"But what about the bear in the woods?" I said. "I had nothing to do with that, and he was able to shift."

"That was different," replied Aunt Vivian. "Obviously that creature had been steeped in spell and potion in order to give him back the ability to shift. A practice run, as I said. But what Cody did, a spontaneous transformation like that, unaided by concentrated spells, and away from any ley structures…that was a beast of a different color."

Aunt Lena nodded her agreement. "I believe that the sudden trauma of being freed from the constraints of your mother's spell triggered the shift in him. The thing we have to figure out is, was this an isolated incident, or has the original spell that forbade shifting been fundamentally damaged?"

"Cody said that he could sense the destruction of the necklace and that it was directly tied to the transformation he underwent," I said. Cody nodded his agreement, mouth too stuffed with chicken to verbalize. "And that's also what allowed me to use my magic as well."

"Yes," said Aunt Lena. "We always knew you had your mother's gifts. We had prayed to the goddess that the day you needed them would never come."

She got up to put on the tea kettle and began rummaging through the tea drawer, bringing out bags with the comforting smell of juniper.

"Three things are of the most importance now," she said. "One, we need to find out who this Mallus is and who these men in black are that work for him. Two, we need to find out why Cody shifted into a wolf; there are no wolves anymore."

"And number three?" I asked when she did not continue.

"Number three is you, my dear," said Aunt Vivian. "The necklace you destroyed was meant to bind your powers, to keep you from accessing them. But that necklace was not the last ward that held the warlocks and the shifters at bay. You are."

Chapter Sixteen

I was so shocked at what my aunt just said that I was actually struck speechless.

"She's a...ward?" said Cody, swallowing a mouthful of fowl. "Cool." The look I gave him made him choke, and he happily returned to the plate of food in front of him.

"Let me clarify," said Aunt Vivian. "You aren't a ward as in you're a veil that is meant to protect us from the realm of the supernatural. What I mean is that in breaking that amulet, you freed yourself to tap into the vast mystical energies that swirl about us. You are capable of more than you know—probably more than even we know."

"My dear," said Aunt Lena, "it's time we told you just what your mother was—what you may yet be as well."

She brought me a steaming cup of tea and I thanked her, taking it in trembling hands. Aunt Vivian sat cups in front of her sister and Cody before she sat down to join us.

"We are all witches," said Aunt Lena. "We were born into a family of witches. We have an affinity with all things supernatural. Magic comes easily to our kind. We are all born with certain gifts that can be augmented with the mystical energies around us when we tap into them. Your aunt—" she nodded at her sister "—has a gift for precognition. She has limited vision when it comes to events that have yet to happen. Myself? I have a connection with the earth, and the flora around us. I can sense the energies that flow around the life-giving plants and trees around us. It lets me know which plants can be combined to make certain potions…and teas." She lifted her tea cup to us and smiled.

"What was my mother's gift?" I asked.

"Like you, your mother was a telekinetic. A very strong one. She had the ability to move energy and direct it into objects to create powerful weapons that were anathema to most supernaturals," replied Aunt Vivian.

"Charging? The way I charged the silver knife the night I was attacked in the coffee shop?"

"Exactly," said Aunt Lena. "That is a singular, unique skill. It's a combination of your natural telekinesis and magic. Your will channels the magic into objects, making them focused weapons capable of disrupting spells and the natural flow of mystic energy. The fact that you were able to channel that ability without being taught is impressive in and of itself. Couple that with the fact that you've been able to project solid magic constructs…the shield that protected you tonight or the orb you conjured in the woods…those are advanced mystical techniques, ones that are beyond the abilities of most witches."

"So I'm a natural?" I said.

"No…more like a prodigy. A magical savant, if you will. Your mother had the same gift as well."

"Then why did she bind my powers? She knew what I was capable of? Couldn't she have entrusted the two of you to teach me?" I asked.

"It wasn't that. She bound you to keep you from becoming something for the warlocks to come and siphon off. They crave a witch's power. It may have been what attracted them to Trinity Cove in the first place..." Aunt Lena's voice trailed off as she said this.

"Lena..." said her sister, her tone low and questioning.

"What?" replied Aunt Lena. "We have come this far. Just tell her the rest. She's taken off her chains now, so she might as well know what she is." She turned to me, reaching across the table to take my hands in hers. "Allie, your mother was a very specific, very special type of witch. She was what was known as a Reliquary. In its truest definition, a Reliquary is a vessel meant to contain holy relics during ancient times."

"You mean like the Arc of the Covenant?" I asked.

"Exactly," replied Aunt Lena. "They were also consecrated to contain holy writings, scrolls, rings...even the bones of saints."

"So...how does a living person become one of those?" I said.

"A Reliquary, a true Reliquary, was created through rituals of prayer and invocation by the leaders of the church. It was reinforced by years of prayer and the application of specific oils and potions until it was deemed worthy of holding the artifacts placed within it for an eternity. Over time, the specific ritual and prayers that created a Reliquary were lost. The art itself died. The church, in its great wisdom, decided that any container could become a Reliquary as long as it was blessed by an official of the church. As a result, there are few true Reliquaries left in the world. While the art of creating these was lost to the church, it was not lost to those who first created the tradition."

"Let me guess," I said, "witches."

"Yes," said Aunt Lena, nodding. "We were the inventors of the lore that the church stole."

"What did you create Reliquaries for?" asked Cody. I looked over at him, and he seemed to be far more at ease now that he had eaten. For some reason that made me feel a little more relaxed as well.

"Originally, we used Reliquaries as part of our rituals. They were meant to contain artifacts of magic that were only brought out for specific ceremonies," said Aunt Vivian. "Over time, witches began to use them to contain dark matter; spirits, fairies, demons…things that were capable of crossing over from other realms into our world and afflict human beings. These malefic creatures were held in certain stones and crystals. Crystals vibrate at the same frequency as the veil that separates our world from the world of the dark ones. Occasionally a denizen of the dark realm would find a crack in the veil and make their way onto our world. Witches would gather these spirits up and trap them in a Reliquary to seal them away."

"Or use them," said Aunt Lena.

"Use them how?" I asked.

"Some witches figured out ways to force the captive spirits to do their bidding. They were called Servants of the Relics, or known more commonly as Gens or Genies," Aunt Vivian continued. "It was that manipulation of power that first gave rise to the warlocks. They had no power of their own, but they could tap into the power contained in Relics, and eventually they learned to harness the energy of a living witch."

"The rise of the warlocks coincided with the birth of the first Reliquary witches," said Aunt Lena. "These witches were born with the innate ability to contain vast quantities of mystical energies that they could draw upon to perform previously unheard-of acts of magic. They could utilize spell and position, of course, but in addition to being able to channel their power into visible forms of energy, they could reduce the most complex of spells to a single spoken word and give it form. Your mother had this power, and now, we believe, so do you."

"And that power is what attracted the warlock to Trinity Cove?" asked Cody.

"Warlocks are attracted to power. It's what they crave," said Aunt Vivian. "And your mother stood out like an all you can eat buffet to a starving man."

"So you think that's what is happening now," I asked. "That I possess the same power my mother did and that's the reason for the sudden increase in supernatural occurrences?"

"I believe that by slowly tapping into your power over the last couple of years, you have…pardon this expression…put your scent out there," said Aunt Vivian. "That necklace your mother fashioned was to keep your powers bound, to prevent you from accessing your full magical potential. And as long as you didn't access that power, you stayed off the grid for all the leeches that have now come sniffing around."

I didn't know what to say. The thought that I was somehow responsible for…

"Don't do that," said Aunt Lena in a stern voice. I wasn't used to hearing that tone come from her. Typically it was Aunt Vivian who carried the heavy emotional weight around the house. "Don't go blaming yourself for something that you have absolutely no control over. Whatever it is that's happening now was destined to happen, no matter what any of us may have tried to do to prevent it." She gave

Aunt Vivian a look that I pretty sure was the period to a discussion they must have been having between themselves.

"A Reliquary, huh," said Cody, smirking. "That's pretty cool."

"Couldn't possibly be any cooler than being a werewolf," I replied before I could stop myself. It sounded less mean in my head, and when I saw Cody wince I instantly regretted it.

"About that," said Cody, turning his face away from me. "How can I be a werewolf? You said they were extinct."

A dark look crossed Aunt Vivian's face as she considered his words. "No. That isn't exactly what I said. I think you need to talk to your father to get that question answered."

"Agreed," said Aunt Lena, "but for now there is another question we need to get answered. Who, or what, is Mallus?"

I nodded. "How do we do that?"

"Well, that's simple," said Aunt Vivian with a smile. "Most likely this is all centered around the warlock that your mother defeated and imprisoned at Singing Falls. The easiest thing would be to ask him what he knows."

Cody and I looked at one another, neither of us trying to hide the shock on our faces.

"I thought you said he was dead," I said.

"Oh, I'm sorry. I guess I need to be a little more succinct with my words," said Aunt Vivian. "We will hold a séance and ask his spirit."

Chapter Seventeen

We follow the aunts up the stairway into the large study that they shared, opposite an open loft that was used as a reading room. This was the second time in one day that we been in their study. To my knowledge that was two times more than I had ever set foot in it as long as I lived in this house. This time I took stock of what was around me. With the exception of the large walkout basement, the room was easily the largest in the house. It was dominated by three nearly floor-to-ceiling windows along the far wall that opened to a view of the street in front of the house. Cream-colored drapes had been drawn across them, and in front of the windows sat two leather club chairs that faced one another with a small cocktail table between them. There was a bar on one wall that appeared to be nicely stocked with a selection of bourbons and whiskeys. Along the opposite wall there was a large, comfortable-looking, well-worn orange sofa. As we entered the room we walked by a wall that was dominated by a custom bookcase running the entire length of it. The open shelves were covered by a multitude of leatherbound tomes. Each row of bookshelves was separated by a row of small jars, vases, and ornate pillboxes, as well as hundreds of mason jars that were filled with dried and fresh herbs. The very bottom shelf held large wooden bowls, ceramic bowls, and what looked like apothecary mixing pieces. A single large area rug dominated the center of the room. The only other item of furniture in the sparsely decorated space was a large wardrobe closet that was tucked into the farthest corner of the room.

"Are you sure this is a good idea?" I said.

"Not at all," said Aunt Vivian. "But right now it's really the only option that we have."

"Make no mistake," said Aunt Lena, "we are doing this for you. In all honesty I would just as soon put you on a plane and ship you off to the opposite side of the country if I thought it would make a difference. But if we have learned anything from the past, it is that some things need to be stopped before they can get started."

I chose not to ask what she meant by that. Instead I looked around the space and smiled. "So what is the big deal about this room? Why is it that Gar and I were never allowed in here?"

"You're about to find out," Aunt Lena said. "This is our sanctum. Every adult with grown children in the house should have one."

I ignored the sarcasm as the aunts directed Cody and myself to have a seat on the couch. It was surprisingly comfortable as we settled in to observe what the aunts were doing. The first thing they did was go to the area rug and roll it up until it lay flush against the two club chairs and the cocktail table by the window. The exposed floor beneath the rug was not hardwood like the rest of the room. It was a single dark gray square that fit just inside the boundaries of the area rug.

We watched silently as they both made their way over to the bookshelf and began gathering various objects. Aunt Lena retrieved one of the large apothecary bowls and a mixer from the lower shelf. She placed them on top of the bar and reached inside of the closed cabinet portion below it to withdraw a couple of vials of a gray, powdery substance. She then returned to the bookshelves and gathered more vials and what looked like a mixture of herbs and dried plants from a few mason jars. Returning to the bowl, she added this to the gray powder while softly reciting an incantation. While I could make out the words, they were in a language that I didn't understand. I had a strong desire to ask her what she was saying, but instinct told me to keep my mouth shut.

From one of the shelves Aunt Vivian removed a large piece of white chalk. Stepping over to the now exposed gray part of the floor, she began to draw a large circle roughly four feet in diameter. Chalkboard paint on the floor was a brilliant idea. Gar and I would have had a blast with that when we were younger. When the circle was complete, Aunt Lena placed the bowl that she had been working on in the center. They each went back to the shelves and retrieved two candles apiece. Moving quietly, they placed the four candles on opposite points of the circle with Aunt Lena's bowl perfectly placed at the intersection. They stepped back to stare at their work. It must have passed inspection because they each nodded and stepped away. Aunt Vivian went to the tall wardrobe, opened the creaking door, and withdrew one last object. It was a gnarled staff roughly five feet in length. While it was ornately carved, the dark wood made it impossible to tell what the shapes along its length were.

Aunt Lena walked over to where Cody and I sat and looked at as both. "Listen to me; this is very important. No matter what you see, no matter what you hear, do not say a word. And no matter what happens, do not move from this spot." We both nodded in agreement, and she turned her back to us and moved to consult with her sister. Whatever they whispered about, they came to an agreement, and Aunt Vivian stepped over to the bar and picked up a box of matches. She set about lighting the four candles as Aunt Lena withdrew a large leatherbound book from one of the shelves. She thumbed quickly through it until she found what she was looking for.

I noticed there was no smell coming from the candles, not even the scent of smoke. The flickering light became the only source of illumination as Aunt Vivian turned off all the lamps in the room. The play of their shadows along the walls created an eerie backdrop as Aunt Lena moved to the head of the circle and sat cross-legged, the large open book on her lap. Aunt Vivian stood at the base of the circle, and cast one last look at her sister.

"Ready?" she said.

Aunt Lena did not respond, but merely nodded her head and began reading from the book she held. She chanted in a language that once again I didn't immediately recognize. I could, however, make out some of the Latin phrasing. I guess three high school years spent studying a dead language was coming in handy after all. No sooner had she finished a couple of phrases when Aunt Vivian raised the staff in front of her and slammed the heel of it down onto the floor. In response, the bowl in the center of the circle immediately caught fire. Orange flames erupted in the bowl, catching both myself and Cody by surprise. Just as quickly as they had appeared, the flames subsided, only to be replaced by a thick cloud of swirling gray and white smoke. It billowed outward and rose into the air but stopped about six feet from the ground, almost as if it were trapped beneath a glass dome.

Aunt Lena once again began chanting, and Aunt Vivian twice brought the heel of her staff down onto the floor again. The room grew cold and I began to see the flames of the candle flicker as if an invisible wind were licking at them. I became aware of a pressure around my hand. I looked down and could see that I had gripped Cody's hand at some point during all this and we were now squeezing tightly to one another, our knuckles white. I glanced at his face, but he was fixated on the scene playing out before us. I followed his eyes to the smoking bowl in the center of the circle and covered my mouth with my hand as I noticed the smoke was taking on the ghostly form of a human being.

Chills broke out along my spine as a wind picked up and began to wail lightly inside the room. Those chills turned to rivulets of icy sweat that ran down my back when I realized the wind was no wind at all. It was raspy breathing, heavy and drawn out, coming from the figure that was made of smoke and trapped within the circle. It changed to a low, wheezy rattle and reminded me of someone with a severe case of emphysema compounded by walking pneumonia. With each distressed exhalation I could feel the hair on the back of my neck stand up a little more.

With each deep breath the smoke seemed to coalesce more and more into the shape of a figure. While it had no recognizable features, it seemed to pulse in and out, one minute whispers of smoke, the next the form of a human being. It floated forward and seemed to strike a boundary when it encountered the circle line drawn on the floor. It withdrew once again back to the center, hovering above the bowl. Just when I thought it couldn't get any creepier, the blasted thing spoke.

"Who?" the shade seemed to whisper at all of us. "Who calls me?"

"You are bound by the will of Nekris," said Aunt Vivian, "and like all those who are so bound, you must speak the truth."

There was a long rambling sigh that seemed to emanate from the wispy figure. "Of course. Witches. Who else would call me forward like this?"

"I command you, spirit, identify yourself," said Vivian.

There was a drawn-out wheeze, and the chill in the air thickened. Aunt Lena increased her chanting, and in response the spirit grew more restless.

"You know who I am," it said. "Just like I know who you are."

If the aunts were shocked by what the shade just said, they didn't let on. Aunt Lena continued chanting, nonplussed by the words that were just spoken.

"Again," said Aunt Vivian, "I remind you that you are bound to the will of Nekris. As such, you must answer our questions and you must answer truthfully. Who are you?"

"My birth name is William, but you will know me by the name Zin."

"Are you the warlock who came to our town of Trinity Cove and killed so many of our kind?" said Aunt Vivian. "The warlock who is known as the Bringer of Pain and the Maker of Monsters?"

"I am. Would you give me the pleasure of knowing who you are and how you know me?"

"I will not. I have questions for you and you must answer," replied Aunt Vivian.

I must have been hearing things, for the shade within the smoke seem to chuckle.

"Ask whatever you want, Vivian," said the shade.

"You do not know me, spirit," said Aunt Vivian. "You are forbidden to speak our names, and you must answer only the questions we ask."

"Do you think that I don't recognize the stench of your magic?" said the shade. "You put me in this dark place. You took away my pets. You took away my fun. I can hear Lena chanting. I would recognize the taste of your magics anywhere. But I sense you're one short…"

Aunt Vivian showed no emotion but continued her questioning. "Do you have any knowledge of new warlocks being in Trinity Cove?"

"No. It would not be a surprise if there are, however. The only surprise would be that it's taken them so long to find this treasure."

"Do you yourself have any knowledge of dark magic being worked to undo the balance in Trinity Cove?" said Vivian.

The shade did not answer but seemed to grow restless, if that was possible for something comprised primarily of smoke. "If I did, do you think it would be in my best interest to tell you?"

"Need I remind you, spirit, that you are bound? You must answer truthfully."

"No, I don't have to. There's something different about you now. Your magic isn't what it once was. You cannot compel me. However, I will answer your questions because it amuses me to do so. There are whisperings on this side of the veil."

"What kinds of whisperings?" said Vivian.

"Whisperings that the forbidding is crumbling. That it has weakened in places and allowed old, dark things to creep through. But something tells me you already knew that."

"Is there a force actively working to bring down the forbidding?" said Vivian.

"Yes."

"Is it another warlock?"

"No. The signature is of something much older than that."

"Tell me what you know of the name Mallus and the Order of Nine," said Aunt Vivian.

The spirit seemed to pause, withdrawing back into the smoke. Aunt Lena again increased her chanting, drawing the shade out.

"Do you know who or what Mallus is?" said Vivian.

"Mallus is your death. If Mallus has come then darkness will surely follow. The Order of Nine are his apostles. They will pave the way for him to consume the light."

I could see Aunt Vivian looking at Aunt Lena with concern in her eyes. Aunt Lena's eyes were closed as she continued to chant, but there was a line of sweat breaking out on her forehead. It was obviously a strain for her to maintain control over the forces that had summoned this ghost. But to her credit, she did not give up.

"Tell us, warlock, how do you know this Mallus?" said Aunt Vivian.

"That is simple. Mallus is the one who taught me the ways of the dark. He is blackness and glory beyond your comprehension. And where he walks, the light will fall."

"Tell us how to find him," said Vivian.

"I have a better idea. Why don't you release me from my prison, and I will be happy to take you to him."

"You don't know where he is, do you?" said Aunt Vivian. "And if he was your teacher, you must not have been a very good pupil. After all, he didn't seem to care enough to come to your aid before all this time. I think that you have been forgotten. You will never leave that dark half world that you are trapped within."

"How about I make you a deal?" said the spirit. "Release me, and I'll do something for you."

"Treacherous spirit," said Vivian, "we would never make deals with your kind. There is nothing you can do for me."

"Really? I suppose you never want to see your sister again? Free me from this prison, and I can reunite you with her."

The shock of what the spirit said reverberated through the air. I heard Aunt Lena stopped chanting. Before I could stop myself, I let out an audible gasp and stood up. Wrong move, and I knew it as soon as it happened. Instantly the tone in the room changed. The temperature dropped enough that I could suddenly see my breath in front of me. The smoky form of the spirit had become so dense it was nearly solid, and it stood at the edge of the circle, slowly tracking its featureless head back and forth. I could tell it was trying to lock in on me.

"Who is that?" the spirit said. "What tasty morsel is here with you, Vivian? I sense...so much power."

"We are done here, spirit," said Aunt Vivian. "I command you return to the—"

"No!" I shouted before she could release the spirit. "Did this thing just say it knows where my mother is?" I took a step forward, fists clenched. Only Cody's hand on my arm stopped me as he stood and held me back.

"Allie, no!" he said.

The reaction of the spirit was immediate and violent. A rumble passed through the room as the smoke comprising the shade went from wispy gray to jet black. A face that had until now been entirely formless condensed into a single glowing red eye. It turned and locked onto the two of us.

"My pet!" the spirit shouted. "You have one of my pets! Give it to me! Give it to me now!" The black form charged at us only to rebound from an invisible wall when it struck the boundary of the circle. The spirit roared in rage and launched forward to strike the barrier yet again. The flames of the four candles seem to erupt, belching yellow fire three feet into the air. Still the spirit continued to strike at the barrier. This time a small crackling could be heard folioing each blow it landed.

I saw Aunt Lena slam the book closed and leap to her feet. Immediately she began chanting, arms outstretched, doing everything she could to keep the barrier in place.

"Enough!" screamed Aunt Vivian. She raised her staff above her head and brought it down with smashing force in a two-handed blow. The head of the staff landed in the chalk circle as she said a single word: "Esconde!" The chalk outline of the circle glowed brilliantly before erupting in a dome of bright white and blue light. Aunt Vivian stepped back as the dome melted away, taking with it the wailing form of the warlock.

The silence that rushed to fill the room was all too brief.

The disturbance that had been created by the spirit was suddenly replaced with a sound even more terrifying. The ragged wheeze of the ghost was gone. In its place I could hear a deep, threatening growl. The sound was almost painful, like the combination of a warning, a threat, and fear. I looked slowly to my left at Cody. His body was rigid, his head bowed forward so that his chin rested on his chest. He was breathing heavily with a deep, rumbling growl emanating from his chest. My eyes traveled down the length of his body and I could see his hands squeezed into trembling fists. Blood dripped from his palms where his nails had suddenly extended into claws and were piercing his own flesh. He turned toward me, his face misshapen with glowing yellow eyes. His mouth, only beginning to change, silently spoke one word to me.

"Run!" he was saying, although his thrusting jaw and the rows of jagged teeth that were punching through made reading his lips all the more difficult.

Chapter Eighteen

I fell backward onto the couch, slapping my hand over my mouth to silence a scream. I watched in horror as Cody's back arched painfully. The cracking of his bones sounded like gunshots in the suddenly too small space. I wanted to move, to run away, but I was frozen in place. The gruesomeness of the sight had me transfixed. Slowly, as his jaw began to elongate, Cody turned to look at me. He was beginning to salivate, and the intensity in his yellow eyes kept me from reading what his intentions might have been. His only word echoed loudly in my mind: *Run!*

He turned his body to face me and reached forward, razor-sharp talons glinting in the flickering light. Before either of us could make a move, I heard a sharp thwack as Aunt Vivian's staff struck the side of Cody's head. It wasn't a hard blow; it was only meant to get his attention. It worked, as he turned to face the older woman, a snarl forming in his throat. As soon as he locked eyes with my aunt, he froze in place.

Aunt Vivian held his stare, the tip of her staff inches

away from the bridge of his face. Neither of them moved, and neither looked away, although I could see Cody's nose beginning to twitch as if he were tasting something in the air. The sudden quiet and stillness in the air snapped me out of my frozen panic. I concentrated and reached down for my magic, pulling it up and channeling it into my fist.

"Allie, no!" It was Aunt Lena. Before I could do anything, she rushed to my side, facing Cody. She held her small fist in front of her face, opening it with her palm up to reveal a white powder resting in her hand. She blew hard, blasting the substance into Cody's face.

Instantly the wolf gasped and swatted at the space before him with a gnarled hand. Whatever the substance was, the effect was immediate, as Cody dropped to one knee and then all fours before finally collapsing in a heap on the floor. In the brief second it'd taken him to collapse he reverted fully back to his human form. I felt a hand gripping my forearm and looked up to see Aunt Lena as she held tight to my arm.

"It's okay, girl. Reel it back in," she said.

It took me a second to realize that she was talking about my magic. A blue orb still shimmered around my closed fist. I close my eyes to calm my breathing. As I relaxed I felt the magic flow back into me and settle at a point just behind my navel.

"That's it," said Aunt Lena. "The touch of your magic would have just completed his transformation. And no matter what my sister might think, none of us are a match for a fully shifted wolf at this point."

"No kidding," said Aunt Vivian. "We barely managed to contain one spirit. We are definitely getting too old for this."

I didn't answer, and I could feel their eyes watching me as I stared at Cody's unconscious form.

"Is he okay? What did you give him?" I said.

"A concentrated form of animal tranquilizer," said Aunt Lena. "That dose would've dropped a charging rhino."

"That sounds like a lot," I said. "How long will he be out?"

"You never know with werewolves," said Aunt Lena. "Couple of hours, maybe a couple of days. We'll have to wait and see."

"Should we?" said Aunt Vivian.

"Should we what?" I said.

The aunts exchange looks before meeting my eyes. "And stop doing that," I said. Before they could question me, I continued, "That thing that you two are doing when you look at each other. Whatever that silent communication is. If it involves everyone else in the room then just speak up."

"Very well," said Aunt Vivian. "We were just wondering if it wouldn't be better if your friend here didn't wake up."

I didn't try to hide the look of shock that fell across my face, or the shadow of anger that quickly took its place.

"I can't believe you would just say that," I said, trying to control the tremble in my voice.

"Take it easy, Allie," said Aunt Vivian. "It was just a thought."

"No, it wasn't," I said. "But whatever it was, it's not something that we should ever consider again."

"The warlock referred to him as one of his pets," said Aunt Lena. "Do you know what that means? Because if you don't, I will happily spell it out to you."

I didn't say anything. I didn't feel that I had to. I wasn't around the last time werewolves prowled the streets of Trinity Cove. But what the aunts were suggesting left a very bad taste in my mouth that I just couldn't swallow. I looked down at the unconscious form at my feet, and shook my head.

"There's another way. There has to be," I said. "Otherwise, who are really the animals?"

Neither of them said anything as I took the blanket off the couch and covered Cody with it. I didn't mean to, but I couldn't stop myself from lightly stroking his hair as I lifted his head and eased one of the pillows under it. When I stood up I could see that that small sentiment had not been lost on the aunts.

"What did he mean about your sister?" I said. "He was talking about my mother, right?"

"Honestly, I have no idea," said Aunt Vivian. The fact that she did not hesitate before answering told me that she was not holding anything back. "But I assume, since we have no other sister, that's exactly who he meant."

I hesitated before asking the next question. Truth be told, I wasn't sure I wanted to know the answer. "Is my mother dead?"

"We don't know," said Aunt Vivian, taking me by the hand. "When we faced the warlock, and we created the forbidding that holds him and all of his ilk at bay, your mother sacrificed herself to ensure that he would never walk in this world again."

My legs were numb and would no longer hold me up. I dropped onto the couch, still not letting go of my aunt's hand. She sat down next to me and reached up to push a stray strand of red hair away from my eyes and tuck it behind my ear.

"The spell that we created to lock the warlock away, and keep the world of the living separated from that of the supernatural, could only stand for so long. The magic that created the forbidding needed constant feeding. Without a continual influx of new magic it would have eventually fallen. Your mother knew this." Aunt Vivian's voice faded away. She swallowed an immense sadness and could not look me in the eye.

"Your mother was the only one of us who could maintain such a wall," continued Aunt Lena. "She chose to seal herself away on the supernatural side of the forbidding." She watched me closely to make sure that I was following what she said. "As a Reliquary, your mother could tap into a nearly limitless reserve of magic. She used that power to continually reinforce the forbidding, ensuring that no warlock, no supernatural being of any kind, could cross over and terrorize our world again."

I let what my aunt said sink in. "So you mean to tell me that my mother, your sister, was trapped on the other side of the dimensional wall with warlocks, demons, spirits and all manner of supernaturals all this time?"

Neither of them said anything. "If that's the case, then why did the warlock say there were holes appearing in the forbidding? Why am I suddenly been attacked by bear shifters? And why is Cody suddenly transforming into a werewolf?" Neither of them spoke, so I decided to push the envelope a little. "I'll tell you why. It's because magic is returning to the world. I don't know what that means for my mother, if she's still alive, but it can't be good."

"It doesn't mean anything good for us, that's for sure," said Aunt Lena. "If there truly are cracks appearing along the forbidding allowing the darkness to seep into our world, then all of us are in danger." She turned and spoke to Aunt Vivian. "We need to make a trip tomorrow."

"Where are we going?" I said.

"*We* aren't going anywhere," said Aunt Vivian. "My sister and I need to make a trip up north. There are other communities, covens of witches, farther up the coastline. We need to see if this is localized just to Trinity Cove, or if it's more widespread."

"And if it's more widespread?" I said. "Will these other witches help us?"

"There's no way of knowing," said Aunt Lena. "Many of these communities were settled by witches who fled the warlock's attack on Trinity Cove. There weren't many of them, but at the time they wanted nothing to do with magic or warlocks. I don't think that they will welcome us with open arms considering we're showing up bringing both of those back into their lives."

"And what about my mother?" I said. "Aren't we going to try and save her? Is this even the right course of action?" They both looked at me, their eyes encouraging me to continue. "I mean, if this is just the start, wouldn't they be wise to try and stop this new threat now? Before it gains in strength or more supernaturals are released? Running off to ask for help from someone that you've already said wants nothing to do with us doesn't seem the wisest. I'm sorry, I don't mean any offense, but that's just how I see it. If there is any chance my mother is still alive, I have to find her."

Aunt Vivian sighed before speaking. "Did you not see what just happened? It was all we could do to contain a single spirit. That spirit did not have access to the warlock's powers. If that were to happen, my sister and I would be no match for anything conjured against us. And you are not ready for any of this." She glanced down at Cody before looking back to me as if to press her point home. "And your mother knew the risk she was taking. That's why she never wanted you to know anything about any of this. No magic, no supernatural world, none of it. She didn't want you to ever face the sacrifices required of her."

"So what am I supposed to do?" I asked. "Just sit around here waiting for you guys to decide what we're going to do?"

"Yes. That's exactly what you're going to do," said Aunt Vivian. "Right now your job is to protect Gar. You said it yourself: whatever is happening is just beginning. When we return we will discuss training you in the use of your magic. But until then, your power is too unpredictable. You may feel strong, but any warlock worth his salt will drain you before you even know what hits you."

"We have something for you," said Aunt Lena. She walked over to the corner wardrobe were Aunt Vivian had kept her staff. She rummaged around it briefly before returning, holding something in both hands which she offered to me. It was a length of silver cord about four feet long and weighted on either end.

"What is it?" I asked.

"It is a belt woven of silver thread," said Aunt Lena. "It belonged to your mother. I think she would want you to have it."

I took the shiny cord in hand, examining it closely. It looked like a belt I had seen the girls wearing on *That '70s Show*. It wasn't exactly the height of fashion now. I think the aunts could see the way that I eyed it suspiciously.

"Just wear it for the time being," said Aunt Lena. "It's pure silver, and you have seen the effects that silver can have on anything supernatural. It's a lot easier to hide than a silver dagger in this day and age." I hadn't thought about it like that, but it made perfect sense.

"At least take me with you," I said.

"And what about Gar?" said Aunt Vivian. "He's human and far too vulnerable to all of this."

She knew I would never argue that point. No matter

what else may be happening, I would never let anybody or anything hurt Gar.

"Besides," said Aunt Vivian, pointing at Cody, "you have other duties as well. You need to keep an eye on him. And no matter what, do not expose him to your magic. Or better yet, tell him to lock himself in one of his jail cells until we can figure out what's going on."

Yeah, like that was going to happen. I smiled and nodded but didn't say anything. I smiled not in agreement, but because she had just given me an idea.

"He's too big to move," I said, looking at Cody. "If you sure he's okay, why don't we just let him sleep it off right there?"

"Fine," said Aunt Vivian. "I'm too tired to argue at this point. We will leave first thing in the morning, and you need to make sure that he is out of here as soon as he wakes up. I'm serious, Allie. I don't want you hanging out around a werewolf until we know exactly what's going on."

And that, I thought to myself, was exactly what I was going to figure out as I watched the aunts walk out of the room. I took one last quick glance at Cody to make sure that he was still sleeping, and then headed over to the wall of books that covered the shelves across from me.

Chapter Nineteen

I listened for the soft click as the door to the aunts' study closed behind them. Then I waited, listening for any sign that they may have been standing outside of the door with their ears pressed against it. Once I was satisfied they had retired downstairs, I padded softly to the bookshelves and began looking through everything. The books were all arranged neatly with their binders facing outward. There must have been hundreds of them, and not a single one had any writing on the binder, or the book cover for that matter.

I pulled down one particularly heavy volume, the one that I thought Aunt Lena had been reading from, and upon opening it I realized that it was filled with hundreds of handwritten pages. But of course, it was also in whatever language Aunt Lena had been chanting, not English. Again, it looked familiar to me. I could make out a small tug in the back of my mind. I had seen this before, but I couldn't remember when or where. Just as I was about to put the tome back I felt an itching somewhere behind my eyes. It was accompanied by the now familiar pull of my magic that seemed to be housed behind my belly button.

Instead of putting the book back, I stared harder at the page, letting my magic reach out and caress the words written there. Maybe it was my imagination, but the writing began to take on a golden glow, and the strange markings and symbols started to move around on the page, rearranging themselves into something that more closely resembled English. It wasn't quite the same, but I suddenly realized I could read the words. I hadn't wanted to risk disturbing Cody, so I deliberately left the lamps off, instead relying on the soft glow from the candles that still lit the room. The candles, combined with the glow from the book, were soothing in the dim room. The book itself reminded me of a large Kindle Paperwhite; the light given off was perfect for reading without causing eyestrain.

The Words of Calling was the title of the page I had opened. The paragraphs that followed described how to use the certain esoteric phrases and words, coupled with the intent and will of the witch, to bring forth truths and items that were lost or hidden. That would definitely come in handy, especially with the way I was always forgetting where I left something.

I looked around for something to write on; no way I would remember all of these. But of course the aunts had no pen and paper that I could see on the shelves. I looked around and saw the wardrobe in the corner. Tempting, but no. This was bad enough, but opening a closed door and rifling through what was behind it felt too mush like a betrayal of the aunts' trust. Not that what I was doing was completely on the up and up, but at least I would be able to justify the actions to myself. I mean, the books were all out and sitting right there.

So, nothing to write with. I briefly considered taking out my phone. Would the camera capture the phrasing in a way I would still recognize when I looked at the pictures? Before I could test that, I again felt the tug of my magic. This time it whispered to me, almost like a breeze blowing gently in my ear. I wasn't exactly sure what it wanted me to do, but I gave in to the feeling and let my body move of its own accord.

I held the book open in one hand and placed my other hand on the page. The glow from the writing flared briefly before settling back to its golden glow I had become accustomed to seeing. As soon as it settled back down, I realized that I remembered the phrasing on the page verbatim. Somehow, I had absorbed the spell almost instantaneously, no memorization required.

"Cool! Where was this power when I spent all those nights trying to memorize periodic tables?" I whispered to myself.

I flipped trough the book, taking note of a few more interesting spells that I thought might come in handy and absorbed those as well. I looked at the shelves and realized that there must be more spells present than I would have time to peruse, even if I spent an entire summer locked away in the room. There had to be a reason that the first spell that presented itself to me was a spell of calling. I placed the book I was looking at back on the bookcase and thought about the type of information I wanted to learn. My aunt had mentioned ley stones and ley lines before. I had an idea of what they were, but I wondered if there was anything present here that might explain just what they were and how they worked. I concentrated on what I wanted, and recited the first incantation I had memorized.

"Ephesis gran retiree," I said, holding out my hands.

Instantly a small, tattered book appeared in my hands. I smiled, proud of my small accomplishment. I flipped open the book only to find that it was written entirely in English. Granted it was handwritten and the penmanship of whoever had written it was a little lacking, but at least I could read it without any type of magical assistance.

The book appeared to be a written history of Trinity Cove and the system of intersecting ley stones and currents that ran throughout and under the town and surrounding areas. Apparently, Trinity Cove was built over a rare intersection of Telluric, or Earth current. Those were naturally occurring electric currents that moved through the earth and the sea. The early mystics that settled in Trinity Cove had been drawn by the area's abundant radiant energy that they were capable of sensing. Those early mystics scoured the earth and stone around Trinity, creating the ley lines that corresponded to the Telluric currents. The lines enabled the mystics to tap directly into and direct the energies that bubbled around Trinity Cove.

Over the generations, the combination of their magics and the natural energies found in Trinity combined to create the magical eddies and currents that seeped into the stone, soil and eventually the waterfall that became known as Singing Falls. As a result, the area attracted all manner of supernatural creatures who came to live in peace and harmony with the earth. The mages, mystics, witches, shifters, fae folk, and shadow dwellers all resided in and around Trinity Cove, living in peace and harmony.

The book also warned of the attraction of darker, more malevolent energies that were summoned. It warned that a time would come when the energies of the ley could become corrupted, and when that happened…

"What are you doing?" came Cody's voice drifting out of the darkness.

The sudden sound startled me so much I slammed the book closed.

"Umm, studying I suppose," I said. I placed the book back on the shelf and walked over to Cody. He had managed to drag himself up off the floor and was sitting on the couch.

"What happened?" he asked, rubbing his head, his voice groggy and weak.

"You made with the old presto-change-o and tried to eat us. Well, you started to change at least; the aunts stopped you."

He had a blank look on his face, and then I could see something moving in his features. He was remembering something—something unpleasant.

"What is it?" I asked.

"I remember the voice. The ghost, when it spoke there at the end…it was like he was speaking directly to me, calling me. And I wanted to respond. But in my other form, like I knew what he wanted from me and I wanted to reply in kind." He shivered at the memory. "It was like a master calling his dog. I wanted to go running to him." He looked down, and I could see his shoulders begin to rise and fall quickly as he tried unsuccessfully to hold back tears. "What the hell is happening to me?"

I didn't know what to say because I didn't know the answer to his question. I ached for him, because deep down, I wasn't sure that the answer would be anything good for him. I might not be able to soothe him with my words, so I did the only thing I could think of that might help us both. I reached over and took Cody in my arms, whispering softly into his hair that it would all be okay as I gently rocked him back and forth until his sobbing subsided.

He looked up at me, his dark eyes red and swollen. I smiled and brushed one hand across his cheek before softly kissing his lips and caressing him. His mouth came alive and kissed me back, drawing me closer as the heat between us began to grow. Jesus, had I just whimpered? What the hell was I thinking? That was it, I wasn't thinking…I was feeling, responding to a need that I didn't even know was buried inside me. My hand grasped his shoulder, sliding down his well muscled arm to fumble at his belt buckle.

He gasped. The sudden blast of breath against my face only served to raise my desire. Then he took my hand and moved it away from him, holding it gently in his as he broke our kiss and rested his forehead against mine. I knew what he was thinking; it wasn't the right place or time. While I felt safe with him, I knew that was exactly why we had to stop. A witch who couldn't control her power and a werewolf that couldn't control his shift—it was a potential recipe for disaster.

I pulled away, breaking our embrace. I was sad, but happy at the same time. Cody smiled at me and lay back on the couch, pulling me down on top of him, one arm thrown protectively over me. He was so warm, so comforting that I didn't even remember drifting off to sleep, enveloped in warmth and skin.

I woke up a couple of hours later, greeted by the first ray of daylight creeping into the room. We sat up, each a little sheepish about our actions a short time ago. Cody took my hand and kissed it gently, letting me know that everything was all right. I smiled and we stood up, stretching out cramped muscles, and made our way to the door.

I stopped, another idea crossing my mind.

"What is it?" he asked.

"Just a second," I said, moving back to the bookshelves. I recited the incantation quietly, summoning yet another book to my hands. I flipped through, found the information I needed and absorbed it.

"What was that?" Cody said when I returned to his side.

"Just some insurance," I replied. "Hopefully, like that dusty old bottle of ipecac the aunts keep in the cupboard downstairs, it will never be needed."

Chapter Twenty

Even though it was early, the smell of waffles and frying bacon greeted us as we entered the kitchen. Aunt Lena was manning the cooktop, and I could see Aunt Vivian out on the deck, watering her plants. A smell I wasn't used to filled the air, and I looked over to see a full pot of coffee brewing.

"Coffee, Aunt Lena?" I said. "To what do we owe this pleasure?"

"Your aunt and I have a five-hour drive ahead of us. We need energy, not the relaxing calm of tea." She glanced briefly at Cody as he walked up behind me, but didn't say anything. "Besides, I'm betting you could use a little caffeine as well."

Cody only smiled, then went about removing two mugs from the open cabinets and began filling them with the steaming brew. I like the fact that he didn't ask for cream or sugar but instead took a sip of the piping hot liquid black. I liked him twice as much when he handed me my cup the same way. I raised my cup to him in a small salute before blowing gingerly at the coffee and taking the first warming draw.

"Wow," I said. "I know teas are your specialty, but you really should explore your calling for making coffee. This would be an instant hit at the shop."

Aunt Lena returned the compliment with a smile just as Aunt Vivian was walking in the door from the deck. She looked at me and then Cody before settling her gaze on me.

"I know, I know," I said. "He's on his way out."

"Well, he's here now," said Aunt Vivian. "No pointing him leaving without trying to choke down some of these dry waffles your aunt is making."

"Dry?" said Aunt Lena. "Are you seriously going to criticize my cooking? Allie, do you remember what happened the last time my sister cooked? Was it you or Gar who ended up calling the fire department?"

I wasn't falling for that. I knew better than to laugh. The aunts could jibe at one another all they wanted, but I didn't dare give the appearance of picking sides. I just smiled good-naturedly and said, "To be fair, she did say she was making blackened fish." For some reason that made Aunt Vivian smile and lightened the mood in the room considerably.

"I thought you two were leaving at first light?" I said.

"Oh, we'll be leaving soon enough," said Aunt Lena. "We just have a few loose ends that we want to tie up before heading out." She squinted her eyes and looked closely at me. "Why? Is there reason you want us out of the house?"

"Not at all. I just need to plan the day as far as what to do with the coffee shop and Gar. I suppose I can see if a couple of the part-timers can run the shop today. That will allow me to stay here with Gar until you return."

Aunt Lena nodded approvingly. "Yes, that sounds like a good idea. Until we can figure out what's going on, I'd rather you and your brother stay here where we know you're safe." I wasn't exactly sure we were safe, but I wasn't going to argue that point.

"The only thing I need to do is have Cody drive me back up to the parking lot at Singing Falls. I need to get my car. But don't worry; I will take Gar with me," I said.

"Oh, don't worry about the car," said Cody between sips of coffee. "That lot doesn't allow twenty-four-hour parking, so it's probably already been towed to the impound lot. I can have it brought to you."

I gave Cody a stinging look, pursing my lips for emphasis. For two people who had dodged death a couple of times together, we really were not in sync.

"However," he said, catching my drift, "let me just make a couple of calls just to make sure that the car has been picked up. Even if it has been, it's probably a good idea that I take you to the lot so you can sign for it and make sure that there was no damage to the vehicle." He took his cell phone from his pocket and went to step out onto the porch.

Aunt Vivian walked over and took me by the hand. She reached up and brushed at my hair with her hand before placing both of her palms against my cheeks. "So beautiful. You are the spitting image of your mother." I smiled and reached up to caress my aunt's hand. "I don't want you to ever think that we have forgotten your mother or the sacrifice that she made so that you and your brother could live a normal life. There isn't a day that goes by that I don't miss her. But she made certain requests of my sister and me, and we've always intended to honor her memory by keeping them. There was nothing more important in this world to her than you and your brother. So whatever your aunt and I have to do to keep you safe, well, that's what we're going to do."

I looked down, unable to hold my aunt's gaze. "And I understand that, but I'm not a child, and you said it yourself: we are born into magic. I have these gifts and I feel a calling, like I am meant to use them for something greater. If they can help me find our mother, then I feel like that's what I should be doing." I could feel my frustration mounting. "At the least I feel like I need to help seal the rift in the forbidding. It feels like Trinity Cove is the center of whatever evil is happening, and I need to help set it right."

"I can't argue with you there," said Aunt Vivian. "As much as your mother wanted you to have nothing to do with this life, I don't think that's meant to be. Maybe part of this is our fault for not preparing you sooner, but what's done is done. All we can do is make sure that the past does not repeat itself. And that's why it's very important that you stay safe until we get back."

I nodded and smiled, giving my aunt's hand a caress one more time. She got up and headed into the kitchen just as Cody walked back into the house. He nodded to me and cleared his throat. "So it looks like your car was not picked up just yet. The department is down to only two deputies and they have not had time to open the lot to towed vehicles. So it looks like I'll be driving you back up to the Falls to get it."

"Well you're not heading out on an empty stomach," called Aunt Lena, placing a platter overflowing with bacon onto the island. "Allie, go wake up your brother. By the time you get back from collecting your car we'll be gone, so it would be nice to have breakfast all together before we head out."

I watched Cody move to sit at the island, his face

lighting up at the sight of waffles and bacon heaped before him. I went to rouse my sleeping brother and tried to ignore the slight sense of foreboding that was brewing in the back of my mind.

Chapter Twenty-One

"Hey, I thought we were going to get the car," said Gar. He looked up from his phone and slipped his headphones off long enough to take account of where we were. "Singing Falls is the other way."

"Change of plans," I said. "Cody and I have an important errand to run so I'm going to drop you off with Hope."

"What? No way," Gar huffed. "I'm not a kid anymore. Wherever you're going, I'm going too."

I was sitting in the passenger seat of Cody's car, and I spun around to face Gar. "No, you're not a child anymore. But you're not quite an adult either, and where we're going might be a little dangerous. I would never forgive myself if something happened to you."

"I thought we settled this," said Gar. "Where you go, I go, remember? Besides, I feel safest with you."

He was right, of course; I did feel better keeping him with me, but under the circumstances I knew that wasn't an option. With everything I had just learned about myself, and more importantly what I was learning about Cody, I almost felt the safest place for Gar would be as far from us as possible. But no way was I telling him that.

"Gar," I started, "I promised I would always be truthful with you moving forward. So you're going to have to believe that what I'm telling you now is the absolute truth. You are better off not knowing what we have to go do."

He didn't say anything but seemed to consider the words. "At least tell me where you're going. If it's as dangerous as what you're saying there's a chance you could get into trouble. If I know where you are and you don't come back, I can at least send help."

Surprisingly, I couldn't find any fault with his logic. I really hadn't thought through everything, but it made sense that if something happened to Cody and me, at least the aunts would know where we had gone. I looked over at Cody and he just shrugged his shoulders.

"We're going to see Cody's father."

"That doesn't seem dangerous," said Gar. "Why can't I come along?"

"Because I'm a werewolf," said Cody without taking his eyes off the road. "So we need to ask my father how that can be." He took his eyes off the road long enough to glance over at me. "What? You just said the two of you are being honest with one another."

"Well I didn't think we were being *that* honest," I replied.

"No shit! You're a werewolf?" Gar said. "So when the moon turns full, you get all hairy and fang-ish?"

"No," I said, "he doesn't need the moon to change. But that does raise a question; if you can change against a full moon, what other werewolf stereotypes are wrong?"

"Well as long as the most important one holds true, that's really all that matters," he said. He glanced down at the silver, corded belt I wore around my waist. "Don't think I did notice that."

"So obviously there is more to this than just visiting Cody's father," said Gar. "Is Cody the kind of werewolf that gives into his bloodlust and would kill the both of us given a chance? Or is he the kind of werewolf that remembers who he is, and more importantly, who we are?" He ignored the look I gave him. "What? I do read, you know."

"I think it's a little of both," said Cody. "I remember after the fact. I remember what happened when I'm in my wolf form, but during the act it's like I give in to the feral part of me. I become all wolf, and I'm afraid of what I might be capable of doing."

"We had another run-in with those men that were with the bear shifter that attacked us at the falls," I said. "That was when Cody shifted for the first time, trying to protect me. We are hoping that his father can fill in a couple of blanks and maybe provide some leads as to who's behind this. But I can't go out there knowing that I have to keep an eye on you as well, and I don't mean that in any offensive kind of way. I know you can take care of yourself, but this is something that not even the aunts can explain or prepare for."

Gar was quiet in the back seat. I continued looking forward out the window, hoping that my words had sunk in. "So you're basically going to follow up on whatever information you get from Cody's father, right?" he said.

I nodded, not sure there was any reason to speak.

"Then what you're saying is that you could be…I mean, you promise you're coming back, right?" Gar said, his voice choking off before he could complete the sentence.

I spun around in my seat to look him in the eyes. "No, that's not going to happen. No matter what we need to do, no matter where this takes us, I'm coming back for you. Tell me you believe that."

"I believe you," Gar said. He remained quiet for a moment, staring out the side window. "I know you'll be back, but since we're all sharing, I want you to know something as well." I didn't say anything, just continued to look straight ahead. I swallowed hard, waiting for him to finish his thoughts.

"You should know, I, uh…I've been seeing someone," he said softly.

I closed my eyes, trying to stem the flow of tears that threatened to roll down my cheeks. I nodded slightly before I found my voice. "Thank you for telling me that, Gar. Does this person have a name?"

He was silent for a moment before responding. "Jhamal. His name is Jhamal."

"Cool name," I replied.

"You're not gonna freak out on me, are you?" he asked. "And don't tell the aunts; I want to be the one to tell them."

"I'm not freaking out; I'm just happy for you. I'm happy that you are not only accepting who you are, but you're trusting me to accept you as well. You know I love you no matter who or what you are." I dabbed at the tear that escaped my eye before turning to look at my brother. "And I'm not saying boo about this to the aunts. That's all you, little brother."

"And you?" Gar said in Cody's direction. "I mean, you just shared your secret with me; I figured the least I could do was return the favor."

"Oh hey, it doesn't bother me," said Cody. "I'm all about respect. I say live and let live. As long as you are being true to who you are, who am I or anybody else to tell you otherwise?"

If the tears weren't flowing before, they certainly were after he said that. I reached over and gave his hand a squeeze. "Thank you," was all I could manage.

"I do have a question," Cody said, looking in the rearview mirror at Gar. "I have a cousin who's gay. He lives in the city. His name's Mike. Do you know him?"

"What? You're shitting me, right?" said Gar. "Gay Mikey that lives in the city? Yeah, we all know him."

I couldn't help but laugh as Gar slid his headphones back on and once again returned his attention to his phone and the world that was whizzing by his window.

Cody eased the car to a stop in front of Hope's house. I was happy to see a guard once again stationed in the little house that guarded the gates to the community. Cody had shown the man his badge and we had been waved through without question. Before we got out of the car, I turned to Gar one last time.

"Okay, so Hope knows a little bit about what's going on," I said to him, "but not everything. For now we need to keep it that way."

"Are your wards still in place?" asked Cody.

I close my eyes and reached out, gently probing with my magic. As far as I could tell, everything I had set before we left was still in place and undisturbed. I nodded reassuringly to Cody as we exited the vehicle and headed up the sidewalk to the house. I reached for the doorbell, but before I could press it the door swung open.

"Oh no," said Hope as she stood in the middle of the doorway. "You are not coming back in here. And you most definitely are not coming in," she said, staring at Cody. For emphasis she crossed her arms, lowered her head and stared at him without blinking.

"Hope, I'm sorry," I said. "But I'm in a bit of a bind. Can Gar stay here just for a bit? The aunts are out of town, and Cody and I have business that we need to take care of."

"Is it the same kind of business that came knocking on my door?" said Hope. I nodded, and she softened, but only a little. "Shit. Come on in." She stepped aside so that the three of us could make our way into the house. She leaned closer to me and whispered in my ear, "You're not running from anything, are you? I mean, nothing is going to come after him in the middle of the night, is it?"

I shook my head no. "We aren't hiding from anything. There are some things about Cody that we need answers to, and we're hoping that those answers will lead us to finding out what's really going on around here once and for all so we can put a stop to it." I figured there wasn't really any point in going into too much detail. I had put my best friend through so much already. I couldn't bear the thought of adding to her fear. "Also, the wards that I placed around the house are still active. Whatever those things were that attacked us, they were after me, so you and Gar should be perfectly safe here."

"Hope," came a call from the other side of the living room, "who's at the door?"

Hope dropped her voice to a whisper once again and quickly said, "You owe me big time. You would not believe the shit I caught when my parents came home." She spun around quickly and put a smile on her face. "It's just Allie, Mom. Her aunts are out of town and she has some trouble that she has to take care of regarding the coffee shop. Do you mind if Gar stays with us for a bit?" I smiled politely and waved to Hope's mom as she stepped briefly into view.

"Oh, hello, Allie," she said. "Of course he's welcome here anytime. I suppose Hope told you about the little get-together she had while her father and I were out." I couldn't help but shrink back a little and looked down shuffling my feet.

"She might've mentioned something about having a few friends over," I said, my face suddenly turning red.

"A few friends indeed," her mother said. "She told us that you were unable to make it. I wish you had been here because maybe it would've kept things from getting out of hand. You always were the level-headed one." Hope gave me a look, and in spite of myself I couldn't help but smirk.

"But come on in and make yourself comfortable, Gar," she said. "We were just about to order some lunch. There is a marathon of bachelors in the city playing all day on Bravo. As long as you don't mind sitting through that, we'll be just fine."

"Oh," said Gar excitedly as he pushed his way between us and headed for the living room, "I guess if I have to watch it I'll suffer through."

"Hope, call me if anything at all happens. We will be back tonight but I can't promise what time."

"Don't worry about it," Hope said. "I'll just put all this on your tab." She stopped me as we made our way to the door. "Just be careful, Allie. I hope you know what you're doing." She hugged me, and while the words were directed at me, I couldn't help but think she meant them for Cody's ears.

Chapter Twenty-Two

Cody's father lived an hour and a half north of Trinity Cove in a small town called Susquahana. Cody had told me that once his father retired from the police force he had moved to the middle of nowhere town in order to be away from everyone. He retired at the same time that Cody had graduated from the police academy and joined the department. That fact wasn't lost on Cody. His father had paid cash for a double wide trailer and used his pension to support his alcohol and gambling addiction. Cody admitted that contact with his father had been limited to holiday phone calls and check-ins on his birthday. Other than that, the two of them had had very little contact with one another.

We were fairly quiet on the drive there. Despite the fact that there was so much more to be concerned about, all I could think about was the kiss we had shared in the early morning hours in my aunts' study. Before leaving the house I had swiped the leather journal that contained the history of Trinity Cove. Taking it out of my denim jacket pocket, I spent most of the drive lost in its pages. To my great disappointment, the page following the entry that I had hoped would explain the darkness that was coming to Trinity Cove had been ripped out. There hadn't been much more to learn about our town or the community of witches that settled it.

"Anything else in there that we need to know about?" said Cody.

I closed the book and sighed, placing it back into my pocket. "Not really. Other than what I told you, there doesn't seem to be a lot as far as the history of Trinity Cove."

"Actually, I think that told us quite a bit," he said. "Even though it may not explain what type of dark magic may have been drawn to this area, it still told us how the town was created, and more importantly why supernatural beings seem to thrive here. Or at least they did."

He was right, I had to remind myself. If this tome had been in my aunts' study all this time, that meant that they at some point had read about the history of the Cove. If that was the case, why had they not explained all of this to us in the beginning? I couldn't help but think that there was still something the aunts were keeping from me, some missing piece of the puzzle that might help explain all of this.

"Hearing my mother brought up in all of this has really thrown me," I said. "I was eight years old the last time I saw her. I can barely remember what she looked like, and all this time I had all but given up hope that she would ever return to me or Gar." I was shocked at myself. I didn't know what it was about Cody that was causing me to open up to him this way. I had not even expressed this level of feelings to Hope. He must've sensed something because he reached over and placed one hand reassuringly over mine, giving me just enough of a squeeze to let me know that he was there.

"At least you grew up around someone who cared enough to take care of you," he said. He never took his eyes off the road though his voice seemed far away. "Trust me, having a parent that's right there in the house with you but is never really present is much worse."

I didn't know what to say to that, so I didn't say anything. We made the rest of the trip in silence with me rereading the sections of the journal that I had practically memorized at this point. I looked up as we turned off of the main road and onto a dirt street that went on for a half-mile before dead ending in front of a small, unassuming white vinyl, double wide trailer with a small shed behind it. The property itself was a mishmash of overgrown weeds and shrubbery. There was no way to tell where the property line ended and the wild growth of saplings that marked the entrance to the woods beyond began. To one side of the living structure I could make out an old, broken down Ford Granada sitting on cinderblocks, the hood open and its innards exposed to the elements. All in all, the property had the sad feel of a stereotypical southern redneck dwelling that was on the precipice of becoming a salvage yard.

A surprisingly well-kept German Shepherd greeted us as we exited the car. The large canine padded silently up to Cody, its tail wagging excitedly.

"Hey, Jasper!" Said Cody. "How's my big boy?" He reached down and ruffled the shepherd's ears and head, dropping to one knee to nuzzle the large dog. Cody looked up at me and smiled. "This is Jasper. My dad has had him for the past ten years. He's a great guard dog but relatively harmless as long as you're not here to cause any trouble." I could tell that he wanted me to greet the dog in the same way, but I decided to pass. Present company excluded, I wasn't in the habit of petting strange mutts.

I followed Cody up to the door of his father's house. He knocked lightly a couple of times, and when there was no answer he followed with a harder, more forceful banging of his fist on the front door. "Jesus," he said. He reached into his pocket and drew out a ring of keys. He flipped through a couple before finding the one he wanted and inserted it into the lock. As he turned it and pushed the door open slightly, he said, "Hey, Dad, it's Cody. We're coming in; do not shoot us."

I didn't know if he was kidding or serious, but I wasn't going to take the chance. I held a stab of magic at the ready as we made our way into the small dwelling. The room we walked into was nicer than I expected. A living room with seating for four adults was filled with matching sofas, a small loveseat, a table and drapes that coordinated nicely with an old shag area rug. Off to the right of the space a half wall separated the area from the kitchen. There were dirty dishes in the sink and on the countertops as well as covering a small card table flanked by two folding chairs. The space was dark as there were only two small windows in the living area with drawn shades. The air was heavy with the scent of breeze attempting to mask the underlying smell of cigarettes and more Wick air fresheners.

The sound of the toilet flushing followed by running water came from down the hall where I assumed the bedrooms were. Heavy footsteps announce Cody's father as he walked into the room. I was surprised at the size of the man. He was a full head taller than Cody, and carried an extra seventy-five pounds. Cody wasn't a small man by any meaning of the word, but he seemed to physically shrink in the presence of his father.

"Dad," Cody said, nodding. "We knocked but there wasn't an answer."

"Maybe you should've called first," said the older man. "Of course I knew it was you when I heard the door open and Jasper didn't make a sound."

He turned to face me, stabbing one massive hand out into the air. "Carson Hunter," he said.

I took his hand in mine, greeting him with a shake as I said, "Allie. Allie Caine. Nice to meet you, sir."

"Yeah, I know who you are," he said. His tone was guarded, but beyond that I couldn't read anything coming from this man. He turned and headed into the kitchen, moving toward the full-size refrigerator that dominated one corner of the space. He opened the door and took out a can of Budweiser. "Either of y'all want to drink?"

"Umm, no thank you, sir," I said.

"Jesus, Dad," said Cody. "Hitting it a little hard this early in the day even for you." I followed his gaze around the space and noticed the majority of the dishes cluttering the counter were bowls interspersed with empty beer cans.

"Last time I checked I didn't have anywhere to be today," said his father. "If you came all this way just to rag on me, you can turn around and march your little ass right back out the door."

Cody swallowed hard, and I could tell that he was struggling to contain himself. He looked at me and then checked his temper and continued speaking to his father. "I'm sorry, Dad. I did not come here to fight."

His father seemed to accept the apology as he popped open the can and took one loud swig. "Fine. But I assume you aren't here for a bunch of small talk, so is there something I can help you with?" He moved out of the kitchen and into the living room, settling his considerable bulk onto the couch and dropping the can on the coffee table in front of him. "So? Care to tell me what brings you up this way with her?"

I had only seen this man a few times in the past. I remembered seeing him when we were in school together, and of course I knew him from around town when he was the acting sheriff. While he had never been unfriendly, he also had never gone out of his way to make me or Gar feel at ease in Trinity Cove. As far as I was concerned, he was just an adult version of the same bullies I dealt with day in and day out in high school.

"I'm working a case," Cody said. "I was hoping maybe you could give me a little insight on something."

His father's eyes narrowed as he regarded the younger man before him. "I've been out of the business for a long time now. Somehow I doubt there's anything that I'm going to be able to help you with. I left that life and I don't really want to go back to it."

"You've made that pretty clear," said Cody. "I've never asked you for anything since I joined the force. I wanted you to see that I can handle things on my own and I want to make a name for myself. I would never come to you unless I thought you were the only person who could help."

I watched his father take another long drink before placing the can back on the table and regarding both of us with a steely gaze. "First, tell me why she's here."

Cody glanced nervously at me, but couldn't hold my eyes. "She's helping me. There are things happening in town that are beyond what they taught me at the academy."

"Does it have anything to do with the break-in at her coffee shop?" asked his father. The look of shock on our faces seemed to bring out a smug smile. "Don't be so surprised. Some things still reach my ears even way up here." He finished off the can of beer and got up to go retrieve another from the refrigerator. "Sure you don't want one?"

"No, we're good," said Cody. "It's funny that you mention the break-in at the coffee shop. That's what started all of this."

Again, the older man's eyes flicked from Cody to me before settling once again on his son. "The fact that you were investigating this is the only reason I know about it. You're my son, and I still keep an eye on you." It was the first hint of softness I had heard in his voice. I should've known better; it was quickly replaced with a gruff huffing of air as he settled back into his spot on the couch.

"I can deal with the coffee shop," I said. "That's not what we're here for. We need information of a more… personal nature."

This time the older man stopped in mid-reach for the beer can. His eyes burned into me and his mouth drew back in a sneer. "And just what kind of personal information do you think I'd be willing to share with you?"

"Dad, please just stop it," said Cody. He started to say more, but stopped, seeming to swallow the lump that appeared in his throat. He turned to face me. "This was a mistake. Let's just go."

"I told you to stay away from her and her kind," said Cody's father. "But you wouldn't listen. Ever since you were a child you are always sniffing around after her." This made us both blush, Cody from embarrassment, me from anger.

Cody moved to stand up and head for the door, but I stayed where I was.

"What do you mean by 'my kind'?" I said.

"Just what I said," he replied. "There was a time when you people kept to yourselves and minded your own business. I can't help but wonder if things wouldn't be a lot better if you'd stayed that way."

For some reason this pissed me off to no end. I felt thunder and lightning rolling behind my eyes and it was all I could do to tamp it down.

"My aunts told us what happened," I said, leaning forward. My anger was getting the best of me and I couldn't keep the accusatory tone out of my voice.

"I don't know what your aunts told you as far as we're concerned," he said, his voice equally as angry as mine. "But they know nothing about me or my son, so whatever they said about him is all lies."

"Dad, calm down," said Cody. "They didn't say anything about me." He turned to look at me and nodded toward the door. "Allie, let's just go."

"No. We came here for a reason and we're not leaving until we at least get some answers!" I turned to face his father as our staring contest recommenced.

"You witches just think you know it all," he snarled. "You don't change, and you don't care who gets caught in the crossfire as long as you get your way in the end. I guess this is my fault. I should have left just like everyone else with brains."

"Yeah, I heard how you weren't man enough to stand with my aunts and my mother when the time came," I said. At this point I was seething and unable to self edit.

"Allie!" exclaimed Cody.

Before he could say anything else, his father exploded. One meaty hand grabbed the edge of the coffee table and flipped it end over end, sending it crashing into the kitchen space. He stepped closer, his bulk filling the space before me, his face inches from my own as he glowered down at me.

"Your mother," he began, stabbing his finger at my face, "was one of the bravest people, man or woman, that I have ever known in my life. There isn't a day that goes by where I don't wish to God that I had the strength to do what she had asked me to do that day." He looked over at Cody, and his eyes started to well up with tears. "But at the same time I don't regret it. Not for one minute."

Cody moved closer to the two of us. "Dad, what were you asked to do? Am I... I mean, was I a part of..."

"Is Cody a werewolf?" I said, finishing the sentence that he couldn't.

Carson Hunter looked at me, but this time there was no hint of anger or aggression on his face. He suddenly looked like a man who was resigned to the fact that he was broken. He sank back onto the couch and motioned for us to have a seat as well. "No. My son could never be one of those monsters."

I sat down on the small loveseat and motioned for Cody to join me. I measured my next words carefully. "He's already changed once. The more we know, the more I may be able to help him." When he didn't answer, I knew that I had his attention, and that maybe, just maybe, he was ready to talk. "My aunts told us about the day that they worked with the townspeople to drive the warlock away."

He nodded, closing his eyes as if to shield himself against painful memories.

"We were so young then. Most of us were about the same age as the two of you now. And yes, we agreed to help the witches. Trinity Cove had always been such a peaceful place. Everyone lived together, and everyone helped everyone else. Of course there were secrets; what small town doesn't have them? But they weren't secrets that made anybody hate anyone else. But when the witches started to go missing, and the bodies of shifters were turning up in the woods torn into pieces, we knew something wasn't right.

"I don't know what all your aunts told you about that day, and I'm not sure I want to know," he said to me, "but all of those humans who remained in the town knew that if we didn't help stop this evil, there would be no town left for us. So yes, we banded together with the witches and with the shifters to drive this darkness out of the Cove. Did they tell you everything that happened?"

"They told us what they knew. They told us everything up to the point where the townspeople, and you among them, found the children of the wolves."

Carson Hunter leaned back and tried to swallow the unpleasantness of the memories that we had dredged up. I looked over Cody and could see that the blood drained from his face. His olive toned features had suddenly gone waxen.

"Yes, we found them, all right. And your mother told us to put them all down."

He let that hang in the air, twisting and churning the tension until it matched the feeling I was getting in the pit of my stomach.

"The spell they cast prevented any shifter from changing. One of the witches who stood with us said that these babies had never shifted into their wolf form, that they were innocent. But your mother said with werewolves there was no such thing. She continued on with the others deeper into the cave to confront the warlock. Me and the rest of the humans gathered up the babies and made our way back outside. We knew what we were supposed to do, but none of us, not a single person, could bring ourselves to do it." He looked at Cody and tears rolled freely down his face. "I don't care if it was the right thing to do or not; I could not bring myself to smash you with a rock. I just couldn't do it."

The elder man leaned forward, his elbows on his knees, one hand supporting his head as his body became racked with spasms. Cody and I exchanged glances, neither of us knowing what to do or say. I had never even seen my younger brother cry, so I could only imagine what he must be feeling seeing his father so overcome with emotion.

"I couldn't do it to you," Carson said, looking at his only son through teary eyes. "None of us could do it; we just couldn't bring ourselves to do what she asked us to do."

"Mr. Hunter?" I said. "What did everyone do?"

"You have to understand, my wife and I... we had just lost our daughter. I was carrying you out of the enclosure, Cody, and the way you moved in my arms, the small sniffling cries you made, reminded me so much of her." He paused here, swallowing the dryness in his throat and trying to make himself say what needed to be said. "So I kept you. I brought you home and asked my wife to love you just as she would any child that she had born. The rest of the town folk did the same thing, those who had maybe lost a child and couldn't have another, or those who were way too compassionate that day; they all kept one of the babies."

"So all this time... I mean... I've never..." Cody's words tripped over one another. I could tell he was trying not to ramble but at the moment wasn't really capable of forming a coherent thought. His eyes cleared and his voice steadied. This time his words were crystal clear. "Am I the reason Mom left us?"

"She couldn't take it," his father replied. "She said that

she couldn't bond with you after what we had just been through with your sister, Rebecca." Cody's gaze seemed far away as he listened to his father. "Your sister was everything to her. I believe deep down she really did love you. But after everything that happened, she knew that staying in this town would never work for her. Just like I knew that leaving here was not an option. Many of the others who… adopted, for lack of a better word, the rest of your siblings did leave town. They just wanted to start new lives where no one knew who they were or questioned their children."

"So all this time…" I said, "has anyone ever come around asking questions about Cody? Does anyone else know?"

Carson shook his head. "We made a pact never to reveal this to a living soul. That's another reason why so many left town, so the children would have no contact with one another. We never even told one another the names we gave them."

"Has he ever shifted in the past?" I said. Time was of the essence here and I couldn't afford to drag this out.

"Never once," said Carson. "After all the mess with the warlock was settled, one of the witches told us that because the children had never shifted to their other form and because they were locked to human shape by magic, shifting was impossible for them. It was no longer part of their makeup. And for the most part, as far as I know, they've all led normal lives."

My ears pricked up at that. I looked at him questioningly. "For the most part? You just said for the most part they were normal. Does that mean there was something abnormal at some point?"

Cody's father looked down, his feet moving restlessly on the outdated shag carpeting. Finally, with a heavy sigh he got up off the couch and walked to the back of the home. When he returned he had a large manila folder with a red rubber band around it to try and contain the fading, dog-eared, loose-leaf paper stuffed within it. He handed the bundle over to Cody.

"There. It's all in here. I've kept all your medical records since the day I brought you home. I can't speak for the others, but everything I know is in that folder."

Cody stared at the packet for a full minute before he finally handed it over to me. He stood and nodded for me to follow him out the door. His father reached for his son's arm, stopping him in his tracks.

"You're still my son," he said. "I don't care what you find in that packet, or what she tells you. You will always be my only son." He looked at me one last time, his eyes narrowing. "But I wish to God you had listened to me and stayed far away from those witches."

I started to turn the doorknob but had a last question. "Mr. Hunter, does the name Mallus mean anything to you?"

"No. Should it?" he said. I shook my head and started out the door, but was stopped by Cody's voice.

"How about Alexander Tilden? Do you recognize that name?" he said.

His father visibly paled at the question. I could see all of the blood drain from his features so quickly that the man had to sit back down to keep from passing out.

"Dad? How do you know that name? That's the body that was found at Singing Falls a couple of days ago."

His father drew a deep breath before looking up at us. "He is... was... one of the other parents. He was raising one of the children as well. He moved away right after everything happened, and had vowed to never set foot in this town again. What about his son? He had taken one of the boys as well."

"There were no other bodies found," said Cody.

"Mr. Hunter," I said, "is there something you're not telling us? Because the look on your face says that something just terrified you."

He didn't hesitate to answer this time. "A few of us have been in touch as of late," He slouched back into the couch and heaved a sigh as if just saying the words brought on so much relief. "A message has been going around to all of us, so we reached out to one another to try and decide if it was real."

"What kind of message?" I asked.

"Someone had been contacting us saying that they have a cure," he said, his eyes cutting to Cody. "Of course I didn't believe it, plus you and I had not been speaking when I received the message. It seemed fishy; whoever claimed to have this cure left a contact number and nothing else. Alex was one of the ones who said he responded and was hopeful about this."

"From everything I understand, werewolves are born the way they are. There's no curing them, because what they are is not a disease," I said.

"Yeah, well you haven't seen what I and some of the other parents have seen. And in all honesty it's something I never want to see again," he replied.

Cody and I looked at one another, trying to contain our excitement. This may have been the break that we were looking for

"Dad, we need that contact information," Cody said.

His father sighed heavily and reached into his back pocket, pulling out his cell phone. He keyed in a code, made a few swipes, before tossing his phone back onto the couch. "There, I just sent it to you."

Cody checked his phone before nodding to his father. "Thank you."

As we were walking out the door, his father made one last plea. "Cody, take my word for it: if you get involved with these witches, I can only hope that you live long enough to regret it."

Chapter Twenty-Three

"Trust me, they're the best," Cody said as he tugged at the steering wheel.

After we had left his father's house and Cody had said goodbyes to Jasper, we made our way back to Trinity Cove when Cody decided we should stop and grab a bite to eat.

"I'm really not big on hot dogs," I had said. Cody had told me he knew where a diner was on the way home that served the world's best grilled hotdog and chili fries. To say the least, I was skeptical; I mean, had he really tried every hotdog in the world? But I agreed to it partly because my stomach was starting to growl, but also because I wanted a chance to talk about what our next steps should be.

As soon as we got into the car I started reading the contents of the manila folder. Cody made me promise to read anything out loud that I found alarming. I had to give his father credit; his record-keeping had been meticulous. Everything was arranged in chronological order starting with a full checkup of Cody beginning at four days old. While I was no expert on medical matters, everything I was reading seemed pretty cut and dry. It was borderline boring. I was into his teen years when suddenly it hit me.

"Hey," I said just as Cody was pulling the car into the parking lot of a silver trailer with a neon light flashing above it that said "Red Dogs." "Have you ever had a cold? Or serious injury?"

"Not that I remember," replied Cody. "Why?"

"Because that's what's missing from this chart. Illness and injury."

"So? I've always been healthy."

"Yes, but you're also a male, and you were active in sports. Gar has had multiple sprains and injuries and he only runs cross-country. Boys are naturally more danger-prone because they take more risks physically. But according to these records, you've never so much as twisted an ankle or sneezed."

"Huh, you're right," Cody said as he turned off the ignition. "I guess I never really thought about."

I contemplated bringing the file into the diner with me to read some more as we ate, but then thought better of it. I tossed it back onto the seat but then reconsidered leaving it exposed like that and decided to slide it under the seat before following Cody through the door of the fifties-era establishment. The diner was small on the inside, consisting of a bar top with an open kitchen behind it, and rows of banquette-style booths of red faux leather faced one another across a narrow white laminate table that was bolted to the floor on a single pedestal. Cody waved, signaling to one of the waitresses by pointing at a booth in the corner near the rear of the diner. The waitress nodded and Cody smiled and led me to the back of the restaurant.

We had barely sat down when the same waitress

The Girl with the Good Magic

appeared next to us with two menus and an ear-to-ear smile.

"Well, well, if it isn't Cody Hunter," she said. "Where you been hiding?"

"Oh, you know, work's been crazy. I don't really get to come up this way much anymore," he said sheepishly.

"Well we're just gonna have to work on that," she said. "You want your usual?"

He looked at me at the corner of his eye before replying, "Yes, make it two orders please."

She winked, picked up the menus, tossed her mane of hair to one side before giving Cody a coy look and heading back to the kitchen. Cody looked at me, the slightest of blushes creeping up his neck.

I arched an eyebrow and tried not to laugh. "So that's what passes for flirting up here?"

Cody laughed. "She's an old friend of the family."

"Should I be worried?" I asked half-jokingly.

"Not at all," Cody said in a very serious tone. He reached across the table and took my hand in his. I was caught off-guard at the intimacy of the small act. Before I could say anything, the waitress reappeared and sat down two iced glasses of a dark liquid in front of us. She didn't acknowledge anything, but the way she turned on her heel and walked away without speaking told me that she saw his hand covering mine. "It was real, you know," he whispered. "The kiss I mean. As much as I wanted to take things further, I want to do that when the time is right for both of us."

I swallowed hard and took a drink of the soda before I trusted my own voice. "Wow, and I thought I was the girl," I said jokingly. "But I like that. Plus, we still aren't entirely sure what other shifting triggers you may have, so that might not be the best time to find out." I had the insatiable urge to kiss him right then and there in front of everyone. But instead I just leaned back and stared longingly into those big brown eyes. He smiled at me, and licked his lips. Christ, was this man a telepath as well as a werewolf? I needed to say something to break the tension.

"So what we do about this lead your father gave us?" I asked.

"I was thinking about that," he said, taking his hand away from mine. He reached into his pocket and pulled out his phone, opening it to the text his father had sent him. "All we have is a number here. I'm going to email a buddy of mine in the department and have him run a trace on the number and see what he can find."

"So you're not afraid of getting in trouble anymore?" I said smugly.

"Oh, I'm sure I'll have a lot to answer for when I get back to work," he said. "But as far as we've taken things, we might as well go all the way." He began tapping out a message on his phone and I waited for him to finish.

"Speaking of, how are you explaining your absence from work?"

"I've asked for a few days of personal leave," he replied. "With the body that was found and everything that's going on, it's not the best time for me to be away, but until I know more about what's going on with me I'm not sure I trust myself to be involved in certain situations."

I started to confess that I knew exactly what he was feeling, but at that moment the waitress returned with a platter containing our food. She set the plate in front of us and looked at Cody. "Anything else?" she said, only a hint of ice in her voice.

"No, this is perfect," Cody said. His eyes lit up and he

smiled ear to ear, but I wasn't sure if he was smiling at the waitress or the food. Either way, it was all I could do not to laugh as I looked down at the massive pile of French fries smothered in chili and cheese, and a large, spiral cut hotdog on a bun with a single pickle lying beside it.

"This doesn't look very healthy," I said suspiciously as Cody picked up his hotdog and took a large bite. He just looked at me, the twinkle in his eyes growing brighter. At least he didn't try to talk with his mouth full of food, so I was grateful for that.

I shrugged. "Oh well, when in Rome..." I picked up the dog and took one tentative bite. It was surprisingly good, with just the right amount of crisp to the outside but perfectly cooked in the center. I dug into the mound of fries and found them equally as delicious. "Okay," I said between gulps, "I suppose this isn't bad as a once-in-a-while treat."

Cody's phone pinged and he picked it up after carefully wiping his hands on a napkin. I saw him stop chewing mid-bite as he stared at the screen. He swallowed hard before slowly moving one finger up the screen to continue reading the message.

"Cody, what is it?" I said, dabbing in my mouth with my napkin. When he didn't say anything, I finally added, "Okay, you're starting to make me a little nervous here."

"My buddy at the precinct just sent me the information on the phone number. It's actually a landline, not a cell phone."

"So whoever is sending out the messages is either very stupid, or..." I said. "Or it's a trap for anyone that follows through on it."

"The phone number is registered at 127 Delphine Way. That's one of the more secluded areas leading up to the Falls."

"Okay, so that's where we're going next. Unless there's more to this than you're telling me?"

Cody reached for his soda and downed it in a couple of gulps. Then he looked up at me and said, "It's registered to a Eugenia Garner."

Why did that sound familiar? I could feel my eyebrows knitting together as I searched my memory, trying to figure out why that name was ringing a bell with me. It hit me at the same time Cody spoke.

"Dr. Garner is the pediatrician my father always took me to," he said.

"Holy shit," I said. "So that would explain why one of the parents would be trusting enough to show up if they received the same messages. Do you think this pediatrician treated the rest of the..."

"Shifters? It's okay, you can say it." I could tell he tried to keep the hurt out of his voice, but it was still there. "When I was growing up she was the only physician in town. So it stands to reason that's where they would've gone, at least the ones who didn't leave town."

"When was the last time you saw her?" I asked.

"Just after I turned eighteen. It was right when I was leaving for college and I decided to join the police force."

I pulled out my own phone and began tapping quickly at it.

"What are you doing?" Cody asked.

"I'm trying to see if she still practicing. I've been here most of my life, and I've never even heard of this physician. The aunts always complained about having to take myself and Gar into the city to see our physician. I would think if there was a local option they would've taken us there." I stared at the screen in shock at what I was reading and then looked up at Cody, mouth agape.

"What is it?" Cody asked. When I didn't answer, he pressed the question: "Allie, now you're the one scaring me."

I had Googled Eugenia Garner and cross-referenced it with practicing MDs. I handed my phone over to Cody so that he could see the results for himself.

"Are you kidding me?" he said in shock. "This says her specialty is in veterinary medicine. She's a vet. All this time my father's been taking me to a fucking vet?"

Chapter Twenty-Four

For once it didn't take a lot of convincing to get Cody on my side. He agreed waiting for the aunts to return was not the smartest play. Granted, what we were about to do might not of been the smartest play either, but I'm pretty sure it was all we had going. We decided to drive out to Dr. Garner's house and pay her a visit. This was the only truly concrete lead we had come across, and we were both afraid to let it go cold.

Delphine Way was a windy, two-lane stretch of road that carved its way through the foothills leading to Singing Falls. Cody pulled the car over to the side of the road and parked it just before reaching the driveway to 127.

"The house sits about another quarter mile up the drive," he said. "I was thinking maybe we should walk the rest of the way just in case we don't want to attract attention."

"Good idea," I said. "If we don't advertise our presence, maybe there won't be time for anyone to prepare any nasty surprises for us."

"Okay; so when we get there just let me do the talking. No magic, no intimidation, nothing like that. I still remember how incredibly nice this woman was to me growing up. I can't believe she's wrapped up in anything dangerous."

I just nodded and didn't say anything. Cody might be very trusting, and he had had enough heartache thrown at him for one day. But if this woman had answers, and could lead us to my mother, then I would do whatever I had to in order to get her talking. But I kept that tucked away in the back of my mind and just smiled and nodded at Cody in agreement.

A few feet off of the main road and we stepped into darkness. There were no lights along the driveway, and the crunching of the gravel surface seemed to be the loudest sound in the world at that moment. I thought about telling Cody that we should walk along the side of the driveway to stay as quiet as possible, but then I remembered the way that the roots from trees grew in gnarled, crooked hooks that danced along the surface of the ground in this part of the town. A little bit of noise was better than risking a fall and a broken arm.

"I should've grabbed the flashlight out of the back of the car," Cody said. "I'm pretty sure it's a straight shot up to the house from what I remember."

"Now that's something that I can help with," I said. I held up my hand and concentrated, willing magic to pool around it in the form of blue light. The glow from the circle illuminated the path in front of us in flickering warmth. I looked over at Cody and returned his smile.

"Well," he said, "I guess I'll keep you around. You certainly come in handy in the dark."

I tried to hide my blush. Part of me hoped that he

meant that in the pervy double entendre way that I took it. But then I felt it, and all of the brevity drained out of me. I dimmed my light and motioned for Cody to stop. We stood there motionless. I could feel his eyes burning into me. I held up a finger and just as he started to speak pressed it to my lips.

Peering through the darkness, I could make out the shape of the large center hall colonial just through the clearing ahead of us. I could feel it, the itch behind my eyes, the tingling that raced down my spine and pooled in that spot behind my belly button. Magic. And we had almost walked right into it. I closed my eyes, centered my breathing, and pulled my own magic up and let it burn through my vision. When I opened my eyes I could see it there ahead of us, shimmering softly in the darkness and surrounding the house.

"What is it?" Cody asked, no longer able to contain himself.

"Wards," I said. "There are magical wards surrounding that house."

"So what does that mean? Is it like... a force field?"

As silly a question as it seemed, I realized that I didn't know the answer. My aunts and I had used wards to keep out supernatural beings. But I never really thought about the mechanics of how that happened. Could they pass through the field? Did it simply alert the person who cast the spell that someone was there? Or did the person vaporize on contact with the ward like they did in cheesy sci-fi movies when someone would reach out and touch a crackling energy barrier? I also wondered if it would keep me out if I didn't have my magic flaring. Technically, I was a human, so the ward shouldn't have any effect on me. But what about Cody? He wasn't human, and if this ward was set to repel supernaturals, what would happen if he tried passing through? I was also assuming that this ward worked the same way as the ones I had used. What if a much more skilled practitioner cast these wards? Who knew what they might be capable of doing.

"Why would a veterinarian have mystical wards around her house?" I asked. "More importantly, how are you going to get past them?" I was speaking rhetorically, processing my thoughts aloud, and I didn't really expect an answer from Cody.

"Only one way to find out," Cody said. "Why don't we just walk up to the house and see what happens?"

"You know, for somebody trained as a police officer and who always seems to look before he leaps, you really can throw caution to the winds at the worst time."

He shrugged his shoulders and looked at me. "We're running short on options here. Unless you can think of something else…"

"Maybe, just maybe," I said. "Wards are typically set in place to keep out something supernatural. But they also function like an alarm system, alerting the person who cast them that they've been breached. What if the good doctor inside is not the person that cast these wards?" I thought for a moment and then reached out and took Cody's hand. "Maybe these wards are in place to notify someone else whenever a wolf arrives."

Holding Cody's hand, I let my magic flow again. The soothing blue light spread from our joined fingers up our arms until it outlined both of our bodies. I took a step toward the house, pulling Cody along with me. The closer I got, the more wary I was becoming of the house. Something was triggering my fight or flight instinct. My magic was reacting negatively to the magic that flowed through the wards. Whoever had created these had seriously dark intentions. Still, we pressed on, and I hesitated for a second just as we were about to pass through the threshold of the wards. I concentrated even harder, focusing my will on the shield around us. I wasn't sure I could pull it off. But the intention was to pass through the ward without setting off the alarms.

I wasn't sure what Cody might've felt, but for me passing through the ward felt like stepping through a beaded curtain made of entrails and bits of bone. They scraped across my own shield in a way that made me feel violated and sick to my stomach. But in an instant we were on the other side of it and standing at the base of the stairs that led up to the porch. I let out a deep breath and let my magic drop away. I could feel the slight warning flash that signaled the onset of a possible migraine. It might have seemed like a simple idea, but maintaining that shield had taken a lot out of me.

"You okay?" said Cody softly. I nodded yes and gave his hand a squeeze. He smiled back at me, and together we walked up the steps and rang the doorbell. There was no overhead porch light; the only illumination came from the small windows to either side of the door. Despite the fact that we would have appeared as vague shadows, the door opened almost immediately; there was no question as to who we were, and that told me we, or someone, was expected.

A short, dark-skinned woman of indeterminate age was suddenly standing in my face. She were stylish, frameless glasses, and her dark eyes scanned me up and down before she turned her back and motioned for me to follow her into the house.

"You're early," she said. "And I thought you were going to call when you arrived."

A quick magical probe confirmed what her nonchalant attitude already told me. She was not the one who cast the wards around her house. Her attitude told me that she didn't even know they were there. I glanced to Cody, who only shrugged in response, and we both stepped into the house. I mouthed the words, "Is that her?" at him. He nodded but didn't speak.

"You told me you had him under control. What happened up there was anything but control," she continued. "And I don't know why you think meeting in person is a good idea. This is on you." She led us through a well appointed living room that led into an office that consisted of a large exam table, and shelves that lined the walls filled to overflowing with glass mason jars as well as stethoscopes, surgical blades, and what looked like electronic monitoring equipment all arranged neatly in rows and columns. "I told you I had no idea what would happen if you tried to shift one at this point," she said, finally turning to face us.

The office was brightly lit, and this was the first time the doctor was able to get a clear look at the both of us. She adjusted her glasses and seemed to take me in with a single toe-to-head sweep. She glanced over my shoulder at Cody and froze in place.

"Cody? Cody Hunter?" she said, reaching to place one hand on the table to steady herself. "My God, boy, is that you?"

"Hello, Dr. Garner," Cody said. "It's been a while."

Dr. Garner looked at me, her eyes beginning to well up.

"I didn't know he was the one you were going after," she said. "I thought it was one of the others. You should have given me more notice." She turned from me, shaking her head in disbelief before spinning back around again. "My God, his father! I've known that man since we were in school together."

Finally I spoke up, unable to take the confusion any longer. "I'm sorry, but I don't believe we've met."

The doctor looked at me, her eyes narrowing with suspicion. "Who are you?" she asked. She moved quicker than I would've anticipated for someone of her age. She opened a drawer at the foot of the exam table, reached in and withdrew a shiny scalpel blade which she held pointed at me. "You're not one of the Order of Nine."

"No, I'm not," I said, pulling up a dagger of blue light and holding it out in front of me.

"Hey, hey," said Cody, raising both hands and slowly stepping between us. "Dr. Garner, we're not here to hurt anyone. We just want some answers. Please, just put the knife down."

She was staring at the blue power signature that flowed within my hand, and her eyes were wide. I stepped back and recalled the magic and opened my hand palm out to show her that I meant no harm.

"Who are you?" she asked again.

"My name is Allie," I said. "Allie Caine." I could tell by her demeanor and the stiffness in her neck that she recognized my name. But I had no idea if that was a good thing or a bad thing.

"Dr. Garner," said Cody, "I *know*. My father confirmed who and what I am."

"What brought you here?" said Dr. Garner. She slowly placed the blade back in the drawer and eased it shut.

"You sent a message to my father," Cody said, "telling him that you had a cure. It was the same message that went to all of the parents of us wolves."

Eugenia Garner's head snapped up sharply to look Cody in the eye. "It wasn't me who sent that message. You have no idea how much danger you are in."

"Then tell us," I said. "Tell us how much danger we are in and help us figure out what's going on around here. Starting with who did you think we were and who or what is the Order of Nine?"

"The Order of Nine are the servants of Mallus," she said. "They want to bring down the forbidding that keeps magic from flowing freely in this world."

"The same magic that keeps the shifters locked in form, right?" I said.

She nodded her head, and the fact that she didn't question how I knew that told me that she knew who I was.

"Yes, that's right," she continued, "but it goes beyond that. That forbidding has locked the natural flow of the ley energy in Trinity Cove. The mystical energies that flow through the bedrock underneath the town, as well as the ley lines, are a natural occurrence in this world. Your mother created a spell that altered that flow. Over time the energy has become vulnerable to outside corruption—corruption in the form of black magic."

"So the person you've been dealing with," I said, "what is her stake in all this?"

"The forbidding has become frayed," Dr. Garner replied. "Some of the magic that it contains is seeping out into the world again. The Order of Nine want to restore not only shifters but bring back other, older forms that lived in this world at one time. Trinity Cove will be the aperture for that magic. It will also, once again, serve as the wellspring for all things supernatural on this plane."

"Including the warlock that is locked behind it," said

Cody. "And any other power-hungry warlock that fancies themselves a boss, I'm betting."

"Exactly." Dr. Garner nodded. "If the forbidding can be brought down then there's no telling what manner of creatures can once again walk the earth."

"But I don't understand," I said. "If my mother created the forbidding, where were all these creatures before she raised the barrier?"

"A couple of decades ago there were more witches than there are now," she said. "It was their job to maintain order and keep the darkness relegated to the shadows. Your mother had a greater role than you probably know among those who practiced magic."

"Yes, I know," I said. "She was a Reliquary."

"The meaning of which I'm sure goes far beyond anything your aunts would have told you," she said. "Did they tell you that the truest translation of that word is 'warden'?"

"Sorry to butt in here," said Cody before I could answer. "But these cracks in the forbidding that you spoke of, are they why we're seeing shifters again? Are they why I was able to shift?"

Immediately Eugenia was focused on Cody as she rushed over to him. "You've shifted?" She took his hand and pulled him over to the table and bade him to sit down. She hurried over to her shelf and picked up an ophthalmoscope and began shining it in one of Cody's eyes. "How were you able to manage that?" She turned to look at me, her mouth hanging open.

"I think it was my magic that caused his shift," I said. "Magic is also what brought him back. Isn't that how it works?"

"No, not normally," she said. "An adult shifter who

transforms into a wolf for the first time is completely at the mercy of his bestial self. Shifters learned at an early age how to control and channel their energy. They learn this from their pack. But Cody, and the others like him, were never exposed to that. Therefore, as an adult their wolf is savage and feral. That's what I warned her would happen."

"You mean the member of the Order of Nine that you've been in communication with?" I asked.

"Yes. She wants the wolves. She told me I could either help her to gather them or she would hunt them down and kill them and their adoptive family one by one. She had a list of everyone and I didn't know what else to do. But I warned her that forcing a werewolf to shift like that could have unforeseen consequences."

"The body at the Falls," I said. "That was one of the parents, right?"

"Yes," she said. "The Order of Nine have learned how to force the werewolves to shift, but it can only be done at the Falls, where the energy leaking through the forbidding is the strongest. When she forced that transformation, the wolf was uncontrollable and savaged its own human parent." She placed the instrument she had been examining Cody with under the table and covered her eyes with one hand. She seemed to be weeping uncontrollably at the thought of what she had helped bring about.

"That's why you have to help us if you can," I said. "You seem to know an awful lot about what's going on here, more than anyone else that's been willing to talk to us, and that includes my aunts. All I want is to find out if my mother's alive, get her back if she is, and make all this, whatever it is, right again. And stop this Order of Nine from letting demons back into our world."

Dr. Garner whirled around to face me. A look of abject

terror suddenly crossed her face. "No, you need to stay as far away from all this is possible. Don't you understand, this is exactly what Mallus wants."

"No, I don't understand any of it!" I replied. "That's why I want you to tell me. And who is this Mallus? I know he's the teacher of the warlock that's trapped behind the forbidding, right? So what's one more warlock that we have to take out in the grand scheme of things?"

"No," said Dr. Garner, shaking her head emphatically. "Mallus is not a warlock. Who told you that? Mallus is a…"

That was as far as she got with her statement. She was cut off mid-sentence by a sharp thud that suddenly pierced the air. The doctor's head and arms arched backward as her chest suddenly thrust forward. I could see a good six inches of a shiny metallic blade, now streaked with blood, exiting her breastbone. Cody was able to catch her in his arms as she collapsed forward.

"And that will be enough of that," said a voice from behind her.

I looked up and saw a tall, thin woman with jet black hair dressed all in black standing ten feet behind Dr. Garner. The woman raised her hand in the air, and the knife that had just impaled Eugenia Garner flew backward to the woman with enough force that a line of dark blood coated the ceiling and the walls as it was cast off the blade.

Chapter Twenty-Five

Whoever she was she didn't waste the precious moments of shock that her sudden appearance, and bloody action, caused. She held the dagger that had just seconds before been thrust into the body of Dr. Garner out in front of her face. I could see her lips moving rapidly in incantation, and in response the blade lit up with orange flames. Grasping it by the hilt, she once again hurled it. This time it was headed for my heart. Without much conscious thought on my part, my magic flared to life. A hastily erected blue shield appeared before Cody and me, taking the brunt of the attack. The knife struck it and bounced harmlessly away before it once again zipped through the air to land in the stranger's hand.

"I don't know who you are," the assassin said, "but you've just made me waste a perfectly good asset, and I'm gonna make you pay for that."

She took a step forward, and for the first time I noticed she was not alone. In her right hand she held her flaming dagger; in her left she held the end of the chain. It was fastened to a collar around the neck of a tall, muscular man that stood behind her. He was half concealed in the shadows that divided the office from the kitchen, but I could make out that he was shirtless, wearing only a pair of nylon basketball shorts.

"Who are you?" I said. "What are you doing here?"

"I might ask you the same thing," she said. "But honestly, I don't care." She dropped the end of the chain from her hand, reached up and unfastened the link from the collar around her companion. "Kill," she breathed.

All I could think at that moment was, *Oh God, no. Not again.* I watched in horror as her companion pounded fully into view, his body contorting as his limbs twisted painfully back on themselves, his neck elongating, his face melting into something filled with gnashing teeth and harrowing yellow eyes. He dropped to all fours just as he finished shifting into the form of a large gray wolf. The space between us was covered in a single bound as the wolf launched himself claws first at myself and Cody. I poured more magic into the shield, hoping that I could strengthen it to withstand the impact. Three hundred pounds of gray fur and fury smashed into the barrier. It felt like I had been physically struck, but the shield held, flaring beneath the weight of the werewolf.

I was focused on the wolf so I didn't even see the woman as she approached. One minute I was trying to keep Cujo from biting through my force field, the next minute the woman who I assumed was a member of the Order of Nine was at the shifter's side, her fiery blade stabbing at my shield. With both hands on the hilt of the knife, she was attempting to cut through my magic barrier, and I could feel the sweat gathering on my forehead as I concentrated to keep my shield in place. Despite my newfound levels of power, I wasn't exactly sure I could take even one of these attackers, and I knew that I absolutely could not take on both of them at the same time.

"I'm sorry," I said between gritted teeth to Cody.

Cody was on one knee and was withdrawing a small pistol from an ankle holster he wore beneath his khakis. "Don't be. We're not going down without a fight."

"No," I said, "I'm sorry that I have to do this."

"Do what?"

"I have to cash in that insurance policy," I said. I was worried I wouldn't have the strength to do what I had planned and still maintain the force field. I looked over at Cody and held one hand up in his direction. I closed my eyes and breathed without the incantation that I hoped I would never have to use. Instantly my magic stabbed into him, triggering his body's most primal response.

"No!" he cried, dropping his gun. Both hands went to his head as his back arched and his voice became a guttural growl escaping his now expanding chest. As he began to shift, I focused one last invocation his way. "Saierre nephrem!" I shouted.

Know yourself.

The shift in my concentration seemed to be all the woman needed to take advantage of the situation. She raised her blade high overhead and plunged it down with all her strength into my shield. There was a flash of blue light around us as my shield splintered into fragments raining down all around Cody and me. It felt like someone had just punched me between the eyes, and I fell backward, momentarily disoriented.

Through the haze of pain I vaguely made out a gray blur streaking across the floor in my direction. I knew I didn't have the time or the strength to erect a barrier, so I raised one arm hoping in vain to protect my face from the gnashing teeth that were about to descend on me. Thank God I didn't close my eyes, or I would've missed the jet black blur that rammed into the side of the gray wolf with the power of a locomotive. The gray was flung sideways and out into the kitchen. I looked up into the yellow eyes of Cody. He stared at me briefly for a second before unleashing his own growl and sprinting after his adversary.

I had wanted to say I was sorry, but the truth of the matter was I was pretty sure we would have both died had I not just pulled that trigger. My attention returned to the here and now just in time for me to avoid being stabbed in the chest by a red-hot knife. I rolled to one side just as the glowing blade plunged into the floor where I had been lying just a second before.

The woman stood slowly, drawing herself up to nearly six feet of intimidation. Her arms hung loosely at her side, one hand gripping the knife she had nearly just gutted me with.

"My name is Katrina," she said. "And you are?"

Yeah, right. Good try, bitch. I knew there was power in knowing your opponent's name. No way had she just given me her real name, and I could only hope that she was stupid enough to think I would give her mine.

"Nice to meet you, Katrina," I said. "I'm Glenda, the good witch."

She either didn't care or didn't get the reference as she advanced on me, her eyes growing pale and milky as she adjusted the grip on her knife. I saw her lips moving silently, invoking dark magic. Immediately the room began to swirl, and I felt an overwhelming sense of vertigo. She was trying the same tactic as the man we had encountered at Hope's house. This time I was ready.

"Fool me once..." I said, waving my hand at her. I summoned an augmentation spell and threw it at her. It was a type of magic that was meant to be used internally by a witch to boost her senses as needed. When used correctly it would allow me to see at night, or follow an enemy by their scent. When I had read about it, it seemed kind of gross at the time, but I had memorized the spell, thinking that it might come in handy. This time, instead of focusing it inward, I cast it outward in Katrina's direction. I focused it on her ears, increasing their sensitivity a hundredfold.

The roars and the howls that accompanied the crashing bodies of the two wolves fighting in the next room hit her like sledgehammers. She screamed and whirled to face the sudden onslaught that was assailing her. The break in her concentration also broke her spell. The room stopped spinning and clarity returned to me. The magic I had cast on her wouldn't last long, so I needed to make the most of the distraction.

I rushed forward and grabbed her from behind, reaching around to grasp her throat in my hand. I fully intended to summon a blast of magic and use it to rip open her neck, but before I could take action I felt a sharp jolt as she drove her elbow backward and into my stomach. The blow knocked me backward a couple of steps as she screamed in rage and swung around, slashing the knife horizontally at me. I heard a slight rip and looked down to see my T-shirt had been split in a searing cut across its center. I briefly touch the flesh beneath it and breathed a sigh of relief when I realized my skin was still intact. Still, that was a little too close for comfort.

I danced forward and slammed my fist into her jaw. Her head snapped backward, but the pain that suddenly flared up in my wrist told me that I could've just done as much damage to myself as I had to her. I stepped back and looked around, trying to find any object that I could charge with magic and use as a weapon. The augmentation spell was starting to wear off and I could see Katrina regaining more control of her body. She looked around, trying to locate me as she touched one hand gingerly to her ear. She looked down at the dark, red stain on her fingertips and then up at me.

"Bitch!" she spat. "I was going to make this fast, but not now."

She started toward me but stopped as the entire house seemed to shake on its foundation and the two wolves crashed through the wall and tumbled into the office where we stood. I marveled at the sheer size of the beasts. They were far larger, and far more ferocious, than any wolves I had ever seen or heard of. They were each well over three hundred pounds, nearly twice the size of the largest wolves on record. The old wooden floorboards in the office creaked under their combined weight as they circled one another.

I watched as Cody lunged for the gray wolf, the snap of his jaws landing a bite on his opponent's haunches. The gray wolf howled in pain and anger and wheeled about to slash at Cody's ears. The snarling of the two massive animals deepened as they latched onto one another, rolling in a ball that caused the entire room to shake. I took full advantage of the distraction and dove behind the exam table. I began pulling drawers open, trying to block out the horrific sound of teeth gnashing, claws raking against bristled fur, and the mad growls that accompanied bone-crunching teeth snapping together.

I could hear the woman cursing and screaming at the two wolves in a language I didn't recognize. I wasn't sure if she was invoking more magic to work against Cody or was simply caught up in trying to help her wolf survive the encounter. Either way, she had taken her attention off of me for just a second, and that was all I needed. I rummaged through the content of the drawer, looking for something, anything, that I could use.

I picked up something that looked like a small mallet. I wasn't sure what it was, but it looked vaguely familiar, tickling at memories from childhood physicals in the city. I held it by the handle and wasted no time charging it with magic. I stood up from behind the table just in time to see the woman advancing on the two wolves, her flaming knife drawn back to attack. She must've sensed my presence and whirled just as I threw the mallet at her.

She had time to turn her face to the side and throw her hands up in front of her before the mystically charged instrument struck her in the chest. There was a loud grunt as she lost all the air in her lungs, accompanied by a flash of blue magic that lit up the room. She was driven off her feet and across the room, where she struck the far wall with an impact that dropped her to the floor.

"Wow," I said to myself, "eat your heart out, Thor."

A roar thundered across the room and struck my ears. I turned in time to see the gray wolf shaking off Cody and gathering himself to launch at me. I scrambled away from him, feeling along the floor for any object that I could charge. I turned in time to see him bounding across the floor at me, but before he could reach me another shape latched onto the wolf.

It was Cody, but he was no longer in wolf form. He wasn't human either, but had somehow managed to shift into a form that was an amalgamation of both. He was a good foot taller in this form, heavily muscled and still covered in jet black fur. His arms were long and powerful, ending in razor-sharp two-inch claws that glistened at the end of his fingers. His sinewy legs seemed to have lost their flexibility at the knee joints and gave him the appearance of standing in a slight crouch. He was balanced on the balls of his elongated feet, and they too possessed preternaturally lengthened nails. While there was no sign of the black tail that he possessed in his wolf form, his head and neck still resembled the elongated canine shape complete with high, pointed ears, an elongated snout, fangs, and those intense, yellow eyes.

This new form gave him the speed and dexterity to reach the gray wolf before he was able to close in on my throat. He was close enough that I felt the spray of saliva from his jaws when they snapped shut as he came to an abrupt stop. He howled in real pain as Cody latched onto his tail and haunches, hauling him back away from me. He whirled, lunging for Cody's neck. Cody was ready for this, and his humanoid form, while not quite as strong, still gave him weapons that he did not possess as a lupine.

One jet black hand stabbed forward, grabbing the wolf by his neck. Cody's claws dug in as he lifted the beast and slammed it to the floor. He threw his weight on top of the struggling wolf, exerting more pressure on the creature. He placed his other hand on the gray wolf's jaw and pressed his head into the floor. Once he had it pinned down, he leaned forward, opening his jaws as wide as possible, and clamped onto his prey's throat. I heard a horrible sound of muscle, tendon and bones snapping has Cody reared back, bringing half of the creature's neck with him. Arterial blood sprayed Cody, the walls and the ceiling as the wolf's body began to spasm in its death throes.

"No!" came an anguished screen from behind Cody. It was the woman I had sent crashing into the wall. She was on her feet, one hand braced against her rib cage, the other holding her blade. The knife was no longer aflame but instead appeared to be jet black. Before I could warn Cody, she hurled it at him and the blade buried itself in one of his powerful thighs. He howled in pain, arching his back and throwing his face upward at the ceiling. For a horrible moment I imagined that was what he would look like if he were outside, baying at a full moon. He reached one bloodied hand down and grasped the knife by the hilt. With a savage twist, he pulled it out of his leg and dropped it on the floor. Instantly the woman held out her hand for the blade to fly back to her yet again. She faced us, knife in hand, her eyes narrowed in hate as she took in the form of her dead wolf.

I still didn't have anything to throw at her, but in the time it had taken Cody to kill the gray wolf, an idea had come to me. I removed the silver belt from around my waist, holding it in the middle so the two weighted ends dangled at equal lengths toward the floor. I poured my magic into it, charging the belt, and began to whirl it over my head. Rather than the usual bluish magic that infused objects that I charged, this time the belt took on pure white glow as the magic was magnified by the innate nature of the silver threading.

Just as the woman took a single menacing step toward us, I hurled the belt. It spun and crackled through the air, wrapping itself around her neck bolo style. Unlike most of the objects I charged, I felt a tactile connection to the belt; I could feel the woman's neck beneath it. I held my hand up in front of my face, palm toward me, fingers splayed open. I concentrated and closed my hand into a fist quickly. The belt responded in kind, constricting with the same force that I closed my hand. There was a sickening gurgle as it tightened suddenly around my assailant, cutting deep into her flesh and nearly severing her head. She slumped back against the wall, her head at an awkward angle against her shoulder, eyes open and unseeing but still focused on the two of us.

I stood there next to Cody, shocked and amazed at what I had just done. I held out my hand and willed the belt to return to me. It unwrapped itself from her neck and flew back to me, the white-hot magic searing off the residual blood before it reached my hand. I began to rewrap it around my waist as I looked up into Cody's eyes. He was breathing hard as he stared over me, his yellow eyes flickering all around my face. I reached up and tentatively placed one hand on his heaving chest, reveling in the feel of his silky black fur as my fingers moved through it. Slowly I felt this form shift, the hair retreating back into his body as he slowly once more became the man I was becoming accustomed to having stand at my side.

"That was... very intense," he said through deep breaths.

"Are you okay?" I asked. "How did you do that, Cody? You took on the form of a true werewolf."

"Honestly, I have no idea. That wolf was getting the better of me and I just needed a way to get the upper hand, so I willed myself to start the transformation back into a man but then stopped halfway. I was in complete control the entire time. I assume I have you to thank for that?"

"I wasn't sure, but I hope that's how the spell would work. It gives you control over your shifting and allows you to maintain your memories and thoughts in either form."

I stepped from behind the table to survey the damage. "I'm going to try a tracking spell to see if—"

"Allie..." Cody said from behind, cutting me off. "I

don't feel so good." I turned to face him in time to see him place one hand on his head, the other on the edge of the table to balance himself.

"What is it? What's wrong?" I raced to his side, trying to steady him.

"I don't know," he said, his voice thick and groggy. "I feel like my body is on fire and I'm having a hard time focusing my vision." He looked down at his naked thigh where the knife had wounded him. While there was no blood, the skin around the wound was red and swollen. Spidering outward from the spot where his flesh and been torn were jagged black lines that were slowly spreading across his thigh. He looked up at me questioningly and opened his mouth to say something. Before he could speak, his eyes rolled into the back of his head and he collapsed naked on the floor.

Chapter Twenty-Six

"Cody! Cody!" I said, dropping to my knees to shake him by the shoulders. He was very still and I began to panic, thinking that he was dead. But then I saw the slight rise and fall of his chest, and I reached out two fingers and placed them along the side of his neck, feeling for a steady, yet faint, pulse.

"Okay, not dead," I said to myself. "He's not dead, just unconscious. So what do I do?"

I reached out, drawing on the only thing that I had going for me right now: my magic. I placed both hands on his chest and slowly focused my energy into him. I could feel my magic spreading through his body, thick and warm and searching. I was not exactly sure what I was looking for, but I prayed that the magic would know. And then I felt it. It was as if my magic was suddenly funneled to a narrow passageway and then hit a brick wall. I probed harder, wanting to command the magic to break through the barrier, but when I began to exert force I could feel Cody's body stiffen beneath me in response. Whatever was going on, his body wasn't reacting in a positive manner to my deeper probes.

"Stop; you'll kill him," I heard a weak voice say. I turned my head, looking around for the source, and could see Dr. Garner sitting propped up against one wall, one hand stained in blood as it tried to cover the open wound in her chest.

"But it feels like he's dying," I said.

"That's because he is," she said. "But he's dying slowly, and there is a way to help."

I rushed over to her side and kneeled down to examine her wounds. I tried to move her hand from her chest, but she shook her head emphatically.

"No," she said. "It's too late for me, but I need you to listen closely." She was racked by a coughing fit, and I couldn't help but notice even more blood coming out of her mouth with each ragged breath. "Listen to me. The source of the poison that's killing Cody is magical in nature. The fact that he's a supernatural is the only thing keeping him alive right now, but eventually that won't be enough to stop the poison."

"Tell me what to do," I pleaded.

"In the last cabinet on the wall behind the exam table, top shelf, there are some preloaded syringes of high doses of adrenaline. Inject a full syringe into his heart. That, combined with his own nature, will help his body to fight off the poison. But that will only last for so long." Again she was overtaken by a fit of coughing, and this time when she opened her eyes I could see that she was drifting away. Her breathing became shorter as her eyes began to cloud over. "You have to get him to the Falls… That's the source of the black magic they infected him with."

"But what do I do once I get there?" I said, batting away the tears that were filling my eyes.

"That, I can't help you with," she coughed. "I'm a vet, not a witch. Once you get there it's up to you. Listen to me..." She grabbed my sleeve in one bloodied hand and pulled me close as her voice faded ever softer. "He's a good boy. But remember, not all wolves were raised by the hand of a good man."

"What? What do you mean?" I said, looking into her face. There was no reply, and the blank look on her face told me that she had nothing left to offer. I didn't know why, but I reached up and gingerly lowered her eyelids.

There was nothing more I could do for her, but hopefully I could still save Cody. I rushed over to the cabinets that she had spoken of and flung the door open. On the top shelf I found five syringes, each individually wrapped in a protective plastic sheath. I tore one open and removed the protective cap from the needle as I stepped over to Cody. He was not moving, and his breathing seemed even shallower than before. I looked at the syringe in my hand and then his chest. I had no idea what to do, but then I remembered that scene from *Pulp Fiction* that freaked me out when I was younger.

I squatted down, straddling Cody's form, my knees to either side of his waist. I placed a hand on his chest, feeling for the faint heartbeat. As soon as I located it I raised the syringe above my head, one thumb on the plunger. I knew if I thought too long about it I wouldn't do it, so I took a deep breath, plunged it into his chest, and depressed the syringe, emptying the clear liquid inside into his body.

Nothing. I had expected a Thurman-like reaction in which he would suddenly sit up, gasping for air. I waited a second, wondering if maybe I needed to use a second syringe, when I suddenly noticed his eyes open and begin to flutter. He took in a very deep breath, and I slid off of him, awash with relief.

"What happened?" he asked, sitting up.

"That bitch poisoned you," I said. "The knife was coated in some type of mystical poison. I just gave you a shot of adrenaline that's working with your body's own immune system to fight it off. But I don't know how long it will last."

"How did you know to do that?" he asked.

I pointed over to the form of Dr. Garner propped up against the wall. Cody just nodded, and I could see his eyes well up.

"What now?" he asked.

"Right now we go up to Singing Falls," I said. I stood up, reaching down to haul him to his feet. I was careful to make sure that he was steady before letting go of his arm. "She told me that was where the source of the black magic that infected you is from. It seems like all signs lead to the Falls. I think it's time we deal with whatever's up there once and for all."

Chapter Twenty-Seven

There was one last thing I had to do after I helped Cody to the car. I needed to burn that house. I wasn't sure if Dr. Garner was a good woman or not, but in the end she had helped us and I didn't want someone finding her body and rummaging through her life. Plus I had to make sure that the other bitch and her wolf was dead. They certainly looked dead, but I was beginning to realize that maybe dead to a supernatural wasn't really dead at all.

The house was big, and I wasn't sure I could manage to create a fire that size. But it was also old, mostly wood and probably asbestos. Fire was fire; I only had to get it going and then it would give in to its own the hungry nature, consuming everything around it. I walked back up the drive just until the structure was in sight. Then I concentrated, mentally picturing the four corners of the house and commanding them to light. Before long the entire house was engulfed in bright orange flames that lit up the night sky. Even if there were neighbors to see the conflagration, by the time the fire department arrived there would be nothing left.

I made my way back to the car and strapped myself in behind the wheel. Something told me that Cody knew better than to try to argue as to who was driving. I eased onto the highway, making a U-turn, and headed back to town and the road that would take us up to the Falls.

"I can't believe I'm about to say this," said Cody, "but maybe we should wait for your aunts to get back to town. Or at least give them a call and see if they can come back now."

I gripped wheel tighter and shook my head. "Not an option. I only have a few adrenaline syringes left, and we have no idea how fast this poison is working in your system."

"So if Dr. Garner was correct and we're about to walk into ground zero, shouldn't we have some backup if nothing else?"

"We just took out a witch and a werewolf," I said. "Plus I just burned down a four-thousand-square-foot house. I'm pretty sure we can handle ourselves and whatever or whoever gets thrown at us." The truth was I was feeling pretty cocky. Each time I used my magic it was getting easier for me. I could now feel it humming inside of me, waiting to be called up and set into motion. I looked over at Cody as he sat rubbing his temple, his head leaning to one side. "You okay?"

"Just a headache," he said. "I feel cold, like I'm starting to get the chills even though it's not cold in here."

"It's called a fever," I answered. "You'd know that if you had ever been sick like every other normal child in America. It's a sign that there's some type of infection in you and your body is trying to fight it off." He didn't say anything, only turned to gaze out the window as I mashed hard on the accelerator and urged the car forward even faster.

We drove the rest of the way in silence. Cody stopped me before I could turn into the lot at the base of the Falls.

"Not here," he said. He urged me to keep going forward, and we made a right onto a dirt road I'd never really noticed before. He told me to stay on it until we came to a circular gravel clearing with wooden railroad ties arranged around it as a border. I killed the lights and let the car creep to a stop at the edge of the clearing. "This is one of the access roads that medics and other first responders use."

"Is this closer to the Falls?" I asked.

"Much closer. The trail leading to the Falls is a lot wider and easier to manage. We don't advertise this one because we need to keep it clear for emergencies."

I convinced Cody to let me give him a shot of the adrenaline before we got out of the car and made our way to the path. He may not have been at peak strength, but I still needed him focused. I wasn't sure what we might be walking into, but I was sure that I didn't want them to know we were coming. I created a small ball of blue magic and dropped it on the path in front of us. This way the light that was given off at our feet was limited; just enough to keep us from tripping over stray roots and rock clumps, but not enough to be seen from a distance.

"So where exactly are we going?" Cody whispered.

Good question. *No real plan and no destination*, I thought to myself. "Well, both my aunts and your father mentioned a series of caves that run behind the Falls. There had to be something in them that attracted the warlock and by extension the wolves. So I say we try to find those caves, and when we do we'll probably get our answer to what's going on."

"Easier said than done," replied Cody. "I know those caves. As a kid we used to play there. Some of the older kids would use it as a hideout to smoke, drink beer and bring girls. The problem is those caves are labyrinthine; there are probably dozens of them crisscrossing through the mountainside. How do we find the right ones?"

"How else," I said, smiling at him in the dim blue light that shined up on our faces. "Magic."

We were soon greeted by the loud crashing of the Falls and the melodic ping coming off the rocks as water cascaded down the face of the cliff and emptied into the pool below. I suddenly felt uneasy as I remembered the last time we were up here. Looking back on things, it started to make sense. That bear shifter and his keeper did not just happen to stumble upon Gar and me. They were here for the same reason Cody and I were. Either they had been looking for the cave or they had exited from it.

We stopped when we reached the edge of the pool. I closed my eyes and concentrated, stretching out my arms, willing the shimmer of magic at our feet to flow up and gather around my open hands. Then I reshaped the mystical energy, breathing a tracking spell into it. I figured the easiest way to find the right cave was to target the highest concentration of ley energy in the area. Once I set the magic to that task, I dropped the ball of light and watched as it stretched out like a glowing python and began to wiggle its way around the rocks to the back side of the falls.

"Come on," I breathed. "So much for stealth. Whatever's in there will see that thing coming, so we might as will be prepared for anything. How are you feeling?"

"I'm okay," he said as we made our way behind my little magic snake. "My heart is racing and I feel jittery, but I guess that's to be expected considering you lit me up with a syringe full of adrenaline not long ago."

We ignored the back spray of the Falls and hugged the slick rocks as we followed my tracker into one of the openings between the granite. It was a tight squeeze, but soon the passage opened up as we entered the mouth of the cave proper. I paid close attention as my tracker stopped, seeming to curl up like a rattlesnake about to strike as it pulsed blue light in the darkness. Then it seemed to make up its mind which way it needed to go, and struck off through a passageway to our left.

Cody was right: we passed in and out of a half-dozen passageways and I started to wonder if we'd be able to find our way back. We were deep enough that even at midday it would still be pitch black in here. What if my magic faded? What if we got lost? No, I banished those thoughts from my mind. If I had to summon another tracker to lead us out of here, I would. Of course, that would mean we had to survive whatever we were walking into...

I felt Cody tug at my elbow to get my attention. I had been lost in my thoughts with all my attention focused on the tracker and had not noticed where we were going. I looked up and saw that my spell was slithering toward a larger opening that seemed to have a weird, flickering pink glow coming from it. At the same time I saw it, I felt it. It was the same itchy feeling I had gotten in Hope's house when that one member of the Order of Nine had worked his magic on me. The stench of black magic was suddenly everywhere, and I had to steady myself against the assault to my senses. I stretched out a hand and reabsorbed the magic that created the tracker. Wouldn't be needing that again.

Cody stepped up next to me, and together we walked slowly toward the opening. I called up a blast of magic and held it at the ready in my hand. I looked over Cody and he nodded in response and willed a bit of the shift to come over him. His eyes glowed yellow and I could see his teeth elongating into fangs. Looking down, I saw that his nails had extended into razor-sharp claws which he held at the ready. That was as much as he allowed himself to shift, and together we walked into the space.

Chapter Twenty-Eight

The first thing I noticed inside the cavern was that the pinkish glow seemed to be emanating from various points along the floor and the walls of the space. The rock that made up the floor and the walls was smooth and well worn. Rather than dark slate, they were a lighter sandstone color. At various points along the stone there appeared to be tiny cracks that allowed the pink-white light to pulse through in irregular-cadence beats.

I could feel Cody's body go stiff at my side. I glanced over at him and could see that his frame was rigid and tense as his eyes darted to and fro, looking for something that seemed to be hiding just outside the periphery of my vision.

"What is it?" I said. I was hoping it wasn't a supernatural threat; surely I would've been able to sense that as well?

"I'm not sure," he replied. "I feel... something familiar here. I know this place."

"Well you did say you used to bring girls up here," I said.

"No, I said some people brought girls here." His tone

was more serious than I liked; it reflected the gravity of the situation. "I've never been this deep into the caverns. I have never seen this part of the caves. But still…"

He walked forward in the space, moving to an area at the rear of the room. There he squatted down and placed one hand on the floor, his head cocked to one side, eyes closed. He stood up and looked over at me, and even without my magic I would've sensed the waves of sadness that suddenly rolled off of him.

"This is where it happened," he said softly.

I could feel the hair on the back of my neck stand up. "Where what happened?"

"Where I was born," he said. He paced around the room slowly, reading the space in a way that I couldn't. "Yes. It's not like I remember being here per se, but the smells, the feel, the taste in the air; all of it tells me this is where life started for me. For me and many others. And…" He stared at one spot, tilting his head and sniffing at the air. "This is where they killed my mother. Yes, this is where so much started."

Something about the pain in his voice triggered something in me, something that tugged at my magic. I concentrated and whispered a spell of revelation and willed my eyes to see the truth. Instantly everything around me changed. The cave lit up with a new source of light that only I could perceive. Everything gave off a glow, and the spidery lines that had previously been luminescent now stood out as black, tarrish and bleeding lines. They looked like an ebony ichor that crept across the surfaces all around me. They were invasive and dangerous, and I could feel the stone around me crying out for help.

"What is it?" Cody asked.

"There's so much power in the space," I said, "and pain.

Not just your pain, but the entire bedrock here is hurting. I can see the ley stones and the ley lines intersecting all around us, and these pulsing cracks that are giving off the light are what's choking off the natural flow of magic all around us. These cracks are like an infection spreading through everything."

Maybe it was the combination of Cody's enhanced senses and my spell of revelation, but something made both of us turn and face a corner of the cave at the same time. It was the one area of the cave where no light illuminated. But we both knew something was there. A shadow moved within the shadows and seemed to detach itself, taking on a ghostly form that was all too familiar.

It was the shade my aunts had summoned in their study.

"Oh my," breathed the shade in its raspy tones, "now this is interesting. I put out a call, yet I had no idea it would be you that would respond."

I stared hard at the dark shape, but even the spell of revelation couldn't help me see anything in or around the spirit. For all intents and purposes he might as well been invisible to me. I glanced at Cody and he only shook his head as if he read my mind. Even his enhanced vision couldn't make out the form within the darkness.

"I may be trapped here," the spirit said, "but this is still my little piece of the world. You will not be able to compel me or divine anything from me that I don't want you to know in this space."

"What do you mean you put out a call?" I asked. Despite the chill running down my back, I found my courage, and in the immortal words of William Shakespeare, I screwed it to the sticking point. Since it wasn't doing me any good, I dropped the spell of revelation and drew on my more active magic, channeling it into my hands in preparation for an offensive attack. I had no idea what kind of magic worked against a ghost, but I was ready to find out.

"The infection you are referencing," said the warlock, "was caused by the forbidding that was created to keep me locked away in this place. It dammed the flow of magic in order to lock me in place. And now it has seeped into the very wellspring of mystical energies and poisons them."

"You're lying!" I shouted. "My mother created that spell and she would never do anything to harm nature!" Instantly I regretted what I said. Though we were deep enough into the cavernous system that no wind could flow, I suddenly felt a foul breeze swell up around us.

"I knew it," cackled the warlock. "When I heard your voice, felt the magic that it carried, I knew you were the direct descendent of her—the one who imprisoned me here and robbed me of what was rightfully mine."

Every instinct I had told me to run. But we had come too far, and I was determined to see this through. I had come here determined to find a cure for Cody, and I wasn't leaving without one.

"My mother imprisoned you because you are a murdering leech who lived off of the stolen magic of witches," I said.

"Is that what they told you?" the spirit said. A long, dry, raspy laugh followed that statement. He let the laughter die on the air, which had suddenly grown still around us, before he spoke again. "Why don't you ask your mother the truth? She's here with me, you know."

And that was all I needed to hear. I completely lost it.

"You lie!" I screamed. The magic I had called up erupted from my hands in bright blue, searing blunt force. The energy waves struck the shadow with a thunderous crack. I felt Cody's arms wrap around me and could barely make out the words he was shouting in my ear.

"Allie, stop it!" He was saying. "Get a grip on yourself! This isn't helping anything."

Reluctantly, I reeled in my magic. I regretted that outburst because I felt spent and my head was already starting to hurt.

"Well, I would say that tickled," said the spirit, "but in all honesty I didn't feel a thing. But I do thank you for bringing my pet to me." I sensed a pause in his rhetoric, and I could tell he was shifting about, floating from place to place in the confined space. "What's wrong with him? What have you done to one of my pets?"

"I haven't done anything," I said. "He was injured in a fight with one of your Order of Nine bitches."

"Oh yes, I can feel it," he said. "He's been cut by the black blade. Nasty stuff. I'm surprised he's still alive."

"What's the cure?" I said. I could feel my anger starting to build again, and it was all I could do to keep it under control.

"Well I certainly don't have it," said the warlock. "There's a vet in town that specializes in the unique physiology of werewolves. She has a way to stop the spread of the poison through his system."

I stepped forward, hands clenched in anger. He was playing with us, and he knew that we knew it. "Dr. Garner is dead. So that's not an option."

There was a rumble in the darkness as I sensed the warlock weighing my words.

"Well then, my dear," he said, "the two of you are fucked. And not in the good way." If the shade had features, I was certain he would have been grinning ear to ear at us. "While I don't want to see any of my pets suffer, I'm afraid there's nothing I can do. The same magic that infects the ley is the same magic that now courses through his veins."

Again, the spirit paused. I knew there was more he wanted to say, but in this space he was correct: I could not compel him to do anything against his will. However, he had told me quite a bit, whether he meant to or not. I still wasn't sure I understood everything about magic. I assume that like most forms of energy, it followed very specific laws. For every spell that was cast and created an action, there had to be an equal and opposite reaction. For every spell there was a counter spell. So it stood to reason that there was still hope for Cody, and I was going to find it.

"There's only one way to stop the poison spreading through his body," said the spirit. I swallowed hard as I considered that maybe this warlock could read my mind. Either that or he was one hell of a guesser. "The dark magic that is killing him is only possible because of the spell that created the forbidding. Shifting is a natural occurrence in the world, and to block it off requires a twisting of nature. Kind of like the twisting that is infecting the mystic energies you see around you."

I stared hard at the dark shape moving around in front of us. Even without being able to compel him, I could sense that he was telling us the truth—or at least some version of the truth.

"It's pretty simple," said the warlock. "Break the spell that keeps the forbidding in place, and you break the dark magic that is flowing through his veins. Or do nothing and he dies. The forbidding is already crumbling, just not fast enough to save your lover. Eventually I will get out of here. It's just a matter of whether you want that to happen now so that he lives, or later, after he's dead. Your choice."

"Allie, no," said Cody. "This is not something you

should even consider. How do you know that even attempting this won't kill you? I'm not... I'm not worth the risk."

I walked over to Cody and took his hand in mine. He'd shifted back to his fully human form, and I could sense the weakness that was once again surging through his system. I reached up, placing one hand behind his neck, and pulled his face down to mine. The kiss was long and needy and flooded my body with new strength and determination.

"You're wrong," I said. "I would risk anything for you." And before he could argue, I placed my hand on his chest and willed a bolt of magic to flow forward, pinning him against the cave wall. "I'm sorry. I can't risk you trying to stop me." My hand went to my right hip as I grasped the hilt of the knife I had slipped into my belt. With a tug, I freed the blade I had retrieved from the house just before setting it ablaze. It had belonged to the female assassin who killed Dr. Garner, and I could still feel the dark magic she had whispered onto it that infected Cody.

I spun to face the open cave and once again dialed up enough magic to see the ley lines coursing through the stone. There seem to be a central spot five feet to the right of the floating spirit. I was both drawn to and repulsed by the energy coming out of the ground. Every instinct I had told me this was Ground Zero. I kneeled down on both knees and raised the knife overhead, holding the hilt in both hands.

"Allie, no!" screamed Cody. He shifted again, this time into his full lupine form, hoping that his strength would overcome the mystic ties I had bound him with. I couldn't afford to split my concentration to give more energy to the straining chains, so I had to make this quick.

With every bit of strength I could muster, I stabbed the

blade downward into the rock between my knees. I had expected the blade to shatter on impact, but instead it felt like the time I had helped Hope slash her cheating boyfriend's tires. The rubber was resistant, but it eventually gave way to the blade as we found the sidewall.

I hoped that that was where I had stabbed; the vulnerable, dark magic sidewall of the ley stone.

As soon as I felt the blade punch through the rock, I poured my own magic into it, charging it to a degree I had never known possible. The black energy of the knife was burned away, replaced by a blinding white light. The normal blue hue of my magic was bleached away by the amount of raw power I poured into the blade.

I felt the entire cave floor rise up and shake violently beneath us. A column of white light shot upward from the blade, striking the ceiling of the cave some sixty feet above us. Again, the cave rumbled. It sounded like a freight train was tunneling through the rock toward us. I sensed Cody break free just as the column of light exploded in a million daggers of mystic energy that radiated outward in all directions.

Out of the corner of my eye I saw Cody shift again into his hybrid form. One muscular arm closed around my waist and scooped me up as he bounded away from the knife toward the far side of the cavern. Just as he landed, one final explosion rocked the cave, sending a percussive shockwave spiraling outward that penetrated the rock walls in all directions.

And then, just like that, it was quiet and dark once again. But that was just it; it was dark. There was no pink glow, no flickering lines racing across the floor or the walls. Just a blackness that was so inky I almost thought I could reach out and touch it.

I held up my hand and generated a glowing ball of light that allowed us to see in all directions. I was looking for the spirit of the warlock, but it was nowhere to be seen. Just then a breeze picked up in the cave. I could feel the hair on the back of my neck stand up, and I could hear a slight warning growl beginning to emanate from Cody's chest.

"Uh oh," whispered the voice of the warlock, seemingly from all directions. "Something wicked this way comes."

Before Cody or I could say anything, we were both blasted backward by a hot burst of wind. We watched as the wind swirled and began to take visible shape. Another spirit materialized in front of us. This one was tall and menacing, but again without the form of a human. At the top of the shape, two piercing emerald eyes formed, glaring at us with an intensity that shook me to my core.

"Allie, what have you done?" the spirit breathed.

All feeling left my body as the words ripped into me.

"Mother?" was all I could say.

Chapter Twenty-Nine

"You let him out, Allie," said my mother. "What were you thinking?"

I was in shock and completely unprepared to speak. Try as I might, I couldn't make out my mother's form or features; just an amorphous floating blob in front of me with piercing emerald eyes—my mother's eyes.

"Mother?" I stammered. "Is this really you? I don't understand. How are you here?"

"I've always been here," she responded. "This was a decision I made that night so many years ago. When I created the forbidding I knew that eventually he would get free. That's why I've stayed here for so long, continually reinforcing the magic that keeps the forbidding in place. But I am weakening, and cracks between the two worlds have started to appear."

"Mother, are you... are you alive?"

"No, my dear, not in the way you mean. My physical body has died and turned to dust, returning to the bedrock that is the source of all of our magic. I did this because I didn't want you to ever have to go through what we went through. You deserve more."

"What can I do to get you out of here?" I asked quickly. My mind was racing and I was running through spell after spell in my memory, trying to latch onto one that could restore a spirit to the world of the living.

"No, there is nothing you can do," she said. "With the forbidding destroyed, you have freed me to move on. I cannot maintain this state much longer."

I could feel my eyes burning at the thought. "There has to be a way. You've been gone so long and I'm just now finding you again. You can't just leave me all over again."

"Allie, you have no idea how much I would love for that to happen. I miss you and your brother more than anything in this world. But I can't stay on this plane now. You should not have come here, and you should not have broken the forbidding."

I was choking up now, and didn't even bother to stop the flow of tears that began to scream down my face. "I didn't know what to do. He was dying and I couldn't let that happen."

For the first time, my mother seemed to realize that there was another person in the cave with us. She focused her ethereal gaze on Cody before looking back at me.

"Allie! That's a werewolf!" The air around her spirit form began to crackle and heave. I could feel the heat begin to roll off of her in waves. I quickly placed myself between her and Cody, praying that she would listen.

"Mother, no. He would have died!" I screamed.

"He should die, Allie! That creature will herald the beginning of the end if you let it live. With the forbidding down, it's only a matter of time before the warlock figures out how to bring the rest of his kin back into the world."

"It's already happening," I said. "They've already had success creating the wolves. But Cody's not one of them."

"He absolutely is," she said. "It's just a matter of time before he recognizes his master's touch and goes crawling to him. You have made a powerful enemy in that warlock, Allie. If you have the power to bring down the forbidding, then you've attracted their attention. Even now the warlock has gone slinking back to his master, Mallus."

There it was. That name again. "Mother, who and/or what is Mallus?"

"You're going to find out for yourself sooner than you think," came a voice from behind us. I recognized the voice immediately, and spun around to face the warlock.

He wasn't a spirit anymore, but rather was there in all his physical, gangly glory. He was tall and thin, his skin wrinkled and impossibly pale. His long, unkempt hair was a crow's nest above rheumy, bloodshot eyes. He was dressed in dirty rags that hung off of him in tattered pieces, barely clinging to his withered form. He also wasn't alone. Standing behind him were three men and one woman all dressed in what I was beginning to recognize as the signature black garb of the Order of Nine.

"Hello, Angel," he said, directing his cracked, strained voice at my mother. "It's nice to see you from this side again."

"Don't call me that," replied my mother. Again, the air around her began to crackle and blaze as she drew upon her magic and readied herself to throw it at the apparition before her.

"Oh, please," the warlock replied, "you're all show at this point. We both know that you are little more than a light show, all smoke and mirrors as the anchor that tethers you to this world quickly fades." The four members of the

Nine that stood behind him stepped forward so they were all in a single line. Together as one, along with the warlock, they raised their right hand and stabbed it at my mother. I could feel the wave of magic that struck her, threatening to snuff out the mystical flames that she had summoned.

"No!" I screamed. I didn't think; my body acted on its own. I raced forward and placed my body between the warlock's horde and my mother. Before I realized it, I had my silver belt in hand and began whipping it in a figure eight pattern in front of me.

The air between us exploded with light and heat as the magic I generated collided with the force coming from the warlock. My belt hummed with power as it cut through the tendrils of mystical energy that were attempting to get by me. Beside me, Cody had gone full wolf and roared his defiance.

The cave seemed to roll and groan beneath our feet, and the rock wall split under the force of the pressure wave where our two magics collided. I held my free hand in front of me, creating a shield that also parted the mystical energies before us, giving me a clear shot at the warlock. My belt was charged and I let it fly, spinning through the air on a direct course for his neck.

Maybe I only imagined it, but I'm pretty sure the warlock actually laughed. He held up a single hand, palm out, with two fingers raised, and stopped my charged belt in midair.

Just as Cody charged at the members of the Order, fangs bared and claws gouging at the rock as he propelled himself forward, the warlock gestured and redirected the spinning belt at the wolf. The glowing silver wrapped itself around Cody's front legs, sending him crashing to the ground. He howled in pain as the mystical silver began to

The Girl with the Good Magic

cut into him. His sharp cries were enough to divide my attention so the Order of Nine were able to punch through my shield, striking me with a battering ram of dark magic.

The impact drove me backward, slamming me into the cave wall. I felt the breath flee my lungs as bright pinpoints of light began to dance in front of me. I slumped to the floor, struggling to maintain consciousness. I sensed one of them approaching quickly and barely managed to hold up a hand and conjure a blue shield that deflected the knife point that was diving at my face.

It was one of the male Order. His lips were moving quickly, invoking God knows what manner of incantation. He drew back his fist and slammed it into my shield. It felt like I had been struck by a hammer as the glowing force field that protected me cracked and split apart under the force of the blow. Before I could move, he had his knife, the blade crackling with black energy, at my throat. I closed my eyes as I felt the pressure that preceded the cut.

"Stop!" said the warlock. The man continued to hold the blade at my throat, but did back it away from the skin the merest fraction of an inch. "Yes, I understand you had some measure of success against two of my neophyte members. But these..." He gestured about the space. "...are my more seasoned acolytes of the Order. Your parlor tricks will do you very little good against them, as you can see."

I looked around through the blinding pain and saw two of his accomplices squatting down next to Cody's struggling form. Their knives were drawn and held at the ready to plunge into his dark shape.

"Your aunts really should have prepared you more for this," he said. "Maybe I should say your mother should have done a better job. Maybe, if she had been there to teach you the true ways of magic, you wouldn't be in the predicament you are right now."

He walked up to me and crouched down until his face was inches away from mine. His friend with the knife backed away but still remained close enough to step in if I tried anything. The presence of the warlock so close to me was offensive in every way. I felt sick to my stomach, and his warm, fetid breath threatened to make me lose all control of my gag reflex. His pale, filmy eyes flitted across my features. I turned my head to one side as he raised his hand and gently placed it against my cheek.

"You're lucky," he rasped. "You're lucky that Mallus still has a need for you. Otherwise I would let them slit you open and feed on your insides in front of your mother. It would be the last memory she took with her on her journey into the netherworld."

He stood up and looked down at me, and then motioned for the male to put his knife away and step back with the others. He walked over to Cody and regarded him with a blank stare.

"I should put you down," he said. "But I respect the lives of all my pets. Even the turncoats. I have faith that you will be returning to the pack before too long." He bent down and ran his hand through Cody's fur, mindless of the harsh growls his contact elicited. "Indeed, I have a feeling that you'll be begging to rejoin my army before long."

I managed to draw myself up to my knees. I ignored the stabbing pain that seemed to be leapfrogging around in my skull, and summoned a flicker of magic in my hands.

"Do not try me, girl," said the warlock. He gestured, and that small movement caused my body to be racked with pain that snuffed out the mystical energy I was trying to create. "We will meet again, and rest assured, when that happens I won't have to hold back with you. Mallus will have what he needs from you and I will be the one to reunite you with your mother's shade."

He turned his back and walked, flanked by his minions, out of the large space toward one of the tunnels that led out of the cave. As he disappeared through the opening, I heard him whisper one last thing, the words carried to my ears on wispy remnants of magical energy.

"War is coming, little Allie, and you're standing on the wrong side."

And just like that they were gone. I didn't try to probe for them mystically. Instinctively I knew that that would prove futile. Instead I rushed over to Cody's side and began removing my belt from around his legs. Once the silver was off of him, he was able to transform and once again take on his human shape. The cuts to his arms where the belt had entangled him were deep and worrisome, but he shook me off when I reached for them, and I watched as the cuts began to close as tissue and skin slowly began to knit whole again.

Together we walked back to where I had last seen my mother's spirit. She was still there, but her form, which had previously been so dense, was now wispy and pale, like a barely there shimmer in the summer air.

"Mother, what's happening...?" My voice was raspy, and my head hurt so bad I could barely form coherent thoughts.

"I'm passing on, Allie," she said. Her voice sounded disjointed and ethereal, and seemed to be very far away. "Unlike the warlock, I had no earthly body to remain tethered to on this plane. My time here is done, but yours is only just beginning."

"You can't go," I cried. "Not again, please..."

"Allie, that warlock is pure evil, and the one he serves is worse by far. But he was right about one thing: I should've better prepared you for this. War *is* coming, and you need to make certain that you can trust those around you. Even now, I can sense the world around us changing. Shifters, both old and new, are reemerging. Find them and help them. But never turn your back on the wolf, any wolf. For in the end they all serve Mallus." Her voice was strained and the shimmer of her form was beginning to fade.

"Who is Mallus?" I asked through my tears. "How can I be prepared to fight something if I don't know who it is?"

My mother's shimmer faded, and I could feel her presence slip away. I can only imagine the strength it took for her to utter her final words.

"Mallus is not a who, he's a what. Mallus is a vampire; one of the true ancient ones…"

And just like that she was gone. I felt Cody's strong arms gather around me as he pulled me into his chest just as the tears began to flow unchecked.

Chapter Thirty

The smell of baby back ribs slow roasting in the oven wafted throughout every level of the house. Aunt Vivian stood at the stove, stirring the pot of peach bourbon barbecue sauce that she would later slather on to the racks of ribs before she passed them off to Aunt Lena to finish on the grill. For her part, Aunt Lena was outside, creating an elaborate tablescape on the deck in preparation for the feast to come. I sat at the large island, watching my aunt as she methodically added the secret ingredients to her sauce that would make it, in her words, "bone-sucking good."

It'd been two months since my battle with the warlock in the cave, and since the last time I had seen my mother. I had secretly tried out a couple of communication spells, trying to contact her, all to no avail. While I had wanted to attempt the séance spell that my aunts had cast, I remembered the tone of my mother's voice the last time she spoke to me. She sounded tired, and ready to go. Wherever she was now, she was at peace, and I owed it to her to let her rest.

Trinity Cove had been quiet since that day. No dead bodies had turned up, there had been no mysterious animal attacks, no burglaries or break-ins reported. Our sleepy little cove had started napping once again—only this time it was keeping one eye open.

There had also been a new influx of residents moving to the Cove since the warlock had been vanished. Shifters and a few other supernatural types had slowly moved into town. They were drawn by the energy of Trinity Cove and they sensed somehow that this was a safe place for them, a place where they could explore their newfound abilities. Most of the townsfolk only knew them as strangers, and nodded politely and accepted them into the community.

For my part, I was beginning to recognize the unique bio-signatures and the mystical energy each gave off. It was as unique as a fingerprint, and I cataloged each one in my mind. Surprisingly, there had been no new witches moving to town. My aunts said that was because they sensed the fall of the forbidding, and unlike the shifters they knew better than to come to a town that had been marked by a warlock.

I should've been worried, but in all honesty I was just happy to have my family back together again, and safe. The aunts had begun to teach me more about the history of Reliquaries and how to use my powers. They knew what I had been through, and more importantly they had a feel for what I was in for. The covens they had traveled to recoiled at the very mention of Mallus's name. They told them the same thing that my mother had told me; that he was a vampire of unknown origins and one whose power was renowned in the realm of dark supernaturals.

They told my aunts that if he had teamed up with a warlock, and the two of them had set their sights on our town, then our town was as good as dead and all we could do would be to try and save ourselves. But I wasn't going to run. I had grown to love my friends, my family and this town. And if I had to lay down my life to protect all of them, then that's what I was going to do.

"Allie, would you stop daydreaming?" Aunt Vivian said. I looked up at her and realize that she was half turned from the stove, facing me. I had no idea how long she may have been speaking to me.

"I'm sorry, Aunt Vivian," I said. "What was that?"

"I said go and tell the boys to wash up; dinner will be ready in less than a half an hour. Plus, our guests should be arriving any minute now."

I nodded obediently and hopped off the stool. I made my way downstairs to the large space where Cody and Garland were sprawled on the couch, a PlayStation 4 controller in each of their hands, their eyes glued to the giant screen before them as they argued and jibed with one another about kill streaks and team scores.

"Hey, you two," I said, "time to wash up and get upstairs. Dinner's almost ready."

Just then the doorbell rang throughout the house and Gar jumped up from the couch like a scolded cat. He dropped the controller and bolted up the stairs. I couldn't help but laugh to myself as Cody stood up and turned off the game and the television. He leaned over and kissed me before heading up the stairs with my hand in his. As we ascended, I could see the scars on his wrist where my belt had bound him in the cave. Despite his healing power, those scars would most likely always remain. I felt a pang of guilt, but that was quickly swept away by the reassuring squeeze he gave my hand as we entered the living room.

Garland had already opened the door, and I could hear him speaking excitedly to someone.

"Hey, Allie," his friend was saying, "thanks again for letting me come over for dinner."

"Not a problem, Jhamal. My aunts have been wanting to meet you for some time now," I said, winking mischievously at Gar.

"And are you guys sure you don't mind my cousin joining us?" he said. "She just got into town and doesn't know anyone, plus I think she needs to eat something other than McDonald's for a change."

"Of course not," said Aunt Lena as she stepped into the room to introduce herself. "Where is the dear girl?"

"Oh, we stopped to pick up a pie and a bottle of wine as a thank-you," he replied. "She wanted to bring those."

Just then the door opened again, and the young woman who could not have been too far past her thirtieth birthday stepped into the room. She was petite, barely reaching five feet in her stylish boots. The tan khakis and light blue sweater she wore barely hid her athletic figure. Her dark skin, sparkling eyes and brilliant smile were all capped off with a head of curly hair that spilled out in all directions.

"Hello," she said, stabbing one hand out to make my aunt's acquaintance. "I'm Diana, and I can't thank you enough for opening your home to me. Jhamal has told me so much about you."

"The pleasure is all ours," said Aunt Lena. "It seems like your Jhamal and my little Garland have taken quite a... liking to one another. I'm betting we're gonna spend quite a bit of time together, so we might as well get to know one another."

Aunt Lena took the pie from Diana's hands and headed back into the kitchen. I took the bottle of wine and motioned for her to step inside. "My name's Allie, I'm Gar's big sister, and this is Cody, my boyfriend."

Diana reached out a hand and shook Cody's, flashing that smile once again at him. "Nice to meet you, Cody. I'm Diana Garner."

We both froze slightly at her words.

"Garner?" said Cody. "Are you any relation to you Eugenia Garner?"

"Yes. She was my aunt."

I could see the shock in Cody's eyes, and I tried to deflect as quickly as possible. "I am so sorry to have heard about your aunt."

Diana nodded sincerely, her smile fading only a bit. "Thank you for that."

"Are you in town to settle her affairs?" said Cody. "I mean... Trinity's a small town and I didn't know that Dr. Garner had any relatives."

"You could say that's why I'm here," Diana replied. "I couldn't make it to the funeral because I was out of the country. But I'm actually here to take over her business. I just graduated from veterinary school, so I'll be the town's new vet. I hear that the animal population around here is really booming lately."

She smiled at the both of us as she smoothed her immaculate sweater and headed into the kitchen. I looked at Cody and simply shrugged. It looked like Trinity Cove had just gained its most interesting new resident.

Next in the Shifter Wars Series

vinci-books.com/entertherwolf

Saving a life sometimes means breaking the world.

Allie Cain's decision to save her werewolf lover has unleashed horrors she never could have imagined. As the shadows gather, Allie's burgeoning magical powers are the only thing standing between her town and total annihilation. But darkness is cunning, and the battle ahead will leave scars that may never heal.

Turn the page for a free preview…

Enter The Wolf: Chapter One

Sure, a forest can be romantic and beautiful... babbling brooks, dappled sunlight flowing through the leaves and all that. But on a night with no light from the moon, and clouds obscuring any stars above, it can also be creepy as fuck.

And creepy-ass woods might be the last place I wanted to be, but for right now it's exactly where I needed to be. I found a good-sized tree to hide behind, one that afforded me a clear view of the path ahead. It was big enough, however, to keep me shielded and out of sight for the moment. The good thing about the woods at night was that there is very little wind, so I didn't have to worry about my scent carrying and warning my prey of my presence.

At least I hoped that was the case. I hoped that I wasn't the prey. I shuddered, and pushed that thought the back of my head. First things first: I had to locate her. I reached down, grabbed my magic, and breathed out an augmentation spell. I focused the spell onto my eyes, and it allowed me to see clearly in the near-dark of the woods. As I peered out from behind the tree, everything around me took on an eerie glow. My vision range was shorter than what my human eyes would perceive in the daylight; about thirty paces ahead, everything faded into a blur. I concentrated again, this time shifting my vision to perceive the thermal range.

There! Twenty feet to my right I made out a red outline pressed against the cold darkness of the trees and leaves. The difference between the body temperature and the coolness of the canopy is unmistakable. Now all I had to do was figure out how to get the drop on her.

I concentrated and cast a shimmer over my body. I had to be careful; the normal blue hue of my magic would have stood out like a signal flare to her eyes. A shimmer was designed to mask one's physical presence as well as dampen sound. As long as it was active I would blend in seamlessly with the foliage around me, effectively making me invisible even to someone whose eyes were accustomed to the dark. I moved quickly across the open path, knowing that the shimmer should mask my sound, and wanting to end this as quickly as possible.

A few quick strides, and I was at her back. I grasped the hilt of the knife in my belt, drawing it and charging it with my magic, while in the same moment dropping the shimmer spell. Just as I raised the glowing blade overhead to start the downward plunge, she turned around and looked at me.

"Allie, wait! It's me!"

I halted the blade inches from Cody's face.

"Jesus! What the hell?" he said, looking up at me.

"I thought you were her!" I replied. "You're crouched down here by a tree and all I could make out was your heat signature. I thought you were trying to flush her out from the other side?"

"I was chasing her, I was right behind her and then... I lost her right in this area."

"What do you mean you lost her? You're a wolf! How can you lose anyone?" I was keeping my voice low and speaking only in hushed tones, although I was pretty sure our location was blown at this point.

A sudden rustling of leaves coming from above told us that she had gotten the drop on the two of us. I looked up just in time to see a black form dropping down from the canopy on top of us. I managed to get my shield up just as her roar filled the air. Sparks flew from my shield where her claws swiped at it. The impact shook me to my core but the shield held, and the heavy body bounced off into the undergrowth. Her massive body hit the ground and rolled, bringing her back to her feet. Almost instantly, a single bound took her up, over the shrubbery, and crashing through the woods once again.

"Now, Cody! Go!" I threw a ball of blue magic in the direction the panther had disappeared, lighting up the night sky and the surrounding terrain. Instantly, Cody shifted to his wolf-form and crashed after the Were-Panther with blinding speed. I followed behind, sprinting as hard as I could, but knowing I was no match for either of them in the speed department. A howl and a crash from ahead told me that Cody had either caught up with her or she had turned to confront him. Either way, I ignored the burning in my lungs and the cramping in my legs and pressed on until I reached a clearing—where the two Shifters appeared to be circling one another.

Despite the fact that in human-form Cody was much larger than Kendra, in their were-shapes they seemed to be equally sized. Just as I came into view, Kendra pounced on Cody. Her sleek panther form was nearly the same jet black as Cody's; the only difference was that her coat was shiny and short compared to the long, double layer of thick black hair that made up Cody's fur. Their large bodies crashed together as they rolled across the clearing, snapping dried logs and timber beneath them.

The collision of bodies brought them closer to me. Cody came up out of the roll and bolted to the side, a split-second before the panther could regain her footing. It was the only opening that I needed. I willed a bolt of magical force into my hand and hurled it at the Shifter. The blue blast hit her square in the side, driving her to the ground. The panther was clearly shaken; she was slow to get back up, and a low, threatening growl emanated from deep within her chest as she eyed me.

I watched as she gathered her powerful legs beneath her in preparation to spring—but that was when Cody struck. In the blink of an eye he had shifted from wolf-form to his hybrid shape. His body grew leaner. A light coat of black fur peppered his sinewy form. His face took on a slightly elongated look, his square jaw lengthening to make room for razor sharp fangs. His ears grew pointed and flattened against the side of his head. His eyes were almond-shaped and glowed bright yellow as he pounced on the Were-Panther, wrapping his powerful arms around her chest and lifting her into the air. The panther wasn't expecting such an attack, and all she could do was roar in displeasure, claws raking at the air, as she sought to twist her supple body free of his grasp.

"Now, Allie! Hurry!" Cody said.

I could tell from his strained tones he was having a hard time holding the Shifter. I lost no time in rushing up beside the struggling pair. I summoned my magic and thrust it into the were-panther, reaching deep beyond her conscious thought into that primal, bestial part of the brain that was beyond her control. There, I found the keys, the mystical pathway that controlled shifting I was looking for and began to play them in a sequence I had recently learned. The panther grew still, her roars subsiding, her flailing limbs going limp as she slowly began to shift, reverting back to her human form.

We released her as her transformation completed, dropping her to the ground. Cody shifted back into his human form as well, and stepped back to regard the both of us.

"Quicker than last time, but still you guys were way too clumsy," said Kendra. "I mean, I'm probably nowhere near as fast as a vampire, and I still didn't really have a hard time evading you."

I sighed and powered down, locking my magic away deep inside of me once again.

"She's right," said Cody. "We never even thought to look up in the trees. She got the drop on us like a couple of rank amateurs, which, if you think about it, is really what we are."

"I know, I know," I said. "But practice makes perfect. I mean, we did way better this time than the first time we tried this exercise."

"You almost stabbed me," said Cody.

I rolled my eyes at his exaggeration. "No way. Not even close to that." This elicited a laugh from Kendra. She looked from one of us to the other, her dark eyes sparkling in the night.

"Look," she started, "I'm willing to play these war games as long as you need. But in all honesty, I've rarely even met other Shifters. I've heard rumors of vampires existing, but neither me nor any other Shifter I've ever spoken to has ever actually met a vampire. If the rumors about them are true, you chasing me around the woods is not really going to prepare you for the real thing."

"See, that's just it," I said. "All we know are rumors. We have no idea what the real thing will be like."

"Well," said Cody, "we can pretty much agree that all rumors aside, vampires are the apex predators of supernaturals. They are strong and fast and effective killers."

"Exactly," I said, turning to Kendra, "and you're the closest thing we can find to that. As a panther, your strength and speed will hopefully imitate what we would be up against."

We were heading out of the woods led by the faint, blue glow of a magical sphere I had summoned. Unlike my two companions, I was incapable of seeing in the dark, and was grateful for the light. As we exited from under the dense trees into an opening, I turned to Kendra. "So, how are you finding things here in Trinity Cove?"

"I'm getting used to it," she replied after a pause. "It's not easy… I mean, it wasn't hard leaving my old life behind. That was a life of pain, and shame. But it was a pain that I knew; a pain I was familiar with. Starting over again here in this idyllic setting was scary. Sometimes the pain you know is more comforting than fear of the unknown."

Something in her tone told me that she wanted to say more, but I sensed that now was not the time.

A year ago, I destroyed the forbidding, an ancient spell created by my mother to contain rampant supernatural and magical energies, and in doing so saved Cody from a mystical poison. Ever since then, Shifters have been reappearing in the world—humans, many of whom had no idea they were Shifters until the whisper of magic touched them, and some who remembered what they were, but had been locked away from their abilities. Many of them made their way to Trinity Cove, the wellspring of the magic that had created them. Like many, Kendra had decided to settle in the woods around Singing Falls. The vast camp grounds were beginning to fill up with RVs where many Shifters were content to create their own little community away from the heart of the town. Eventually, they would probably move in closer, renting apartments, buying real estate, creating businesses, just like any residents moving into a new community. But the fact that they were Shifters, and were new to their abilities, made them wary of humans. It would take some time for them to adjust and trust their new neighbors.

As for the humans that lived in Trinity Cove, most were blissfully unaware of the changes taking place around them. There were some, mostly older, who had been in Trinity since before the Warlock I had mistakenly freed had attacked our community, and those residents recognized and welcomed the return of the supernaturals. Among those few there were a handful that reacted with fear. They remembered the days of the Warlocks and the werewolves hunting in their streets. Still, despite their unease, they welcomed the strangers into town.

Cody and I kept a low profile, taking in the new lay of the land. Cody's work as a deputy allowed him insight into sensitive situations before they became public knowledge. There were members of the police force that knew exactly what was going on; they knew who I was and who my family was. They didn't exactly turn a blind eye, but they trusted Cody when he volunteered to take point on anything that appeared to be of a more supernatural origin.

As for me, things were starting to look up. Business at

the coffee shop I ran had definitely picked up. I had developed a cast of regulars that came in after school or after work that I was beginning to get to know on a first-name basis. Most days between six and nine, the large mahogany leather club chairs arranged around coffee tables with gaming boards inlaid into their centers were all taken. Despite my aunts' initial disagreement about changes made to their store, my upgrades of installing WiFi, adding the new furniture, and offering free coffee refills had brought in patrons that quickly became regulars. Most of them were young, but there were quite a few of the older townsfolk that seemed to enjoy a nightly espresso while reading the local paper and pretending to be annoyed at all the chatter and clatter of laptops around them.

As for my aunts, they would occasionally swing through to see how things were going while squinting and making disapproving clicks with their tongues. But their disapproval quickly faded at the end of each week when I would show them the business tallies for the shop. Aunt Lena had even brought in batches of her homemade teabags to offer up for sale. Typically, they disappeared as soon as she dropped them on the counter, and while she might have acted annoyed, I could tell that she secretly loved the fact that her herbs were so desired.

I attributed the popularity of the coffee shop to free WiFi and refills. However, Cody had once told me that word had spread amongst certain members of the town community about how I had worked to restore the natural balance of magic in Trinity Cove. The fact that many of the new regulars frequenting my coffee shop had the unmistakable air of a Shifter about them attested to that fact. Whatever the reason, I was grateful not only for the increase in business, but for the fact that I didn't seem to be as much of a pariah as I had been before the fall of the Forbidding.

It was almost enough to make me forget that a crazed Warlock, in service to an ages-old vampire, was out to kill me. Almost.

Hence the late-night training exercises. Despite the trove of books in my aunts' library, there were no hardcore descriptions of true vampires and what they were capable of doing. If I was going to be in their crosshairs then I was going to be ready. And since I couldn't find a vampire to fight, a Were-Panther was the next best thing.

A sharp scream in the distance snapped me out of my reverie.

"The camp!" said Kendra.

In the blink of an eye, she shifted to her panther-form, and sprinted in the direction of the encampment she shared with other members of the Shifter community. Cody and I sprinted after her at a much slower pace, making our way through the brush until we reached the clearing at the edge of the woods. There, Kendra and other members of her community had set up RVs and makeshift tents.

Kendra, in human form, was standing next to an older woman who was wailing inconsolably.

"What is it? What happened?" I managed to ask between puffs of breath.

Kendra turned to face Cody and me. "Her grandson. She said her grandson was just taken."

"Taken?" said Cody. "Taken by whom?"

Kendra's eyes narrowed and flashed yellow as she stared at Cody.

"Taken by a wolf," she said. "She said that a wolf came into camp and carried her grandson off into the woods."

"Which way did they go?" I said.

By this time more people had gathered around us, having been awakened by the woman's screams. Everyone looked as she pointed to a break in the trees on the other side of the expanse.

Before I could say anything, Cody had shifted into his wolf-form and shot across the open space, heading into the woods.

"Stay here!" I said to Kendra as I turned and sprinted after Cody. I summoned my magic and willed it into my hands as I ducked into the tree-line, chasing two wolves and a stolen child.

Enter The Wolf: Chapter Two

I crashed through the low-hanging branches, throwing blue-light magic ahead of me so I could see where I was going. I could hear Cody crashing through the underbrush, his lupine eyes not requiring magic to see. I muttered a useless curse at myself for not being able to keep up. I could only hope that if Cody found the Wolf he wouldn't engage until I was there. I stumbled out of the woods onto a small game path in the midst of the thickets. A few feet to my right, I could see Cody outlined in my flickering magic. He was sniffing at the game trail, trying to pick up the other Wolf's scent.

He growled before I could catch my breath or ask him which way to go. He looked to his left, and again took off following the trail. I ran after him, willing the burning ache in my lungs to dissipate. Just when I thought I couldn't run any longer I burst into a small, treeless patch of earth and almost tripped over Cody, who had stopped at the edge of the glen. His body was stiff, the dark hair along his back standing up as he growled, his gaze focused on something ahead. My eyes strained to pick up what he was seeing in the shadows.

"Fuck it," I said. I gathered a ball of magic in my hands and threw it into the air, where it split apart into a hundred sparkling shards that cascaded down like fireworks on the Fourth of July, illuminating everything around them. Suddenly the glen lit up as bright as day, and I could make out the form of a young boy lying on the ground.

I could also make out the form of a large gray wolf pacing back and forth around the boy. His tiny body wasn't moving, and even in the light of magic I couldn't tell if he was alive or dead. But then I heard it: a tiny whimper of fear escaped his little mouth.

The muscles in Cody's haunches flexed as he prepared to spring forward.

"No, wait!" I cried.

The gray wolf must have sensed Cody's intentions. It stopped pacing, and lowered its massive fangs to within inches of the boy's head. The warning growl told us that if either of us made a move, a quick snap would end the stolen child's life.

We were stuck. We didn't dare advance, and the wolf didn't bite. The stalemate did give me a chance to reach out with a slight tendril of magic. I could taste the wolf on the tip of my tongue, the sharp acrid bite of dark magic that surrounded it. There was no mistaking it; this was definitely a Shifter. Other than Cody and the one that had attacked us in Dr. Garner's house, there had been no sightings of wolf Shifters since I had destroyed the forbidding. As far as I knew, a wolf Shifter was always accompanied by one of the Order of the Fell, the mystical henchmen of the Warlock and the vampire Mallis. But no matter how deeply I probed into the surrounding woods, I could sense no other sign of magic. It was just the three of us and one whimpering child.

"Wait for my signal," I whispered to Cody. I spoke in a tone that was so quiet that I hoped even the supernatural hearing of a werewolf would not be able to pick it up. To his credit, Cody gave no indication that I said anything; his attention instead remained focused on the wolf that loomed ahead of us.

I began to lightly whisper a spell. My first instinct was to hurl a mystical hex bolt at the wolf and fry it before it could make a snack of the child. But something about its demeanor and the look in its eyes told me that that wasn't the best of ideas. No, this would call for subtlety, not a battering ram approach.

I concentrated on my magic, and breathed what I needed into existence. It was called ghosting, and it came from a set of glimmer magics that I had been practicing. I willed my magic to form a perfect three-dimensional image of myself that was indistinguishable from the real thing, even by another practitioner of magic. Once I was confident that the image was in place, I stepped back, the magic also shielding the physical me from perception.

I split my focus, using magic to maintain my illusion while also using it to dampen the sounds of my physical body as I circled around to flank the wolf. The closer I got to the Shifter, the more sick to my stomach I felt. Whatever magic had given rise to this being was so dark and powerful that I felt like I was being smothered. I was close enough that I could feel the heat being radiated by the wolf's body. I watched in revulsion as the creature lowered its head enough that its flickering tongue grazed the top of the boy's head.

It was tasting the child. My stomach turned as I sensed

the hunger and desire inside of the beast. Enough of this bullshit. I dropped the cloak of magic that shielded me from the wolf's senses, and channeled it into my hands in a ball of raw power.

I struck with all the fury I could muster, aiming a blast of power at the creature's side. I was surprised at the speed with which the wolf reacted: despite my cloaking, as soon as I dropped my spell to go on the offensive the wolf sensed my presence.

It turned with blinding speed, a mass of gray tooth and claw hurling at me before I could unleash my power. In a flash, the beast was on top of me. I felt like I was being crushed beneath its massive weight as it snarled and snapped for my throat. I managed to get my forearm up in front of my face, stifling a panicked scream. I felt three-inch-long canines bite through my leather coat and deep into the muscle of my arm. The pain sent shockwaves through my body and my magic flared out reflexively. Blue power lashed at the wolf, throwing it off of my chest.

The wolf was thrown backward and hit the forest floor with a heavy grunt. I ignored the searing pain that ripped through my forearm. Instead, I channeled the adrenaline rush into my magic, and cast a shimmering protective field around myself and the child, cowering on the ground beside me. I reached down to place a comforting hand on the poor boy's head, trying to calm him even as I felt the immense weight of the Shifter crashing into my force field. I looked up in time to see the gray wolf take a couple of steps back and then charge forward, slamming its full weight into my shield. My whole body shook with the impact, but one of the things I had been practicing was maintaining protective barriers. No way was I letting this beast get to myself or that little boy.

Just as I was about to draw up more magic to lash out at the beast, a dark shape slammed into the wolf, sending it sprawling away from me. Cody took a second to give me a quick look before hurling his wolven form at the other Shifter. In the blink of an eye he advanced on the gray wolf, and used his bulk and muscle to pin it down before lunging out with his own considerable fangs, aimed at the soft underside of the beast's neck.

But before they could make contact with the vulnerable spot, the gray wolf shifted. In the blink of an eye the wolf assumed a hybrid form, lean, muscular and covered in velvety gray fur with humanoid features that mimicked Cody's when he was in that form. The new shape allowed it to twist out of what would have surely been a death blow. Cody's jaws snapped shut mere inches from the creature's carotid arteries. In hybrid form, the Shifter nimbly rolled out from under Cody, grasping tightly at the fur and skin of Cody's back with a clawed hand. With a powerful heave, the hybrid tossed Cody's massive form like it was nothing, out of the clearing and into the trees beyond.

Almost quicker than I could follow, the hybrid lunged at me, raking razor-sharp claws across the protective blue barrier that kept myself and my young charge alive. Sparks flew from my shield as the creature rained blow after blow onto it. Just when I thought I might not be able to maintain the barrier much longer, the beast stopped and stood back. That was when I got a good look at it.

Except the creature wasn't an "it" at all; it was most definitely a "she".

In hybrid form I could definitely make out the curves, lithe musculature, and breasts of a female figure. Gray fur covered her from head to toe and sparkled in the eerie luminescence of my magic. She stepped back and leered at us, her lips drawing back from impossibly long fangs. Maybe it was the stress of the situation, but I could have sworn that she smiled at me before turning and leaping into the air, her form twisting, transforming back into a full wolf to land on all fours and sprint off into the woods.

I dropped my magic just as Cody came sprinting up. He shifted back to full human-form and stood beside me, just as I was helping the small boy to his feet.

"What happened?" he asked. "Where's the werewolf?"

"I don't know; she just ran off into the woods," I answered.

"She?"

I nodded without saying anything as I looked down at the small child beside us. He didn't seem to be any worse for wear, I decided, examining the puncture marks in the back of his shirt where the wolf had dragged him. Before I could say anything, Cody spun away from us, looking off into the distance.

"What is it?" I said. I could sense Cody drawing on his Shifting abilities, his head tilted to one side as he processed something I could not hear. Whatever it was, it was enough to spring his claws free. That, and the tension in his body, caused me to draw up a flame of blue magic and hold it in my hands.

"Screams," he said, turning to face me, "and… gunfire!"

Suddenly, I realized why the wolf had cut her attack short.

"The encampment!" I said. "This attack was just a ploy to draw us away from the Shifter camp."

Enter The Wolf: Chapter Three

As we got closer to the encampment, I could make out the cries and wails of fear and pain. The acrid stench of smoke hit me as we broke from the last bit of trees and undergrowth right before the clearing.

I was breathing hard, and sucking lungfuls of smoke was causing me to cough almost uncontrollably. The smoke stung my eyes; through the tears I could make out that a few of the tents that had been pitched near the RVs were on fire. The RVs had been the target of the fires, but the sparks from the campers had also landed on top of a few of the tents, setting them ablaze.

Chaos had set in. Many in the Shifter community were running to and fro, some of them carrying small children to safety while others battled the fires with portable extinguishers. Immediately, I was filled with fear, as every movie containing a scene with a burning vehicle played out in my mind. I wasn't sure if cars really burst into giant fireballs after burning for a few minutes, or if that was just a Hollywood effect that was created by one enterprising director, and had since spread to every movie ever shot containing a blazing vehicle. But then I remembered that most RVs contain propane gas tanks of some kind—either as a heat source or cooking source—and that even if the gasoline tanks didn't erupt, those most definitely would.

Three RVs were burning, their flames transitioning from bright orange to white against the black sky. I sprinted toward them, unsure of my exact plan. If they did blow, they would take out a sizable chunk of this camp, and who knows how many of the innocent Shifters would also fall.

I stood as close as I could to the inferno, then closed my eyes and spread my arms wide. I had gotten pretty good at starting fires, but I had never really considered the mechanics of putting one out. Especially not one that had not been created by, or as a response to, my magic. While that thought was frightening, it also gave me an idea. I concentrated, and willed my own magic to pour into the flames. Instantly, I almost regretted it; whatever my magic touched, I touched, and vice versa. I stifled a scream as I was hit with the sensation that every inch of my flesh was suddenly being seared.

Instead I blocked out the massive rush of heat and concentrated on the task at hand. I felt my magic begin to infuse the flames, taking over their warmth and turning them from white-hot to cool blue. However, the effort of corralling the flames was taking its toll. I could feel my teeth grinding together so hard that I was sure they would shatter in my mouth. Every fiber of my being cried out for me to stop, but I was way too stubborn to give in to voices in my head. Just when I thought I couldn't expend any more energy, I started to call my magic back. I could feel it retreating within me, and with it the angry flames that were threatening to destroy the camp.

It felt like my skin was splitting open. Slowly I drew my power, and with it the fire, back into my body. I still didn't open my eyes, but I knew the danger was gone; I could feel the change in the temperature around me. The cool, crisp mountain air had returned, and the acrid smoke no longer clawed at my nostrils. I suddenly felt like a puppet with cut strings as I dropped to my hands and knees, weakened beyond the telling. I began to cough uncontrollably, each forceful exhalation expelling black smoke out of my lungs and onto the ground in front of me.

"Hey, easy there," said Cody. He was standing next to me and had bent over to place a reassuring hand on my back. "You okay?"

"Yeah, I think so," I replied. The coughing and the smoke coming out of me had finally subsided, and I was able to regain my footing.

"Okay, that was impressive," Cody said as he continued to massage my back. "And you are burning up!" He raised one hand and placed it against my face. It felt like I was being touched by a soft, smooth blanket of ice.

"Better me than all of them," I said, nodding at the Shifters that were starting to gather around us. I noticed that the small fires that were threatening the tents had been put out, and most of the inhabitants' attention seem to be focused on me and Cody. "Is everyone okay? What happened?"

I looked around, but all I could make out was confusion and fear on the faces that had gathered to gawk at us.

"They made good on their threat." It was the old woman who spoke up—the one whose young charge was taken by the wolf. She now clutched the young boy fiercely to her side, her tattered old shawl draped protectively around his shoulders, his face buried deeply into her neck.

"What threats? And who made them?" I asked.

The assembly that circled us murmured amongst themselves, but no one spoke up.

Finally, the old woman stepped forward. "Those cult members, or whatever they are, that have been coming around here lately...they're looking for witches and Shifters that are willing to join up with them." She spat onto the ground beside her and stared at me, her eyes narrowed and filled with fury and hatred, but at what, I couldn't tell. "They said that any Shifters that remained here would be sorry. They said a war was coming and anybody who wasn't with them would be treated like an enemy. They suggested that we all leave and go back to where we came from."

"These cult members," Cody said, "were they all dressed in black?"

"Well of course they were," said the old woman. "I told you, they're cult members; what else do they wear?" I would have laughed, except the anger in her voice told me that she wasn't trying to be funny.

"So they did this?" I asked. "They set fire to your camp to try to scare you away?"

"How long is this been going on?" Cody said.

"About a week now," she replied. "They first showed up and started offering fistfuls of money to Shifters who would join their cause. When they didn't get many of us to jump at the offer, they started making threats. Told us we would regret this. I guess now we know they were serious."

"I guess this confirms what we were thinking; the wolf that stole the child was a distraction," I said, turning to

Cody. "That was just meant to draw the two of us away from the camp so that whoever was working with the wolf could do this. Thank God no one was hurt seriously."

"Well, hopefully not too seriously." The voice floated from the back of the assembled Shifters. It sounded weak and filled with pain. Before anyone could reply, a small figure cut its way through the crowd to approach me and Cody.

It was Kendra, her gait unsteady and her head hanging down. Both of her arms were clutched around her waist as she stumbled forward on legs that looked like they could barely support her weight.

"But this—" she held up one shaky hand that was covered something wet and thick "—kind of feels pretty serious."

Cody managed to catch her just as she tumbled forward, lapsing into unconsciousness. She was covered in blood from a wound in her abdomen.

"My God!" said Cody. "She's been shot!" He lifted her into his arms to cradle her frighteningly still figure.

"Somebody get a blanket!" I said, rushing to his side. Her still figure seemed tiny and fragile in his arms.

"We need to get her to a hospital," Cody said as a member of the community ran forward to drape an old, checkered blanket over her.

I placed two fingers on her neck, feeling for a pulse. It was slow and weak, but there nonetheless. The blanket that covered her was already beginning to show a dark spot where it made contact with her torn flesh.

I looked up at Cody and shook my head. "We can't take her to a hospital; it would raise too many questions—the kind of questions that even you won't be able to bury."

"We can't just let her die!" Cody said.

"We're not going to," I said, looking up at him. "She doesn't need a hospital, but she does need a doctor."

Grab your copy...
vinci-books.com/enterthewolf

About the Author

M.J. Caan is an avid reader and writer of all things science fiction and fantasy. Author of multiple science fiction and paranormal fantasy series, M.J. likes to think that there is still magic out there in the world. Even if it's only between the pages of a great book.